Tales of the Were

Grif

BIANCA D'ARC

DEDICATION

First, I'd like to thank my friend, Peggy McChesney, for her sage advice and help. You're a godsend! Thanks for everything!

This book was a long time in the making. I first invented Griffon Redstone in about 2005, then abandoned the story for other projects when I got my first paying writing gig. But Grif and his family were always in my mind and I'd take that old manuscript out from time to time and dust it off, polish it a little, then usually get distracted by another project again.

So Grif is pretty important to me. And I "borrowed" some of his brothers, relatives and back-story for other books along the way. The youngest brother, Matt, plays a prominent (and very naughty) role in my book *Sweeter Than Wine*, for example. And Keith, a Redstone cousin, is the hero of the short story, *The Purrfect Stranger*. Keith plays a supporting role in *Tales of the Were: Rocky*, and another brother, Steve, plays a supporting role in *Tales of the Were: Slade*.

I mention all this to explain how near and dear Grif and his story are to my heart. This book is the foundation of a lot of characters I've used in books since this one was first started. It is also the culmination of about eight years of on-again/off-again work and lots and lots of thought and daydreaming.

When I started writing this book, my mother was still alive and my life was very different from what it is now. I'm still in a state of transition and who knows where it's really going? Certainly not me. But for now, I'd like to dedicate this book to the person who most influenced my life to date—my Mom.

She was a pioneer and a role model. A woman who faced adversity bravely and experienced more than most people can even dream. She was a child of WWII, a Prisoner of War and an immigrant to her adopted homeland, the United States. She made this country stronger for her presence and touched the lives of many of her students, colleagues and friends in profound ways. I owe my love of learning to her and try my best to live up to her standard. I wish I could be as brave, strong and willing to take chances as she always was, and I wish more than anything to rediscover the *joie de vivre* that she took with her when she left this earth.

This book was first released in ebook format near what would have been my parents' 59th wedding anniversary. We should all be so blessed to find a marriage like theirs. This book is also dedicated to them, as a couple, and the example they set for all of us of how to be partners, mates and spouses. It is my wish that all of us find that kind of deep, true and lasting love during our short time on earth.

AUTHOR'S NOTE

The internal chronology of my paranormal stories probably needs a little explaining. In a perfect world, all these books would have come out in the order in which the events in the books happen. Unfortunately, due to publisher issues all along the way, they are coming out in a slightly different order.

The events in my earlier-published book, *Sweeter Than Wine*, actually happen after the events in both *Rocky* and *Slade*. The circumstances of this book, *Grif,* are referred to in *Sweeter Than Wine* and can be presumed to happen somewhat simultaneously.

PROLOGUE

His people were hunted. The hunters didn't always realize the intelligence behind the sparkling feline eyes, but they recognized the challenge. For that reason, his people had always been hunted along with their brethren of the animal kingdom.

But his people were not animals.

Nor were they completely human. They were somehow...both...and neither. They were a people out of legend.

Griffon Redstone was proud of his power and his skill. Proud of his family and protective of his siblings. Growing up, he'd gone off on his own from time to time, as his kind often did, but he always returned to his family, the loving bond between them strong and sure.

So when his family home in Nevada was violated by the stench of evil magic and violent death, something ripped loose in his soul, never to be righted. His beloved mother, the matriarch of their Clan, had been murdered in her own backyard.

She'd not only been killed in the most violent fashion, but her body had been mutilated after death. When threatened, she'd shifted shape to her animal form and the killers had taken part of her pelt as some kind of sick prize.

She'd been skinned. It was the crudest form of desecration in the shifter community.

He would never forgive himself for not being there when the devil came to visit. For only pure evil could have committed such a brutal act. His baby sister, twelve-year-old Belinda, whimpered in one corner of the lush garden their mother had been so proud of. Poor Belinda had found their mother's mutilated body and Grif feared she would carry that emotional scar for the rest of her life.

It was up to him to take her away from the heartbreak, to help her heal as best he could. She was his responsibility now. Griffon Redstone was now the eldest of the Redstone Clan. He was the caretaker who had failed in his duty to protect his mother. He would not let little Belinda suffer alone.

CHAPTER ONE

The woman's divine scent teased his senses, but she was all too human. Grif watched the pretty waitress traipse across the worn linoleum, alternately mothering and flirting with the somewhat questionable, mostly male clientele of Ed's Diner. The men's eyes followed her, but she treated all equally, her very elusiveness part of her charm. She had a great smile too, and killer legs, long and muscular beneath the rather blah uniform skirt.

She was neat and tidy, and if the middle button of her cotton uniform seemed to strain from time to time as she leaned forward to place a plate before a customer, it had everything to do with the superior quality of her breasts and the inferior quality of the one-size-fits-most uniforms Ed's waitresses were made to wear. Grif appreciated the view though, realizing she was pretty much unaware of the covetous looks aimed at her from all over the room.

She appeared naturally outgoing and friendly to all, and he could scent no sexual interest coming off her as she talked with and sometimes teased the other male patrons who watched her with desire in their eyes. Grif had spotted the other werefolk in the diner as soon as he'd walked in. Mostly they were wolves from the local Pack. He'd seen some of them in one form or another as he ranged over his territory.

The wolves had given him a wide berth, aside from their Alpha male coming to his cabin shortly after he moved in to *welcome* him to the neighborhood. The welcome consisted of a half-hour grilling about his intentions and a reading of the riot act about the rules this Pack adhered to, and expected any werecreature in their territory to live with as well.

Grif had taken it all in stride, knowing that the dominant number of werewolves in the Wind River mountain range of Wyoming allowed them to call the shots, even if Grif ran one of the most influential Clans in the country. He was on vacation.

Roaming with his little sister in tow. Seeking space to run and forget their shared troubles for a little while. A place to heal, away—for the most part—from humans.

The Wind River wolf Pack's rules were pretty straight forward. No hunting owned animals, no stalking humans for kicks, and that sort of thing. It was easy to just agree with the Alpha male and get him out of Grif's cabin so he could enjoy his solitude. If enjoyment was something he could still feel.

He spent most of his time now in his fur, letting the aggressive nature of his *were* side help him forget the tragedy in his life. He and his little sister roamed over their new territory for days on end, only stopping at the cabin once in a while. But they had to be human sometimes and as humans, they needed supplies from town every now and again. When he came to town, Grif stopped in Ed's Diner more often than not, nodding to the other shapeshifters that would acknowledge him and enjoying human food he didn't have to cook himself.

This pretty waitress was new, or at least he had never seen her here before on one of his infrequent trips into town. He watched her deal efficiently with the last of the lunch crowd as he settled at the counter. She placed a cup and saucer before him with one hand while holding up a carafe of coffee with the other. A raised eyebrow and questioning expression asked if he wanted some of the caffeinated brew. When he nodded, she filled his cup without a word and sashayed down the narrow space behind the counter to the pickup window, filling another customer's order as he perused the menu.

He already knew what he wanted, but he took his time looking at the plastic covered menu, studying her covertly. What was it about the woman? She was undeniably human, which normally wasn't a big turn-on for him. He'd never had a bed partner that wasn't a shapeshifter of some kind, not for lack of opportunity, but for lack of desire on his part.

But this woman was different. She moved fluidly and her scent called to him. She was strongly built, not some delicate hothouse flower. He liked that. And he found himself admiring her shapely, muscled calves and short-nailed fingers. She had working hands, but they weren't rough. They looked pretty and capable, and he wondered what they'd feel like stroking over his skin. He wondered vividly what she would feel like under him.

Cursing himself for a fool as his libido stirred to uncomfortable life, Grif turned back to the menu, pulling his eyes from the disturbing human female. Her alluring scent wafted nearer as she moved toward him.

Damn it all.

She was coming over to take his order and he had no choice but to look up from the menu and meet her gaze. She stood only feet away behind the counter watching him. Her eyes flashed, her smile somehow innocent and so lovely, she stole his breath.

"The chili's fresh today." Her voice washed over his senses like warm rain in the jungle. "And we have a great pecan pie."

Grif actually *felt* the sound of her melodic voice drift over his senses. He looked down in momentary confusion, staring hard at the menu, trying to get a grip.

With a deep breath that only made things worse as he inhaled yet more of her lovely scent, he steeled himself to look back up at her. The eyes that met his sparkled with intelligence, a surprising innocence, and expectation. She was waiting for him to place his food order, he realized with a bit of chagrin.

He'd been so preoccupied with her mere presence, he'd lost sight of his ultimate goal—lunch. It was a small goal, to be sure, but after the hell of the past few months, he'd learned to take one thing at a time, set priorities and see them through. To lose sight of even such a small goal as this, was a shocking misstep to a man who prided himself on his control of all within his realm.

Grif ordered the steak special without much fanfare, taking her measure and studying the hidden fire in her eyes. He would definitely like to experience that flame more closely, but he knew this was neither the time nor the place. He counseled himself to settle down, even as the fit of his jeans suddenly became almost too tight to bear.

This distracting female was worth examining further, he thought, as she brought him his food a few minutes later. He resisted the urge to flirt with her. The place was busy with the lunch crowd and he would no doubt be interrupted. He had time. He would wait until the place cleared a bit. Then he would make his move.

"Sweetie, I'm going over to Linette's to pick up that cobbler for tonight," Ed called loudly from the back as he left his diner. The lunch rush was effectively over and Grif watched the pretty waitress efficiently putting everything back to rights.

Only the table of werewolves and Grif were left inside now. And the woman, of course.

He watched as she went over to the booth against the window to clear some of the wolves' plates away and ask them if they wanted dessert. He had just turned to set down his coffee cup when he heard her gasp.

Grif turned back in time to see the largest of the male wolves grab her by the wrist and push his sloppy plate at her with enough force to make the food left on it splatter over her chest. The bad-mannered wolf snarled as he let her go and the plate dropped to the floor, shattering at her feet. She looked aghast but somehow submissive as Grif stood, ready to rip the wolf limb from limb.

The other wolves rose, facing him down.

"Stay out of this," one of them warned him in a throaty growl. "It's none of your business."

The leader of the small group stood then too, throwing some bills at the woman's face as he looked down at her. The wolves were all much taller than the small human. It really wasn't fair for them to pick on her.

"We don't want you here." The werewolf openly growled at the woman, surprising Grif again. "Leave while you still can."

He issued his warning as Grif moved closer to stand behind the woman, making his intention to protect her clear, but the wolves stomped out with a few snarls, making no more threatening moves toward her. When the last one was finally gone, Grif turned his attention fully to the woman. She was kneeling on the floor, trying to collect the pieces of broken china, but he stopped her nervous motions by placing one big hand over hers.

"Don't do that, sweetheart. You'll cut yourself."

He could see the tears tracking down her face as she accepted his help to stand.

"You're right." She surreptitiously wiped the moisture from her eyes and turned to get a dustpan and broom kept behind the counter. Grif just stood and watched her graceful moves, trying his best to puzzle out what had just happened.

He watched her, remembering how her hands were even softer than he had imagined, a tactile delight. He also realized that she had done something to piss off the local werewolf Pack and they were trying to run her out of town. Not good.

Something about this petite human angered the wolves, though as a general rule, shifters didn't much bother themselves with the doings of humans. It struck him as odd that the wolves would try to scare off one small human female.

Whatever she'd done, it had to be something big. Something big enough to stir the wolves to anger and action. They'd made no bones about wanting her gone.

Unacceptable, he thought with an inward growl. He had only just met her. She couldn't leave now. He would not allow those cocky wolf bastards to run her off. Not without learning what this was all about, at the very least.

There was something special about this little human and he wanted to find out what it was that drew him so irresistibly to her. He felt inexplicably protective of her, though he knew it was odd in the extreme that he wanted nothing more than to wrap her in his arms and keep her safe from all harm. Still, his instincts were screaming at him like the cat that lived inside his soul and he had learned never to go against his instincts. Every time he did, disaster soon followed.

He watched her, his gaze following her every move. She was shaking like a leaf when she returned to the mess on the floor. Stepping silently forward, he lifted the dustpan and brush out of her trembling fingers, letting his warm touch slide along her hands, offering that little bit of comfort. What he really wanted to do was wrap her in his arms and make love to her the most tender way he knew how, but that would have to wait. For now.

"Sit for a moment while I do this for you, sweetheart."

"Why are you being so nice to me?"

He shrugged, trying to keep things casual while the protective beast inside him roared to life. "Let's just say I don't like to see a pretty lady treated so shabbily." The beast wanted to stand between her and all harm, though he could not understand what it was about this woman that brought out his primitive side so strongly.

She smiled, but it was still a shaky smile. The threat of violence and confrontation had shaken her to the core, but even as he watched, she firmed her spine and a resolute light entered her pretty eyes. He put some space between them as he dumped the remains of the plate and what food he could scrape off the floor into the large waste bin behind the counter.

Snagging a towel, he handed it to her as he walked back, sitting on the opposite side of the booth. With a pointed glance, he indicated the food stains on her voluptuous breasts, charmed when she flushed from neck to forehead.

She used the towel to try to wipe some of it off and he did his best not to watch as the damp towel pressed over her breasts, desperate not to picture his hands taking the same path without any layers of cloth between them. As it was, his jeans already fit a bit too snug, just from the delicious scent of her. He had to focus.

"So do you want to tell me what that was all about?"

She shrugged, keeping her attention on her stained blouse. The way that towel and her hands were rubbing over her generous curves was making him painfully hard, but there were more important matters to settle first.

He decided in that moment, that he would have her—at least once before the wolves ran her off. The cat in him purred at the thought, but he had to be realistic. The wolf Pack ran this territory. There were way more of them than he could counter alone and he was new to the area to boot. By rights, this territory was theirs and if they didn't want this pretty human female in it, they would probably succeed in getting rid of her.

But not before he got in her pants. He hadn't had a woman since moving into the cabin, and even before that, he'd never bedded a human. He knew nothing could come of it, which was good in a way. He didn't need any more complications in his life at the moment—especially of the female variety, but just the idea of a good romp with this woman stirred his senses in a way nothing ever had before. He vowed he'd have at least one night with her in his arms before he let her slip away.

"It's an old dispute," she said finally, shrugging, drawing him back to the matter at hand. It was obvious she didn't want to tell him why the wolves wanted her gone, but he would find out, he assured himself.

He changed tacks. "You're new here, aren't you?" He offered her a friendly smile and noted when she relaxed a bit with the seeming change of topic.

"My grandfather lived here most of his life. He died recently and left me his place. I just moved in."

"So you live here in town?" He tried for a casual tone and apparently succeeded.

6

"No, I live out on the edge of the res."

"You're at least part Native, then?" His eyes roamed hungrily over her fine features, noting the proud Native American genetics in her strong cheekbones and dark eyes. But her eyes weren't brown. No, they were a deep, dark, foresty green. Instantly, he was fascinated by their hue and sparkle.

"I'm only a quarter Northern Arapaho, but grandpa made sure of my status with the tribe when I was born. They're not exactly welcoming me with open arms, but they know grandpa's wishes and I'm so far out from the center of the res, they easily forget I'm there."

"I live in the mountains too." Volunteering information about his life wasn't something he did often, but this woman brought out all kinds of new behaviors in him, he was fast learning. "I don't get into town much except when I need supplies or work."

"What do you do?" Her question was tentative but friendly. He sensed she wanted to talk about anything and everything but the confrontation that had just taken place.

He shrugged, understanding her need to push aside the ugliness of the past few minutes.

"I do odd jobs, mostly. I know carpentry, plumbing, electric, that sort of thing." He didn't mention the scale on which he'd done those jobs before the tragedy that drove him and his little sister into the mountains. That life was behind him now, at least for the time being, but the knowledge remained with him

"Boy, I wish I knew that stuff. Grandpa's house is just about falling down around me." She laughed and a trickle of sensation danced along his spine. "It's all I can do to keep the generator going."

His brows lowered, concern stirring hot and hard. "That's not good with winter coming on." All his protective instincts came to bear as he thought of her all alone out in the freezing cold woods with no heat or light.

She shrugged. "I'm not rich. I don't have much money to put into fixing things up."

He saw his opportunity and dove for it. "How about I come out to check your generator tomorrow. I don't like the idea of a woman alone in the snow with no power."

She looked cautious for a moment and stood from the table. "That's very kind of you but..." she laughed with a hint of nervousness, "…I don't even know your name."

He remained sitting, not wanting to loom over her, needing to put her at ease. Holding up his hands palms outward, he smiled his most innocent smile. If a predator like him could ever look truly innocent.

"I understand. A woman can't be too careful these days. I think Ed might vouch for me, though. I've done odd jobs for him a time or two since I came to town. And for some of the other shop keepers. I could give you a list of references, if you like."

It was all true, too. He stayed in his fur as long as he could, but when he was human, he had to keep busy. Doing odd jobs gave him some sense of satisfaction and kept his mind from the pain that haunted him—at least for short stretches of time. He'd fixed Ed's kitchen wiring a time or two and done carpentry jobs for some of the shopkeepers and homeowners in the area. He was popular, partially because he charged so little for his services, and partly because he did such a good job. He'd earned a decent reputation with the townsfolk and knew she'd find that out easily enough if she asked around.

"All right, I'll ask Ed what he thinks." She moved back behind the counter, almost defensively.

Standing from the booth, he resumed his seat at the counter. "It's good to be cautious." He nodded as she topped off his coffee. "And my name is Griffon Redstone. You can call me Grif."

She smiled then, wiping her hands for a final time on the towel. "I'm Lindsey Tate." She held one petite hand out over the counter for him to shake.

He took it with barely suppressed eagerness. Her skin was so soft. Her neatly manicured fingernails were short and attractive in a way he hadn't expected. His palm tingled against hers for the moment out of time she allowed him to hold her captive. Not wanting to scare her off, he released her much sooner than his inner beast would have wished.

"I'm going to be in town for the rest of the day." He rose slowly, unwilling to scare off his prey before the chase had begun in earnest. "Talk to Ed and maybe Wilma over at the dress shop, or Pete the barber. I've done work for all of them. I'll be back in for a late dinner before heading back up the mountain. You can let me know if you want my help then. Or just leave a message with Ed." Settling his beat up Stetson hat on his head, he dug in his pocket for his wallet.

"Thank you," she said softly. "For before." She came around the edge of the counter to stand in front of him.

He touched her soft cheek with one long finger, unable to resist. Her eyes dilated in a way that told him she enjoyed his touch, but it was too soon to push her, so he pulled back with a smile. "I hate to see anyone hassle a lady."

She nodded tightly at the reminder. "And thanks for the offer to come look at the generator. I'll let you know, but—" She seemed to blush a bit as she hesitated. "Um, how much would it cost me?"

She'd already told him she wasn't rolling in dough, and something inside him softened. "To get your generator running? Consider it my public service for the week. You can pay for parts, if you like, if any are needed. But if you need any other work done on the place, I can give you an estimate after I see what's what. Ask Ed and the others what I charged them. I think you'll find I'm fair."

"Why would you do that for me?" she asked in wonder, her thoughts slipping out apparently uncensored.

He tipped his hat as he left payment for the meal plus a generous tip on the counter by his plate. "You remind me of my sister." Pain lanced through him as he thought of the young woman whose life had been cut brutally short. "I think you've got some of the same spirit she had. If she were in your shoes, I would've liked someone to have helped her if they could."

She stared after him as he left, he knew, though he didn't turn around. His senses were bathed in her scent, and her conflicting emotions. He knew she was intrigued and he hoped she would talk to Ed and the others as soon as possible. All in all, the day had just turned interesting.

Lindsey cleaned up the rest of the mess and had everything shining once again when Ed returned from his errand. She'd had time to think about the tall, handsome, gold-haired stranger as she worked, realizing that she hadn't been so captivated by a man's mere presence in her entire life. His smile affected her breathing and his sparkling golden eyes seemed to see into her very soul.

When he'd touched her hand, she had felt a tingle down deep in her tummy that she'd never experienced before. He had practically made love to her with his eyes, and she'd been secretly thrilled by his unceasing scrutiny. His gaze followed her, devoured her, and promised hot, wicked delight.

She'd been aware of him from the moment he came through the door. His striking looks, lean hipped frame and strange, vigilant watchfulness, caused her to catch her breath. Those locals she knew were different had nodded in respectful greeting, but none offered him a place to sit, and he didn't seem to expect it

So either he was some kind of lone wolf, or he was something else all together. He was definitely an enigma, and could be trouble for her mission, but she really did need to fix up the house if she planned to stay long enough to complete her task.

And complete it she would. She'd made a promise to her grandfather she intended to keep. They could threaten her all they wanted, but she wouldn't back down. Things had to be made right and she was the only one left to do it. She wouldn't let her grandfather's spirit down. She would complete the task he'd given her—the sacred duty he'd entrusted to her alone—and put right what he'd made wrong.

With that thought firmly in mind, she went back to talk to Ed while the place was empty.

"Do you know a man named Griffon Redstone?"

Ed wiped his hands as he retied his apron. "Grif? Yeah, he's a good guy. Was he in for lunch? It was so busy I didn't get to see who all came and went."

"Yeah, he was here earlier." She hesitated only a moment, but Ed looked up from his work with a questioning smile. "He says he's a handyman."

Ed nodded with a wide grin. "Best damn handyman I've ever had. He rewired the fryer and then rigged a new line for that fancy oven I got a few months back. Installed it too, clean as a whistle."

She looked around at the equipment and noted the neat installation job. "So he's reliable then?"

Ed nodded. "I reckon so. Why do you ask?"

She smiled as he offered her a stool in his private domain. "My generator is acting up and he offered to come by to take a look at it. I need a lot of work done on the place actually, but I don't know if I can afford him."

"He doesn't overcharge for his work. In fact, if anything, I think he cut me some slack on the labor costs. He didn't charge much over the parts and he spent a good amount of time on the job. Did it up right."

"Do you think he's...well, um...safe?" She hated the hesitancy in her voice but knew she needed to be careful with things the way they were.

"You mean to go out to your place?" Ed seemed to consider his answer. "Can't say as I've ever heard a bad thing about him. He's been respectful of my waitresses and never put the moves on any girl I heard tell about. I'd say he's on the up and up, but if you're uncomfortable, why don't you give me a call when he gets to your place. If you don't call me back in a reasonable time, I'll send the sheriff."

She laughed as he'd probably intended, somewhat reassured. She used her afternoon break to go talk to the other shop owners Grif had mentioned. They all gave him glowing reviews too. Wilma especially seemed to think he was trustworthy, which meant a lot to Lindsey. It was always good to have a woman's opinion.

The fact that Wilma thought he was "H-O-T, HOT" too was just reassurance that the woman wasn't blind.

So it was with some eagerness that Lindsey awaited his return to the diner. She only worked at Ed's two days a week, but they were long days. She made decent money in tips and wages, and the part-time job helped keep her solvent.

When Grif returned, it was at the height of the dinner rush, so Lindsey had little time to talk to him. Still they managed to set a time for him to look at the generator and she gave him directions. He ate the rest of his meal, lingering a bit over dessert, but the crowd was demanding and eventually he left without much further conversation.

CHAPTER TWO

Grif knew where she lived now, the intriguing human female with the soft hands and a scent that made him think instantly of sex and passion. Her home wasn't all that far from his cabin as the crow flies—or the cougar runs.

He couldn't seem to keep away, and found himself in his fur, stalking the perimeter of her yard. He was clawing trees and putting his mark on the boundaries of her property to warn others of his kind that she was under his protection. He didn't know what good that might do if he ran up against the whole werewolf Pack, but it was something. Maybe it would buy her some time at least.

At most, it would buy him some time to get into her pants. He made a running leap and landed on the lower roof of the slightly sagging back porch. The entire house was dark except for two rooms near the front on the second floor. Stalking quietly upward, he noted the roof was in really bad shape. There were gaps and even two larger holes that allowed him to see right inside the lit rooms. Apparently she hadn't bothered trying to plug them up yet, but the array of buckets and pans located on the floor directly beneath, indicated she was well aware of her roof problem.

Grif, in his werecougar form, sat gently on the cross beams, making sure no noise would alert her to his presence as he waited to see if he could catch a glimpse of her. His supple ears swiveled and twitched, hearing her soft humming growing nearer in the room below his rooftop perch. She was chanting some ancient Native song, her voice rising melodically through the house, wafting up into the starry night. The sound grew louder as he realized he was looking down into her bedroom. He could just make out about half of the large bed if he craned his neck.

She toweled her damp hair as she entered from what must be the bathroom, in a white terry cloth robe that came to mid-thigh. His mouth watered, even in his altered state. His feline senses exploded as the soft scent of her skin wafted up through the rafters. She must've just come from her bath and Grif felt his libido kick into high gear.

Switching on her hair dryer, he noted the dimming of the old light fixtures. The wiring in the decrepit house wasn't up to dealing with all the modern appliances she used. The old place needed some major work, and he was just the man to do it, but first he had to convince her.

He thought over their earlier encounter. He could tell she was a proud woman, though he sensed a soft, feminine side to her that called out to every protective instinct in him. It made his inner beast roar. And when he was in his fur, it made him want to bloody anyone who might dare threaten her.

Odd, he realized somewhere in the back of his brain, the fear that he would fail to protect her, as he had failed to protect his mother and older sister, didn't fight past the overwhelming need to claim this small human.

She was so vulnerable. Human—and therefore frail—when compared to a woman of his own species, she was in much more danger from the everyday dangers of the world than he could even contemplate. But that didn't seem to matter. He wanted her in a way he had never wanted another female, and he would have her.

It didn't matter that she was human. It didn't matter that he was a proven failure as a protector. Nothing mattered but getting inside her and staying there until she was well and truly out of his system.

She dried her lustrous light brown hair, then absently stroked some cream onto her face. He purred deep in his throat, watching her delicate hands smooth over her soft skin. He imagined the way she would feel against him, her softness stroking over his hardness.

Then she took off the robe.

His breath caught, his whiskers twitched and his senses tingled as she smoothed what smelled like baby oil over her arms, legs, breasts and shapely rear. The soft scent was the sexiest thing he had ever smelled.

Grif suddenly realized that the innocent scent had lingered on her skin ever so slightly when he had first scented her in the diner. He hadn't been able to place it then because it had mingled with her own musk in the hours since she'd put it on, becoming uniquely her own.

Her body was magnificent. Lush curves were topped by bountiful breasts that he longed to lick. She was built like the pinups of old—not too skinny to fuck hard—with toned muscles and inviting thighs. He wanted between those thighs. He wanted those shapely thighs cradling him as he mounted her high, hard and fast. He wanted to mold those curvy hips with his hands as he took her from behind, tunneling into her wet passage with a fury she would echo.

She was a truly sensuous woman. The lingering way she stroked the oil into her soft skin told him that. She obviously enjoyed the way her oily hands stroked over her skin, stopping to spend extra time on her nipples, drawing them out and pinching the tips. Closing her eyes and sighing as she did so, she made him harder than he thought possible.

His tongue lolled out of his mouth as her hands worked their way down, down, down, the fingers of one hand tangling in the trimmed curls at the apex of her thighs. She stroked down and inward, her fingers parting the delicate folds and curving around her clit, pressing lightly, then circling and pressing harder and harder as she fell to the bed and spread her legs wide.

Grif purred low in his throat as she used one hand to stroke her clit while the other stroked in and out of her passage. It was quite possibly the hottest thing he had ever witnessed. Her eyes were shut, her mouth panting out little breaths as she neared her pinnacle.

How he wished he was with her, that it was his hands stroking her pussy, his dick forging its way inside her core. He swore then that human or not, he was going to fuck her long and hard, and damn the consequences. He wanted her as he had never wanted any woman before and he was going to have her.

Lindsey came with a small cry, bucking on the bed for a long moment, but he knew the small release was nothing compared to what he would bring her. He would bathe her in his come and she would love every minute of it. She would suck him off and swallow him down and he would lap at her pussy, feasting on her cream.

Then he would shoot his seed inside her, marking her for all to scent. Oh, the humans wouldn't notice, but any *were* that came near enough would know that she was claimed by him. She would carry his scent for days after he came inside her and he would revel in that fact, even if she never realized it.

Below him, Lindsey shut off the light and pulled the covers up, settling in for sleep while he remained on the roof above, making plans.

Good as his word, Grif Redstone showed up at Lindsey's place bright and early on Saturday morning. She greeted him a little stiffly, but he seemed aware of how wary she was and made no overt moves, staying in the yard while she came down off the front porch to greet him.

Wasting little time, he walked with her out back to where the ancient generator was located, just next to the back porch. He made small talk while he started looking over the machinery, calming her nerves with his easy-going manner and charming smile. But he also generated a warm, safe feeling low in her stomach that was hard to explain.

She didn't know this man, except for the fact that he'd come to her defense in the diner. The local folks spoke well of him, which counted in his favor, but something deep down within her said he was a good man. A safe man. Though the precise meaning of the word *safe* was open for interpretation.

He certainly wasn't safe to her peace of mind. The man made her blood pressure rise and her panties wet faster than any man she'd ever seen. Handsome in a rugged, slightly disheveled way, he appealed to her basic femininity. He wasn't sloppy, but the long strands of his hair were artfully tousled in a natural way, though he definitely wasn't a pretty boy who spent hours in front of a mirror to achieve the look. It just came to him naturally.

Whoa, mama! That was a dangerous thing in a man, and he seemed totally unaware of how scrumptious he looked. Sure, he had confidence, but he wasn't cocky. His confidence shone like an aura around him, radiating from deep inside. He was confident about himself as a man and a person, not as some kind of beefcake, though she thought he could give any male model a serious run for his money without even trying.

She left him out by the generator to work. She didn't want to seem too desperate or cloying by standing there, watching him work. He was just too darn attractive.

But men like him were never attracted to her. She had to be deluding herself that she saw interest in his eyes. He was just being a good neighbor. He wasn't coming on to her. In fact, he was doing all he could to make her feel at ease with him—to make friends.

And on some level she was relieved. No matter how gorgeous the man was, she couldn't very well get involved with anyone now. Not while all her energies were dedicated to a life-altering course that would come to fruition in the next few days. She had commitments. She had to see them through, and no matter how much she was tempted to throw caution to the wind with this man, she knew she couldn't.

Still, Lindsey couldn't help but take a look out her kitchen window every few minutes, just to see what Grif was up to. He tinkered and cursed a bit, banged on things, applied grease that got all over his hands and on his already stained jeans, and in general looked like a man on a mission as he worked on her ancient generator. She puttered and looked for excuses to stay near the back of the house so she could catch glimpses of his broad back from time to time, but chastised herself for ogling the man.

"Munchkin." Grif's voice snapped with authority, but not anger. "What are you doing here? I thought I told you to stay at the cabin." He turned his gaze skyward to pin the juvenile cougar cub staring down at him from the shelter of a stout evergreen. The cat lowered her head, well and truly caught, as Grif prayed for patience.

"All right." He sighed heavily. "You can play in the woods behind me, but don't let anyone see you and don't stray far. I'll be ready to go in about an hour and I want you in the truck when I pull away."

The little cougar nodded its head, scratching against the bark of the tree as she yawned, her topaz eyes glowing slightly as they met his.

Grif lifted his head, scenting the wind. He thought for a moment he'd caught a whiff of something...sinister. Something he hadn't scented since that dreadful night his happy family had started to fall to ruins, but then it was gone. He must have imagined it, yet his inner cat told him to be cautious.

"Stay close, kitten."

Grif rapped on the backdoor, noting the surprise in Lindsey's eyes as she came to the doorway. He'd seen her watching him, but he'd still managed to catch her off guard. He licked his lips as her small hand flew to cover her pounding heart. He wanted his hands there, and lower. He wanted his hands all over her, but that would come later.

"You startled me. You're as silent as a cat!" She laughed, trying to still her nerves as he moved closer.

"You have no idea." He paused, enjoying the flush on her beautiful skin. "The good news is I can fix your generator. I think I have all the parts in my truck. Simple stuff, O-rings and oil is about all it needs."

"That's a relief. It was making such strange noises."

"Metal grinding on metal," he agreed. "Not a pretty sound."

She motioned him into the small kitchen. "Want some lemonade? I just made it fresh."

He prowled into the small space, willing to crowd her a bit now that he was sure she was interested. All those heated glances out the window weren't just curiosity. This woman was interested in him as a man. He could smell her arousal.

"Most folks don't take the time to make it from real lemons anymore. My own mother used to buy the frozen stuff, or worse, the powder stuff." He smacked his lips as he took a long, appreciative swallow from the tall glass she handed him. "This is good."

"Thanks. I like it fresh, so I buy a few lemons now and again."

He swallowed down more of the tart brew as she watched him with those wide, sparkling eyes. They followed the movements of his mouth and arms, even the way his throat worked as he swallowed, so he deliberately licked his lips, pleased with the increase of her arousal as she followed the swishing movements of his tongue. He'd plunge that tongue in all her secret places, he swore silently. As soon as he possibly could. And damn the fact that she wasn't *were*.

The thought pissed him off royally.

No law of his kind said he couldn't fuck a human. He'd just never wanted a human woman like this before. Not the way he wanted Lindsey Tate. He knew would have her. Soon. He just couldn't keep her. That was the bitch of it.

He had to get his inner beast under control. This woman needed finessing. She wasn't *were* to submit to his Alpha dominance, and he couldn't pounce on her the way he so desperately wanted to. He had to do this the hard way—the human way.

"So did you want to show me the worst parts of the roof?"

Her lack of concentration amused him, but he had a driving need to see her bedroom from the inside this time. He concentrated on the idea of fucking her and then putting her aside, much as it angered him. But he couldn't let his fickle heart get involved. There was no way he could mate with a human. He needed a strong Alpha female to be his partner, the co-ruler of his extensive Clan. Pretty little Lindsey Tate was a temporary bed partner at most, but he'd be damned if he didn't already want to keep her for much longer.

Lindsey moved toward the doorway that led to the rest of the house, escorting him up the stairs. Just where he wanted to go.

She showed him all the holes in the roof she knew about, but Grif knew from his own nocturnal inspection that there were others she couldn't see from inside. When they got to her bedroom, she tried to hide her embarrassment with laughter. She lived poor, but she was proud and he could respect that.

Shifters were proud folk too, but even though many of his kind had worldly success, they knew what it was to live wild. Hell, he had chosen the cabin in the woods over his family's spacious homestead as a place for his sister to heal. He knew the rest of the family understood. All the luxury in the world couldn't make up for the feel of the wind on your face or the soft loam of the forest under your paws.

His soft heart went out to Lindsey, trying to ease her embarrassment. She thought him a drifter and yet the pots on the floor of her bedroom still obviously embarrassed her. It was clear they were there to catch the rain.

"Any *pot* in a storm, eh?" She groaned at the pun and he was glad to see the tension in her shoulders ease a bit as she laughed with him.

"I try to think of the holes in the roof as skylights. Doesn't seem so bad that way."

Her smile was magic. His breath caught and held as he watched her gaze up at the clearly defined holes above them. The stretch of her graceful neck made him want to nip and suck.

"Well, I can understand wanting to be close to nature, but I guess when nature comes inside, things can get a little difficult." He glanced pointedly at the pots strategically placed under the various holes. "The good news is, I can fix this. No problem."

She turned to him then, a light of challenge on her smiling face. "Maybe so, but what is it going to cost me?"

He paused theatrically as if to consider, though he knew already what he'd say. He liked the flirtatious tone of her question and he decided to push her a little further on the path that he wanted so desperately to take with her.

"How about two tall glasses of lemonade, about twenty bucks for supplies and..." He moved in close, his breath rasping across her cheek as he bent low, "...a kiss."

He didn't wait for her answer, but laid his lips against hers, claiming her gently, not wanting to scare her off. He put his arms around her waist loosely, lifting his head for just a moment to check her eyes. He didn't want to see fear there and thankfully, he didn't.

She was with him. A partner in their kiss. Neither afraid nor appalled. Her warm gaze said she welcomed his overture and was as caught up in it as he was.

"Actually, I'd do it all just for your kiss."

His voice sounded low and dangerous as his gaze held hers at close range. He didn't see any fear at all reflected there, only a stunned sort of submission that brought out the beast in him. The cougar within raised its mighty head and snarled in triumph as he swept downward to take her lips again, seeking with his tongue this time to taste her tender mouth.

She tasted of sweetness and light, along with a wildness that had his inner cat screeching in delight. She was perfect in every way, though he didn't stop to think about how that could be. His cougar had found its mate and it wanted to possess and claim without regard for anything else.

He stepped back.

Whoa, tiger. She was human.

She *couldn't* be his mate. He knew that as sure as he breathed, but his cougar soul was saying otherwise, confounding him, and his feline instincts had never been wrong before.

It was something he'd have to think about. Hard.

He saw his own confusion reflected in her forest green eyes before she turned briskly away from him.

"Don't take this the wrong way..." Her voice was hesitant as she walked to the window, wrapping her arms around herself, "...but I don't want to get involved with you, Grif. Not with you or any man. Not now."

He wanted to go to her, to wrap her in his arms and never let go, but he was feeling some turmoil of his own. His head swam with thoughts he didn't have time or capacity, at the moment, to analyze.

"I'm sorry." He wanted desperately to go to her, even as he pulled back. "I didn't mean to push you, but you have to know how much I'm attracted to you. Won't you give us a chance?"

If he'd whined or begged she could have handled it better, but the stoic, deep tones of his sexy voice made her want to jump into his arms and never let go. Things had been set in motion though, things that she couldn't stop, and she couldn't get involved with anyone until it was over. But how to explain that to him? She had no idea where to start.

"Please, Grif. I just can't right now, but it's not because I don't like you. I *do* like you. Too much, it seems." She chuckled sadly and turned to face him. She didn't like the look on his face. His amazing golden eyes held confusion, tempered by a strong resolution that she feared would mean doom for her plans.

"I don't just like you, Lindsey. I want you."

The bald statement turned what was left of her insides after those hot kisses, to mush. She had to be strong, she reminded herself. Her task was too important.

"I'm flattered. Really." Somehow the smoldering look in his eyes made her mouth go dry. "But I just can't do this now. Please respect my decision."

He stared her down for what felt like an eternity, his gaze watchful but not condemning, questioning but not accusatory. Then his gaze shifted away and the fire in them died down.

"Okay then…" He looked away and a rueful grin stretched his sexy mouth. "Do we have a deal for the lemonade at least?"

She laughed outright. Tension gone for the moment, he was back to the lighthearted rogue she was coming to really enjoy.

"I'll do you one better. I'll provide a whole pitcher of lemonade and the money for supplies, but I think you're letting me off easy."

She moved to walk through the door past him, but his words slowed her steps.

"Well, you could always throw in a kiss or two to sweeten the deal." His tone was back to light and teasing, making her feel safe once more with him.

She decided not to rise to the bait as she made herself walk past him.

"I meant the money. Surely you should get something for your labor? I'm not a rich woman, but I can afford to pay you a little something for your time, you know."

She knew she sounded a little indignant, but she figured that was better than melting into a puddle at his feet. She swept down the stairs to the first floor, glad when he followed her into the kitchen. Putting the table between them, she poured more lemonade for them both and placed the glasses on the table.

He downed half of his in one long, sexy working of his muscular throat, then smacked his lips with a smile. Oh, how she wanted more of his hot kisses, but she just couldn't give in to his all-too-potent temptation. Not until her task was through... if she lived that long.

"Now don't take this the wrong way." He laid his big hands on the table, sitting across from her. "But I can see the condition of this place and I suspect you don't make too much at the diner." He held up his hands to forestall her indignant reply. "There's no shame in that, Lindsey. Just as there's no shame in me putting my time to good use helping you." He paused though his eyes warned against arguing. "You pay for the supplies and I'll do the labor. I expect nothing in return but that you let me hang around, bang on your roof and maybe spend a little time with you during the day as the work progresses. If I can't have your kisses, spending a quiet moment or two with you will have to be enough." The words *for now*, seemed unspoken, but definitely there.

A shiver coursed down her spine at the look in his eyes. It was possessive, sure, and dominating. Her mouth went dry at the intent she saw in his expression but there was also a noble kind of honesty there that warmed and puzzled her. Why would this drop dead gorgeous man want to spend time with her? She was just a drab little waitress with way too many complications in her life right now.

But she believed the look in his golden eyes. She believed in *him*. Somehow, this beautiful man really did want to spend time with her, even when she'd made it plain that he wasn't going to be getting into her pants anytime soon, if at all. It was amazing really, and what girl could refuse a sexy hunk like Griffon Redstone when all he was asking for was a little of her time and companionship?

She nodded without further argument and was pleased, though a little confused, by the triumph that washed over his face.

He moved back outside after draining his glass, resuming work on the generator, and she went back to her household chores. Okay, so her eyes drifted out the window to watch him more than they should have, but she figured he'd never know and she certainly wasn't telling.

CHAPTER THREE

Grif found her in the kitchen about an hour later, after finishing with the generator. She was bustling around, clearly a little nervous around him now. He regretted that, but knew it was for the best.

He'd had time to cool down and think through the haze of desire that surrounded him whenever she was near. He knew in his head it could never work between them. She was human. He wasn't. There was no sense at all in this unreasonable attraction he felt. It'd be better to just not get involved any further than he already was, no matter how his cock screamed for release.

But his *were* side had other ideas. His inner cat wanted to stalk her and pounce, pound into her until she never forgot him and mark her as his own. Never before had the two sides of his soul been so in conflict, and never before had he ever known a woman who could tie him in knots like this. Lindsey was special, and utterly confusing.

"When I come back tomorrow, is it okay if I bring my little sister with me?" He figured Belinda would just follow him anyway, so he might as well bring her along from the start. He didn't like her roaming alone in the woods, even way out here. She was too precious to risk. Plus, a little chaperonage wouldn't hurt. "Belinda doesn't talk much and I like to spend time with her when I can. She won't be any trouble to you. She can play in the yard while I work, if it's all right with you."

"How old is she?"

"Just turned twelve. Our mother died recently and our sister was killed a little over a year ago. Belinda's taking it all pretty hard."

He saw the compassion flare in Lindsey's lovely eyes and it touched something inside him. This woman was gentle and kind—everything he could have hoped for in a mate—but she wasn't *were*.

That was the deal breaker in the human part of his mind. How could he even contemplate getting involved with a female that couldn't share fully in his life and his heritage? What would his

23

Clan think? He owed it to them to find the strongest, most compassionate Alpha female he could find. A shifter. Not a human who would never be as physically strong or hardy as the people she would be expected to help lead.

And Lindsey was too innocent to use and then discard. He knew his own reactions too well not to realize that this comparatively frail, human woman had already touched something deep inside him.

She had told him in no uncertain terms that she wasn't interested. He should have been glad, but instead he was angry. He wanted her and couldn't accept the denial, though he sensed if he ever did make love to her, he'd want to keep her, and keeping her on a permanent basis just wasn't an option. Not unless he was willing to give up his Clan, his family...everything...for her.

Oddly, that thought didn't bring as much angst as it might have. Some small part of his mind was asking, *would it be so bad?*

Never before had Grif ever considered giving up the leadership role in the Clan and the company he'd built from scratch. Lindsey was making him think about all sorts of things he never could have imagined before meeting her. But could he really give up everything he had worked so hard to achieve? Just to be with her?

Grif didn't even want to think about it. He was very afraid the answer might be yes. The *selfish* answer. The one that didn't take into account how much his family, his Clan and his company needed him.

No. He couldn't do that to them. He owed them much more than that. And they still needed him.

Knowing that, Lindsey could only be hurt by him. Grif didn't want to be responsible for wounding such a beautiful soul, even if it was merely human.

"I'd love to meet your sister," Lindsey said, having no idea about his conflicting, confusing thoughts. "She can help me bake cookies if she wants."

There she went, being kind. She was almost too good to be true, but he'd take the offer of friendship for himself and especially for Belinda. That little girl needed some female company and Lindsey would do nicely, even if she was only human.

"I know for a fact that she loves cookies. If it's not too much trouble."

"It's no trouble at all."

He steeled himself to walk away without pulling her into his arms the way he longed to do. Turning, he made himself open the back door and walk through, but he couldn't help turning back for one last long look at her.

Their eyes met and neither spoke, both remembering the magic of their kiss.

"I'll see you tomorrow, Lindsey."

Lindsey watched him walk away, following his progress through various windows as he went back around to his truck. She lost sight of him momentarily as she moved toward the front window that afforded her a better view. The dappled light over the sheer curtains must have played tricks on her eyes because she could have sworn she saw a soft, fluffy tail disappearing into the truck cab just before he climbed in and shut the door.

Shaking her head, she watched him drive away from behind the curtain that hid her presence. She had to be imagining things, but darn if that man didn't confuse and confound her senses.

He was quite possibly the best kisser she had ever met. She knew she couldn't afford to get involved with him, especially not right now with the path she'd committed to following. She didn't know what the future held for her beyond the next few days, but once she finished her task—if she survived it—perhaps then she might be able to pursue a relationship. Whether it was with the mysterious and totally hot Griffon Redstone or not, remained to be seen.

She continued gazing absently down the lane long after he disappeared from sight. The man was a puzzle, and he was doing strange things to her emotions. All in all, she thought it was a good thing he was bringing along his sister when he returned tomorrow. She needed a chaperone. Desperately.

*

Belinda was a pretty child. Just on the verge of her teen years, she was tall for her age and lithe like a young colt, all legs and arms. Her hair was shiny with good health though she was shy beyond what Lindsey considered the norm. In fact, she didn't really talk much at all, but Lindsey did the best she could to make her feel more at ease.

After just a little coaxing, Lindsey had gotten the shy girl to help her bake chocolate chip cookies. Before long, Belinda seemed more at ease, though she still didn't talk a whole lot. She communicated with shrugs and nods of her head, her eloquent big brown eyes speaking volumes for her when she couldn't form the words.

Grif worked while they baked, but Lindsey sent Belinda to tell him when the first batch of cookies came out of the oven. She poured glasses of cold milk all around and shared the first, piping hot cookies right off the sheet. Belinda smiled happily and even spoke a bit with her brother's reassuring presence nearby. Lindsey was touched to see the closeness between the two, especially considering the great difference in their ages.

Grif went back to work whistling after devouring most of the first batch of cookies and the girls went back to work, pulling out the second batch and putting more in the oven. Eventually they began to clean up the kitchen and Lindsey was pleased to see the little girl's manners were as good as her brother's. She didn't squawk at having to help with the dishes and she even seemed to enjoy washing some of the pans and dishes they'd used.

Grif took more breaks than strictly necessary to scarf down more of Lindsey's fantastic cookies and get out of the hot sun. The work on the roof was moving along quickly and Grif was enjoying not only the satisfaction of hard labor, but the good feeling he got knowing that his work would help protect Lindsey from the elements.

He almost hated to see the task completed, but he'd dragged out the project as long as he could. The roof on the old house wasn't that large and patching the holes didn't take much effort. Most of the rest of the structure was sound enough, so he'd only had to replace the broken sections and that didn't take much time for an experienced carpenter like him. Especially not an experienced carpenter with the strength of the cougar within him. He worked harder and faster than normal men and with an agility that never failed to come in handy. He was especially suited to working at height, unlike some of the other *were*. Cats liked heights and handled the rare fall better than most other *were* species, except of course, the raptors.

Werehawks, eagles and the occasional owl worked the really high jobs, walking steel on the high rise buildings Redstone

Construction built from time to time. A little two story house like this was no big deal by comparison.

When he could put off the inevitable no longer, Grif ate his last cookie and took his leave of Lindsey. Belinda waved happily out the truck's window as they drove away from the run down house. For days afterward, Belinda talked about the things she'd done with Lindsey and repeated almost every story Lindsey had told her. It was good to see his little sister enjoying herself again, even in this small way.

In fact, both brother and sister were spending more time in their human forms than in their fur since meeting Lindsey. Grif took it as a sign that maybe the deep grief and sorrow was starting to lift. Belinda had other things to think about now—a new friend in Lindsey—and for his part, Grif was spending a lot of time focused on the human woman as well. She haunted him. Her scent thrilled him and even the memory of her soft voice and kind words made him want to be near her.

The roof might be fixed, but Grif still found reasons to stalk the area around Lindsey's cabin. He knew she was protected from the rain, but who would protect her from those wolves? They wouldn't just let it go, whatever it was that was bothering them about her.

So he crept through the woods around her cabin in the evening, prowling up on her roof and around her yard, hoping for a glimpse of her. He found himself eating at the diner more often too, and he brought Belinda into town with him. His sister enjoyed seeing Lindsey, though she still didn't speak much in public. Still, he could sense the walls she'd built around herself beginning to weaken. It was a good sign and one he'd been waiting months to see.

*

Lindsey was toting wood from the old shed at the back of the property into the house late one evening the following week when she heard the first howl. Dropping the wood, she moved as quickly as she could toward her back porch, but was caught in the open as wolf after wolf padded silently out of the forest and headed straight for her. There was an intelligence in their eyes and a logic to their movements that was not quite wild. She'd bet her last dime that they were all werewolves.

They surrounded her, their bared fangs menacing, their canine mouths snarling in a way that put fear into her heart, but she couldn't let them see it. She had half expected something like this since the incident in the diner last week. The Pack had done all they could to make her feel unwelcome and told her outright to leave. It only made sense they'd try to scare her off in their wolf forms as well. She just hadn't expected the entire Pack to show up.

She figured she could have handled one or two wolves. She would have been scared to death, but she had some nebulous thought about fleeing into her house. But there had to be at least twenty huge werewolves confronting her—ringing her—closing in on her from all sides. There was no chance of escape. No way out of this unless they *let* her out of it. She had been stupid to think she could handle such predatory beings.

"Okay, I got the message," she shouted with some bravado. She couldn't let them see her very real and nearly debilitating fear. "You obviously don't want me here, but I've got a promise to keep and I'm staying until I keep it. After that, I'll be out of your hair and off these lands permanently. You'll never have to see me again, but I have to do what I have to do first."

A huge wolf, obviously the Alpha male of the Pack, judging by his size and clear dominance, separated from the rest and stalked forward to face her. His teeth were bared menacingly. She couldn't back up. First, it would show her fear, and second, it would only put her closer to the wolves behind her. She was between a rock and a very hard, not to mention sharp, set of teeth.

The Alpha paced closer, his eyes glinting hard at her. She held her ground as best she could. The ring of wolves was closing in. Slowly now, they stalked her.

"If your aim is to scare the hell out of me, you've succeeded. You can knock it off now." She tried for bravado and fell far short. The growling of the wolves grew louder and the Alpha snapped his jaws mere feet from her.

Suddenly there was a screech and something golden and fast moved between her and the wolf. It was a cougar, she realized with alarm as the enormous beast put itself between the Alpha werewolf and her trembling body. The wolf moved forward, confronting the cat. It growled menacingly and the giant golden cougar unsheathed wicked claws, swiping the air in front of the wolf's snout. The wolf jumped back. It sat on its powerful haunches and looked from the cat to her and back again. The cougar's message had clearly been delivered.

Reluctantly, the wolves left. The huge Alpha male departed last of all, watching over his Pack's retreat until only Lindsey and her unlikely rescuer remained. The big cat turned its glowing eyes on her with cunning intelligence. She could barely believe what just happened. She was speechless.

Lindsey tried to move, to turn and go back to the safety of the house, but her legs just wouldn't support her. They wobbled and with a small cry, she landed on her butt. The cat hadn't moved, she was relieved to see. His head cocked to the side, watching her as she hugged her knees to her chest and drew shaky breaths.

She held the big cat's gaze, not knowing or caring that it might be some kind of confrontational gesture. The cougar simply mesmerized her. His eyes were dark rimmed with golden irises. His expression was almost compassionate, if she had to put a name to it. And he'd come to her rescue, no doubt about that.

"Thank you," she finally whispered, smiling a bit to see his ears perk up toward her.

He stood and moved ever so slowly toward her. He glided, she thought, watching his feline grace.

He was the largest cat she had ever seen in her life. Easily two hundred pounds, he was bigger than any mountain lion she'd ever heard of. No wonder he'd scared off the wolves. This giant predator was intimidating as hell, but she felt no animosity from his slow movements toward her. He wasn't stalking her. Just moving slowly. If he wasn't so big, she would almost have said he was trying to be gentle with her. Or at least cautious.

She felt little fear, and even if she could have gotten her knees to support her in that moment, she doubted she would have retreated from his cautious advance.

He came right up to her, those glowing eyes pinning her with every sinuous, slinking step he took. He seemed almost pleased when she didn't move away from him, and with her heart in her throat, she saw the great head with its massive pointy teeth moved to her shoulder, butting her gently. Her hand came up and she stroked behind his ear tentatively, gratified when she heard and felt the incredibly loud purr coming from deep inside him. His big head moved down her body, nuzzling her breasts and sliding across her neck as if in affection. She laughed as his soft fur tickled her tender skin and he purred even more loudly.

It was a magical moment, she knew. This wild creature was stroking her with his skin, purring in her arms, accepting her caresses. It wasn't normal, that was for sure, but then nothing about any of this was normal.

"Did my grandfather send you from the land of spirits?" Wonder sounded through her shaky voice as she rubbed her cheek over the back of the cat's neck, reveling in the softness of his thick fur.

His head came up and his magnificent eyes pinned her once more. He held her there for a timeless moment, then the tip of his great pink tongue came out to lick across her lips, shocking her with the feline kiss. His tongue was raspy—like sandpaper over velvet—and she knew he probably could have hurt her with it, but he was gentle, touching her lightly and with great care.

"Is that a yes?" She giggled as he repeated the motion on her neck. Her skin was a little sweaty and she guessed the cat liked the salt of her skin. "Or are you someone's abandoned pet, to be so protective and familiar with my kind?" She stroked his fur more boldly now, taking comfort from his panting breaths on her neck and his powerful paw planted lightly in the middle of her chest, framed by her large breasts. The wicked claws she'd seen were nowhere in sight, and she reveled in the feel of his great strength held in check, seemingly to soothe her.

It was odd, that sensation she got from this huge male cat. She felt like he was comforting her, that he'd known exactly what he was doing as he'd protected her from the wolves. That she somehow belonged to him and vice versa.

She scratched his ears and stroked her hands down his big body, relieved when he removed his weight from her chest, to plant his huge paws on either side of her trembling body. She let the torrent of tears loose as she sank her face into the fur at his neck, letting the terror of the past minutes reign for a wild moment, allowing herself to release the fear and feel the comfort his strong presence brought her. He remained still while she cried, his long tongue nudging her neck and teasing her hair as if in comfort, as he allowed her to cling to him in a most un-cat-like manner.

She didn't know how long she sat there, her face buried in the soft fur of his throat when the tone of his purring changed from something that sounded like comfort to something more intimate.

She had no idea why she thought that, but the odd notion made her chuckle as she drew back, wiping ineffectually at her eyes. Moments later, she felt his rough tongue swiping at her cheeks too, licking the salt of her tears. It was rough, but his touch was light.

"You're a good mountain lion." She kissed the soft fur of his brow. "I don't know what I would've done if you hadn't come to my rescue." She scratched behind his ears as she moved back to look into his eyes. "Thank you, big kitty, I owe you one."

He made a noise deep in his throat that made her jump, but after one last, long, gentle lick, he moved his paws and let her up. She was still wobbly, but the big cat was there, letting her lean on him for support as she made her way back to the house. When he stepped up onto the porch with her and gave every indication of coming right inside, she stopped him. She liked the cat, but having a wild, two hundred pound mountain lion in her house seemed like a dangerous proposition.

"Sorry, big kitty, I doubt you're domesticated and I have enough work to do in that house without any further wreckage. But I'll get you a bowl of water and maybe I have a steak or something from the fridge?" She shook her head with a bemused smile as she wiggled around the screen door, not letting the cat in. "I'll see what I have for you," she promised as she watched him settle on his hind legs as if to wait for her return. His long tail swished lazily from side to side, making her grin again. There was something about this big cat that was quite amazing. He didn't act like any wild animal she'd ever seen.

She watched him as he waited with seeming patience for her. Returning moments later, she held a big metal mixing bowl filled with water and a thick steak she'd intended for dinner. It was raw and only slightly cold from the fridge but the cat bit into it happily when she offered it to him on a thick earthen ware plate. He lapped at the water too, as if he was truly thirsty and she sat down on the step to watch him with wonder.

For his part, Grif was enjoying being so close to the woman who had captivated his senses. Seeing her threatened by that Pack of curs angered him enough to challenge them all—in their territory. He knew he'd have some explaining to do about that when he next met the wolves' Alpha, which he knew would be soon. That arrogant SOB would probably be knocking the door off his cabin as soon as he returned, but this was more than worth it. Even if she didn't realize the beast she cuddled and scratched and let paw her all over was more than just a 'big kitty,' as she'd been calling him. And damn him, if he didn't get a kick out of that too.

Protecting her had made him feel noble in the aftermath, but her tears had nearly broken his heart. The smiles she gave him now were much better to sooth his savage beast, which wanted nothing more than to pad into her home, up to her lonely bedroom and stretch out full length on the bed in which he'd watched her toss and turn deep in the night. He would change, and in his fantasy, she would welcome him with open arms. But this wasn't a dream. She didn't know what he was, and if she ever found out, he feared she'd run away as fast as she could.

Plus, there was the unforgettable fact that she was human. He couldn't mate with her, couldn't have her for anything more than a short fling, lest it break both their hearts. He knew he needed a cougar mate, one that could run the mountains with him and rejoice in their differences from humans. Though this human woman fired his senses in a way he had never before known, he knew it was damned difficult to have anything other than an affair with a human, often ending with heartbreak on both sides. He didn't want that for himself and he sure as hell didn't want that for her.

He finished the steak and lapped up the water she'd brought for him. He'd relinquished the game he'd stalked for the better part of an hour to come to her rescue and he was hungry enough to eat the cold meat with thanks for her thoughtfulness. Licking his chops clean, Grif turned back to her, boldly rubbing his head against her breasts as she sat on the steps of the porch. He lay down, putting his head in her lap, enjoying the caress of her hands as she stroked his head and belly. He was aroused by her touches, but he'd be darned if he'd scare her away. It was delicious torture.

"You're like a big pussy cat," she said softly as she rubbed his soft fur in her delicate fingers. "If I didn't know better, I'd think you were human. But grandfather never mentioned shapeshifters that could take the form of mountain lions. The werewolves are bad enough." She shook her head as he turned in her lap to search her eyes, but she was looking into the distance, as if in memory.

He was shocked. She knew about the wolves. She knew about shapeshifters. She knew!

But she didn't seem to want to admit even to herself, that he could be the very thing she seemed to fear. He licked her throat, drawing her attention back to him.

She smiled and stroked his head back down to her warm lap. He loved the smell of her and he loved burying his nose against the seam of her jeans, fragrant with her woman's scent. If possible, he became more aroused than he already was. He shifted his long body on the porch, hiding his state from her as best he could.

"Yes, those wolves were scary, weren't they? They don't want me here and they've let me know it as men and now as wolves, but I'm not leaving. I promised my grandfather," she said, her voice choking as she seemed on the verge of tears again. "I know what I have to do." Nodding, she seemed to firm her resolve. "And perhaps you were sent to help me. Grandpa always said my Spirit Guide was a mountain lion. And here you are. Now I know I'm on the right path."

He wanted to argue with her, but he couldn't change in her presence. She wouldn't accept the truth now, he could tell. Perhaps she never would be able to accept the truth about him. Though she seemed to understand the werewolves' nature, she was clearly repulsed by it, as if it was somehow distasteful. That didn't bode well for their future interaction. He knew he would never be able to keep her in the dark about his dual nature if they made love. He would slip somehow and she would know—and probably run screaming from the room, never to return.

He stood, not looking at the pain in her eyes as he removed himself from the porch and stalked out into the yard. He couldn't play this game any longer. It was just too painful. He turned once to watch her for just a moment before he slipped into the woods. She was watching him, a look of heartbreak on her lovely face, but he knew he had to leave her. She would never accept what he was, and he had an irate Alpha werewolf to confront. He would protect her as best he could, but she would never know what he was. Never know what they could share.

He stalked angrily into the woods and broke into a run. He needed to burn off the regret he was feeling with a good run before he faced the Alpha that was undoubtedly waiting for him at his cabin.

CHAPTER FOUR

"Just what the hell did you think you were doing, Redstone?" As expected, the Alpha werewolf was there, stalking Grif as soon as he set foot near his small barn. He shifted to his human form as he moved into the stall where his clothes waited, trying for nonchalance.

"I was protecting my woman," Grif answered shortly, facing the other man as he pulled on his snug T-shirt. "I marked her property. You should have respected my claim."

The werewolf growled. "I saw your mark, but this is Pack business. Not yours. We've asked her to leave."

"Why?" Griffon went on the offensive with the big male wolf. "What'd she ever do to you?"

Logan cursed and backed down, surprising Grif. "It's complicated. And I repeat—it's Pack business."

"It'll be my business if you go after my woman again." Grif showed him a cat could growl just as well as a dog.

"She's not your mate." He threw back at him. "She's human."

Grif shook his head. "I know that, but she's mine. For now." He cursed at the wolf who made him face the impossibility of the connection. "She's mine."

"Look," Logan seemed to want to be reasonable about this, "I don't know how it works for you cats, but I've heard your kind like to play around a bit before you settle down."

"And your kind doesn't?" Grif accused with a salty grin.

Logan nodded. "Point taken, but when we mate, we do it for life. I've seen a few of my kind try to do that with humans, and it almost never works. Don't make that mistake here."

"I appreciate the advice, Alpha, but I don't think this is really any of your business."

"The Pack doesn't want her here."

"Why the hell not?"

Logan didn't like the challenge, Grif could tell, but there was a growing respect between the two strong men, perhaps even the beginnings of an odd kind of friendship. "Her grandfather helped one of my Pack members leave. He made it possible for her to be with her human lover."

Grif looked confused. "So what's the big deal? He helped a romance along. While your Pack may not have approved it's no reason to hold a vendetta against his granddaughter."

But Logan shook his shaggy head. "You don't understand. Her grandfather was a Shaman. A powerful one. He did something—" Logan paced the small confines of the aisle. "He took away her ability to shift. He made her human."

"What?" Grif was floored by the revelation. Utterly stunned.

"You heard me." Logan glowered, clearly upset by the very idea.

"I didn't know that was even possible," Grif whispered as if to speak it aloud would confirm the reality of the werewolf's claim.

"Neither did our Pack's elders. This all happened when I was still a cub, but I remember it and I remember the curse they laid on the Shaman and his line. I have to uphold it now that I'm Alpha."

"All right," Grif finally agreed, his agile mind working swiftly. "I understand your position, but Logan, consider this. She's told me more than once that she's here for a reason. Her grandfather gave her some kind of mission before he died and she came here to see it through. I think perhaps the old man sent her to make amends, if that's at all possible. The least you could do is hear her out. See what she has to say."

The Pack leader stepped from the barn and stopped abruptly, faced with a small, growling female cougar.

"Friend of yours?" he asked the man behind him dryly.

Grif stepped around him and bent to the female cub. "Kitten, I told you to stay inside while I was gone." She licked his face, trying to see around him to the big man behind, but he pushed her soft muzzle away. "Go inside. I'll introduce you to the Alpha when we're done talking."

Grif watched her scamper toward the house, then turned back to the male wolf. "My little sister has been through hell," he said shortly, fiercely, brooking no argument from the other male. "My mother and older sister were both murdered within the past year. She found our mother's body. Skinned. Belinda rarely speaks, and if you say one thing wrong to her, I'll rip your face off."

"Fair enough." Logan nodded once, compassion in his eyes. "I don't hurt cubs of any species. And I'll tell the Pack to look out for her in case she wanders off alone again."

Grif eyed him for a long moment before relenting. "Thank you, Alpha. That will put my mind somewhat at ease." Grif started toward the snug cabin. "Might as well come in for a drink. Apparently baby sis wants to meet you, and maybe rejoin the world again. It's a good sign."

The two males walked companionably toward the house, both resigned to the troubling matters of their families and female complications.

*

Grif couldn't stay away from Lindsey. Not after the confrontation with the wolves. So when he returned to the little house in the woods the next day, it was in his human form. He had to talk to her. He had to see for himself that she was all right.

He found Lindsey hard at work out in back of her home, building something. He wasn't quite sure at first what the little domed structure was supposed to be, but as she saw him she smiled and straightened, and he plain forgot about the little building completely.

In cutoff denim shorts that showed off her long, lean, lightly muscled legs to perfection, Lindsey made his mouth water. The little cropped T-shirt that outlined her full breasts sped his pulse rate right along too.

"What do you think?"

"Pardon?"

"What do you think of my carpentry skills—or lack thereof?" She beamed a smile at him, pointing vaguely to the structure that was taking shape behind her, but he couldn't look anywhere but at the mouthwatering sight of her beautiful body, displayed so innocently.

He growled low in his throat, still far enough away that she didn't hear as he stalked toward her, trying desperately to focus on something other than the fact that his jeans were getting tighter by the second in the crotch area. He knew he wouldn't be able to hide his response from her, so he didn't bother. Let her know how much she turned him on, he thought. It might be the start of something explosive.

And he liked playing with dynamite.

He saw her eyes widen the moment she noticed the hard ridge in his pants. She blushed prettily and turned away to look at her little building, but he could scent the instant arousal that dampened her panties as he neared. He had to touch her. Suddenly, feeling her soft skin was the most important goal in his life.

Coming up alongside her, he put his hand casually on her back, stroking upward to cup the back of her neck, thrumming his fingers over the sensitive skin there as he toyed with the tiny hairs on the back of her neck. He crowded her, but she stood her ground. *Good girl.*

He could feel her body's response as her pulse rate increased under his hand and her temperature rose. Her scent was driving him wild. This woman was hotter than hot, and he wanted her. Bad.

"What is it?" He forced himself to speak casually, allowing his gaze to roam over the bare bones of the structure. She had used long branches to form a large dome of sorts.

She tilted her head, examining her work. "Well, it's supposed to be a kind of sweat lodge, but I've modified the design a little so I can manage it myself."

"Looks like you've made a good start here, and it should be sound enough, though you could probably use another support branch just through there." He pointed to the weak spot and she nodded gratefully.

"I think you're right." She tilted her head up to look at him with a teasing grin. "You ever built one of these before?"

He chuckled low as she turned, forcing his hand away from her nape. "No, I can't say I've ever built a Native American sweat lodge, but I have done construction now and again."

How his brothers would laugh to hear him describe the family business in such simple terms, he thought. Good thing they were all tied up at the moment, overseeing various jobs while he took care of Belinda. He had always been the closest to their littlest sister and they'd all agreed that as head of the family, he would raise her now that both their parents were gone. But first he had to give her some time away from the demands of the human world. He had to give her time to heal.

"Well, grandpa taught me this when I was little. I remember

him building larger sweat lodges from time to time, when he was conducting special ceremonies."

"Is that what you're planning?" He reached up to brush the back of one finger over her cheek. She was so beautiful she stole his breath. "Are you going to do some kind of shamanistic ceremony up here all by yourself?"

She smiled and ducked away from him. "Mmm, something like that." She headed toward the front of the house. "So what brings you all the way out here?" Her voice carried back to him as he followed after her, enjoying the sway of her hips in those wonderfully short shorts.

"Last time I was here, I noticed your porch needed some work. It's been bothering me that those loose boards could be unsafe. I don't want to see you hurt, Lindsey, out here all alone." His dark expression conveyed the deeper meaning of his words and his very real concern.

He heard her breath catch in her throat, her eyes widening like a deer in headlights before she got hold of herself. He liked that he could rile her.

"You don't have to do that, Grif."

"I want to. It would make me feel better to know that possible hazard was taken care of."

"I can't afford—"

He stepped right up and placed his fingers over her lips, leaving them there as their eyes caught and held.

"You don't owe me a thing, sweetheart. I had some extra wood in the barn and plenty of nails. My time is my own and I want to spend it on you."

She looked about to protest, but he only wanted her kiss. Bending, he replaced his fingers with his lips, licking away her words with his tongue. Delving deep, he thrilled to her little moan of pleasure as she gave in, wrapping her hands around his neck, drawing him closer. She kissed him back with all the longing he could have hoped for, matching him stroke for stroke, fitting her lithe little body neatly against his as if she wanted to crawl all over him.

He was hard with wanting her, but he wanted to take things slow. She was human. She wasn't used to *were* ways. For that matter, she had no idea what, or who, he really was. He'd have to curb his appetites as best he could or he might scare her off.

38

So he counseled himself to calm—as much as he could with her in his arms—and gentled the kiss that had threatened to turn from fire to inferno. Instead, he wrapped his arms around her loosely, stroking her back as his lips played with hers, their tongues twining and licking, frolicking in a lazy way as pleasure blossomed slowly through his system.

He'd never really kissed like this. He'd never really had a human before—or any partner that needed such gentle care. He liked it. He liked the challenge and the incredible payoff. He found he enjoyed the slow savor. The easy tingle in his blood. The lingering promise of more... If he played his cards right.

The end game firmly in mind, Grif managed to let her go by slow degrees. He rested his forehead against hers, both of them breathing hard for a moment while the sun shone down around them, warming everything in its path. It was an idyllic moment out of time. Something special had just happened here and he knew it.

"Are you okay?" he asked, hoping she was on the same page.

She smiled and made a little hum of agreement that set his nerves at ease and his body on fire. She was so damn sexy. Unconsciously attractive in a way he hadn't expected in a human. She was downright *hot*, but not in an obvious way.

"I'm fine," she replied on a breathy whisper. "It's fine."

He felt more at ease with her reply. She was all right with him kissing her. Maybe she'd be up for more...in time.

"Just *fine?* That's not exactly a glowing review. I may have to try again, just to up my rating."

She laughed and drew away from him so she could look up into his eyes.

"Fine as in, *oh, yeah, that was fine.*" She drew the word out, each syllable dripping with pleasure. "Not just *fine.*" This time the word was short, uninteresting. And her humor overlaid it all, warming him from the inside out in a joyful, gentle way.

"I see. Glad you cleared that up for me, but we're going to have to work on your vocabulary. Would you be up for me trying to improve my score sometime?"

She stepped out of his loose embrace and tilted her head, smile firmly on her luscious lips as she pretended to consider. "Yeah, I think I'd like that."

He couldn't help but reach for her again, but she danced out of his reach.

"Later," she promised. "I have work to do and I need some time to catch my breath."

He smiled with her, enjoying her playful attitude. He hadn't screwed up with the human. Not yet, at least. He'd been so afraid his natural intensity would frighten her. He was changing for her. Making himself wait. Trying to be gentle.

And so far, it was worth the effort. In a way, he thought it was making him a better man. One who put others before himself— which he did every day as Alpha of a large Clan—but this was different, somehow. This little human was teaching him things about himself that he hadn't known.

"All right then," he agreed, letting her go while he backed away toward the task he had come here to work on. "Rain check. For now." Their gazes met and the playfulness turned to a feeling of promise. A serious acknowledgement of what had just happened— and would happen again soon, if he had anything to say about it.

She nodded and he swallowed hard. He wanted her in his arms again. Now. But he pushed back the instinct of the hunter that lived within him. She wasn't running. He didn't need to pounce. If he did that, all he was working toward would probably disintegrate. No, he had to play the long game here. He had made his move, now he had to let time pass until he could repeat the action and take it further.

The cat in his soul prowled impatiently, but the man knew he would win in the end. She was already under his spell. If he continued to romance her and treat her gently, she would be his sooner rather than later. Whatever time it took to convince her would be well worth the wait.

Grif went around to the front of the house to fix the front porch while she continued working in the back. A little distance was in order, he thought, while they both came to terms with what just happened.

A couple of hours later he'd finished in the front and moved around to work on the back porch stair while Lindsey continued to build her sweat lodge. His gaze followed her and she couldn't help but noticing the tight fit at the front of his jeans. The man was built.

She thought about that kiss again and again as the day got hotter and he removed his shirt. He had the most amazing physique. Sleek muscles made him long and lean, not stocky. She loved the look of him, and from the way his gaze followed her constantly, she suspected the feeling might be very mutual.

It had been so long since she had experienced the kind of attraction she was feeling for this powerful man. He'd come to her defense in the diner, helped her out with the generator without expectation of anything in return and shown true care and love toward his little sister in a way that had touched her heart. He also had fire in his eyes when he looked at her and she was oh, so tempted to burn.

She dropped her tools and just looked at him, thinking hard.

The sweat lodge was almost done. She was going to perform the ceremony tomorrow night—the night of the full moon. She might not be alive the day after, if the Great Spirit demanded her life as payment for her grandfather's actions. Shouldn't she enjoy these possible last few moments in time with a man who attracted her like no other ever had? That couldn't be wrong, could it?

She wanted him. So badly. She'd wanted him almost from the first moment, and she could tell he wanted her in return. Oh, maybe not in any sort of long-term or permanent way, but she honestly didn't know if she had more than just this one day left. So why not spend a few of her hours with him? She could afford the time. The lodge only required a few more boughs and it would be done.

He must have felt her watching him because he dropped his tools as well and walked straight up to her. He pulled her into his arms and stared into her eyes.

"You shouldn't look that way at me, baby, unless you mean it." His breath teased her senses as his head lowered. "Do you want this, Lindsey?" He gave her a fleeting chance to say something before his head dipped to take her mouth with his, but didn't say a word. She wanted his kiss. She wanted *him*. And she knew he could read it in her eyes.

His kiss was hot and hard and she melted into him, flowing against his body as he pulled her close. He shifted backward a few inches to meet her gaze.

"Do you want more? Tell me now, kitten. Tell me no and I'll leave you be."

His eyes seduced her. His voice thrummed through her soul. She wanted him. She wanted this time with him, no matter how short it might be.

"I want you," she whispered, loving the way his eyes lit up with pleasure. And the promise of even more to come.

He reclaimed her mouth, kissing her savagely, squeezing her body closer to his. His arms felt so right around her, his embrace so warm. How could anything that felt as good as he did be wrong. She knew she was doing the right thing, even if they could only have this one moment in time.

Having Lindsey in his arms was like holding lightning. Capturing thunder. It was momentous and earth shattering. She turned him on like no woman in history.

She also made him want to be a better man—a gentler man. One who could claim a fragile, human woman and not scare her off. Grif made himself slow down. He definitely didn't want to frighten her. Even though she'd given him the verbal go-ahead, he didn't want to blow it. He was a gentleman. She could still change her mind and he'd have to live with that.

They were out in the open, groping each other like a couple of horny teenagers, but he couldn't stop himself. She felt too damn good in his arms. Her breasts were soft and full, pointed at the tips conveying her excitement in terms he could truly appreciate. Her skin was like velvet under his calloused fingers and he almost worried about bruising her. He'd have to temper his natural strength to be certain he kept her safe.

He would do anything he had to do in order to have her. She was all that mattered. Lindsey and the desire that sparked like wildfire between them.

He lowered them both to the soft grass, covering her body with his. She was so small under him, so soft and feminine. So perfect.

He was lost in her kiss, loving the feel and taste of her. The scent of crushed grass, wildflowers, the sawdust and tree sap that clung to her skin teased his nose. The scent of woman. Warm, perhaps a little dusty, and definitely aroused.

And the scent of...danger?

Grif lifted his head, his instincts taking over, breaking the moment of passion into one of confusion. He sniffed again, catching a faint hint of...something...on the wind. A dangerous scent. Predator. Familiar, yet...

He'd already lost it, but the threat was real. It made him stand, lifting poor, confused Lindsey up from the ground with him. He couldn't look at her. If he met her beautiful, troubled gaze, he'd be lost and her safety was too important to take any chances.

"Get inside, Lindsey." He put one hand around her waist, guiding her toward the back door of the house while he scanned the woods and tried to reacquire the scent.

"What?"

He couldn't resist. He looked down at her and damn him if he wasn't tempted to take her back down to the ground and fuck her like there was no tomorrow. But he couldn't.

If he gave into temptation, the predator he believed was out there might catch them unawares and then there really would be no tomorrow. She'd be dead. He'd be dead. No more passion. No more pleasure. No more anything.

He leaned down and kissed her. Just a quick kiss to try to wipe some of the hurt off her face.

"I'm sorry, kitten," he whispered. He couldn't explain the danger he sensed on the wind. She would never understand his instincts or why he trusted them so greatly. Hell, he didn't even understand why he was reacting so violently to such a small hint of threat.

Still… something was telling him to take this seriously and he'd learned over the years to trust that sixth sense gifted to him by the cougar that shared his soul. It might not make sense now, but in time, he'd bet understanding would come, as it had in the past.

"But—"

Bless her, she wanted to argue. Grif picked her up bodily, knowing she wasn't about to move to safety under her own steam. She didn't understand the imperative that was riding him. The *knowing*. Danger was out there, stalking them and he had to keep her safe.

He walked briskly through the backyard and up to the back door, pausing only briefly to open it with the hand that was under her legs. He bustled her through the door, depositing her on her feet just inside the small kitchen.

"What was all that about?"

Grif thought fast. He had to come up with some kind of explanation for what, to her, must seem like utterly bizarre behavior. Telling her the truth was out. What else could he say that might sound plausible?

"I'm sorry, Lindsey." He ran one hand through his hair in frustration. "This is happening too fast." It wasn't. He'd wanted to jump her bones from the moment he first caught sight of her—but maybe she'd buy it. "There have been some things happening in my life lately that make me want to take things slow. It's been a rough couple of months." That was closer to the truth. Life had been shit for months. The only bright spot had been Lindsey and his undeniable attraction to her.

Before meeting Lindsey, Grif was almost afraid his dick didn't work anymore. It hadn't been interested in a female in far too long, which wasn't exactly normal for an Alpha male in the prime of his life. He would've worried—if he'd had time to worry about himself during all the upheavals of the past few months.

Lindsey eyed him suspiciously, but she seemed to be willing to listen to his lame excuses.

"After the tragedy of losing my sister... And then my mom's murder... And poor Belinda. I'm sorry. I worry about any female that gets mixed up with me." Now that was true. Truer than he liked to admit.

Lindsey seemed to cave. She stepped close and put her arms around his middle, giving him a squeeze. His arms went around her out of reflex, and he basked in the hug of affection and sympathy she gave him.

"It's okay. I think I understand." She drew away and he had to fight to let her go.

She patted his chest in a comforting way before leaving his embrace completely. Her smile was still a touch confused, but he read acceptance of his ridiculous excuse in her stance. She was letting him go.

It was one of the hardest things he'd ever done in his life, walking away from her. Forget that. *He* was hard. And wanting. Desperate for her. But the cougar in his soul needed to protect and defend. It needed to stalk the stalker and discover what was waiting out in the darkness of the forest...watching.

Until the cougar's curiosity was satisfied, the man couldn't get satisfaction either. Grif sighed and left with a few last words of farewell. He had his phone out even before he heard her lock the door behind him. He needed help to keep his woman safe, and he knew just who to call to get it. Not the local wolves. No, this was a job for family.

"Steve, I'm glad I got you," Grif said into his phone as the call was picked up on the other end. "I need some help out here in Wyoming. It may be nothing, but I could swear I've caught the faint scent of Jackie's killer in the wind. It's happened more than once."

"I'm on my way," his brother, Steve, replied without hesitation. "How much backup do you need?"

"Let's keep this informal for now. Who else can you spare to come out here?" All four of Grif's younger brothers were supposed to be running different aspects of the family business and Clan while Grif was away, but he wasn't really clear on just who was doing what. He'd just trusted them to get the job done.

"I'll ask Matt. Bob's going to have to take on my work. Matt just finished the Wallace Towers job. As for Mag," Steve sighed. "He's been more away than here lately."

"All right. You and Matt. As soon as you can."

"We'll be on the next possible flight. Meanwhile, watch your back, bro. Timmons is dangerous. Just hang tight until we get there."

"I know, Steve." Grif shook his head. "It might be nothing…"

"But it might not." Steve's voice was very firm over the satellite connection. "Don't take chances."

"Hey, I called you, didn't I?" Grif tried to inject a little humor into a situation that could very well be prove to be deadly.

Timmons had killed their sister. He'd evaded the best trackers Grif could hire for months now. He was both skilled and treacherous—a very bad combination.

"I'm glad you called. We'll be there shortly." Steve's voice was solid and reassuring.

Of all the brothers, Grif and Steve were probably closest, not only in age, but in temperament and experience. They'd both served in Army Special Forces and had trained in ways, and with weapons, the other brothers had not. All in all, Grif was relieved that both Steve and Matt, their youngest brother, were on their way.

Once out of sight of Lindsey's house, Grif loped into the woods, on the trail of the elusive scent, but it was lost. Could he have imagined it? Was he losing his mind? This was not the first time he thought he had scented Bill Timmons's unique brand of evil, but every time he searched for the trail, the scent soon disappeared. It was entirely possible he was imagining things. He hated to think what that could mean to his sanity.

One thing was sure, he definitely needed backup. If he was losing it, someone would need to look after Belinda. If he wasn't losing it and Timmons really was somewhere nearby, he would need help protecting the women. Not only did he have to take care of his little sister, but now Lindsey, regardless of her humanity, was under his protection as well. He refused to let either one of them down.

Steeling his resolve, he headed for the cabin at a lope. His brothers were already on their way. As far as he was concerned after this last scare, the sooner his brothers got here, the better.

CHAPTER FIVE

When the cougar reappeared the next night as Lindsey was finishing up the sweat lodge in the backyard, she took it as a good sign.

"Welcome back, Spirit Guide," she said aloud to the cat. "I've decided that's what you must be. It's as good an explanation as any, I guess."

The cat just sat, watching her for a moment, and if she had to name the expression on his face, she'd call it amusement. But perhaps that was just her imagination. Cats were pretty inscrutable. Even the big ones.

He started to move around the ceremonial building she'd put together out of tree limbs and other greenery, as if inspecting her craftsmanship. She watched as he moved around the perimeter, sniffing here and there, then moving back to look at the whole.

"Grandpa told me how to do this, but except for that one time, I never saw it in person." She stood back from her somewhat lopsided creation. "How does it look?"

The mountain lion made a noise low in his throat that she had no way of interpreting.

"I'll take that as approval." She smiled and crawled inside the small structure, dragging some of the extra provisions she thought she might need later. Clean towels in a closed basket, jugs of water and fire-starting tools all went in and she took a moment to set things up to her liking.

She shouldn't have been surprised when the cat followed her inside, taking up a position across the ring of stones she'd made for the fire she would start later and just watching her.

"I'm getting this ready for tonight. Grandpa gave me very specific instructions. Tonight is the full moon. I'm going to start this fire at sundown and begin the ceremony he taught me before he died." She sat back on her haunches and surveyed the small environment she'd created. "It's been a long time coming, but

47

maybe after tonight, if I do this right, he can finally be at peace."

A silent tear rolled down her cheek, but she brushed it away, smiling.

"No time for the sentimental stuff now." She worked her way out of the small building. "I've got to get ready. And hope those werewolves leave me be long enough to get through this."

Grif followed her out of the small building, puzzled but willing to see where her actions might lead. He knew he'd bought her some time from the Alpha of the wolf Pack, so she'd probably have the time tonight to complete whatever odd ritual her shaman grandfather had committed her to do. But he knew he had to be there, watching over her. If she got into any kind of trouble, he would be there to drag her out of it.

Maybe he was her Spirit Guide, in an odd sort of way, he considered. He was watching over her in his fur. She was a small human woman, way out here alone, and attempting a purification ceremony that could be dangerous to large, healthy men. She needed someone to watch over her.

And he'd appointed himself her guardian. He'd come back tonight and sit with her, making sure she took care with her health. But he had some things to do first back at the cabin, namely getting Belinda to agree not to go anywhere tonight. She was roaming alone more and more and he didn't like it. She was too little and there were predators out there who didn't care if she was *were* or just a regular little cat. He didn't want to lose her too. So he'd tie her down if he had to, or at worst, he'd see if the local wolf Pack would let her run with them tonight.

The moon was full tonight, so they'd all be running. Maybe there were some werewolf cubs who wouldn't mind a werecat in their midst too much. She'd enjoy the challenge and she could always sprint up a tree if they got too rough with her.

That thought in mind, Grif left Lindsey and headed at some speed for the cabin. He had a lot to do before sunset, when he would return to watch over the little human woman who meant far too much to him.

At sunset, Lindsey entered the small sweat lodge she'd managed to construct. She was dressed ceremonially, in beaded buckskin that she'd made herself. The outfit had layers so that as the heat started to build in the small building, she could take off the shirt and long, split skirt that kept her warm and still be somewhat covered in a soft leather bikini-type outfit. It wasn't very traditional, but it was functional and her grandfather said it didn't so much matter what style she wore, so much as that it was hand made, by her own hand, of natural materials.

So she'd arrived at this rather unorthodox, but highly functional attire. Besides, no one would see her. Only the Great Spirit and It didn't care what you wore, or so her grandfather had told her. It only cared what was in your heart.

She shouldn't have been surprised, she thought later, when she entered the dim building to find the mountain lion already there, waiting for her. He sat stoically, across the ring that would hold the fire, staring at her in that very solemn way he had about him. His eyes were a gorgeous, bright golden light that tracked her movements. She'd never realized how a cougar's eyes glowed before, and it was almost mesmerizing.

"Good evening, my friend. Have you come to keep me company on my vision quest?" She sat across the fire pit and started working to get the blaze going. It was easy enough, since she'd preset everything earlier in the day. All she needed to do was light it up and wait until it caught, heating everything in the small building.

The cat didn't shy away from the fire. He just sat there, silently, watching all. The thought crossed her mind again that this cat was unlike any cat she'd ever seen, but that only confirmed in her mind that he was sent to be her Spirit Guide. He was a mystical cat, that was for sure, but she felt no threat from him. He was there to protect her, as he'd already proved, and she felt safe in his presence.

She began the ceremony, as her grandfather had taught her. It wasn't anything like the ceremonies she had witnessed as a child when she'd visited her grandfather and attended tribal gatherings. No, this was completely unique. A shaman's secret, passed down in her grandfather's lineage, now to her. She was the last of the line. The last one left who might possibly have the power to restore the balance her grandfather had unknowingly disturbed.

He hadn't been able to tell her what the outcome of the ceremony might be. He only knew, if she had the power, and the Great Spirit favored her, the wrong would be righted and the balance would be restored. Exactly how that would happen remained a mystery.

She was willing to risk whatever the Great Spirit might demand of her if it meant completing this work, entrusted to her by her grandfather. He'd impressed upon her the fact that this work was bigger than herself. Bigger than just their lives. It was a monumental thing that needed her selfless act to repair.

She began thinking of the chant she would perform and started to feel the heat from the fire as it warmed the stones. Normally there would be a fire pit outside to heat the stones, but since she was doing this alone, she'd had to compromise on the design. There was a chimney of sorts in the roof of her hut and though it did let some of the heat escape along with the smoke, it allowed her to breathe fresh air. She'd also created an intricate design with rocks around and over the fire that she put into use now. She would add water to the stones, creating steam, without dousing the fire. She was sort of proud of the design she'd come up with and was happy when it worked just like she'd hoped.

The steam began to gather in the small structure and she removed her buckskin top, reveling in the feel of the moist air against her skin. Her cougar companion moved around a bit, dropping his head to his paws, but stayed on his side of the fire, so she paid him no mind. He would bear witness to the ceremony. She took it as a good omen that her Spirit Guide would come to her in her time of greatest testing.

As the heavily laden air thickened even more, she took off the long skirt and bundled it up behind her. The air was charged with the power she was calling. It was almost time. She ducked her head to check the small bit of the sky she could see through the chimney opening and was gratified to see the moon full overhead.

It *was* time.

Breathing deeply of the heavy air inside her ceremonial chamber, she began the chant her grandfather had taught her. She called on the Great Spirit, the power without and within, and was amazed when she felt the energy gathering in a way she'd never experienced before. It was awesome. And it was more than she'd ever imagined.

The cat must have felt something too, because he perched on his front feet, his eyes alertly glowing out of the dimness. She felt more than his presence in the darkness, and she knew her chant had called forth the Great Spirit. Now she had to say what her grandfather had taught her and plead for divine intervention.

"Great Spirit, I seek your counsel, I ask for your help in righting the balance that my ancestor put wrong. I come before you now, in his place. I offer myself to your wisdom." She began to chant again, feeling the power grow in the small sacred space. If something was going to happen, it was going to happen soon.

Suddenly, she was hit with a blinding white light as she felt the bones in her body shift and change. It was agony.

It was ecstasy.

And it was totally unexpected.

The Great Spirit had acted all right. It had turned her into a wolf!

Wait. No. Not a wolf. She could hear them howling outside her shelter, but she couldn't understand them. Not really. But she could smell them. And she smelled their anger and their joy. They were summoned to this place to witness her transformation, she realized as the Great Spirit nudged her. The male cougar was still there too, but now she was looking at him through eyes that saw more than she had as a human. He wasn't just any old mountain lion. He shone with the Great Spirit's Light within his eyes as well.

He *was* a shapeshifter! She'd thought only wolves could share their souls with certain special humans, but here was proof that mountain lions could too. She could see it in the Light that shone around him.

She could smell him now in a way she couldn't have before. He was familiar to her. She knew him as a man as well as a cat, she realized, but she didn't have any idea whether she'd ever be able to speak again. She was in a cat's body. A cougar, she guessed, judging from what she could see of her...paws! And fur!

What she didn't know is if she was going to be a cat forever, or if she was also going to be some kind of shapeshifter. She had no idea how to change back—or if she even could. Right now though, she didn't want to change. She wanted to run!

But first she had to face the wolf Pack.

She'd be lucky if they didn't tear her limb from limb. They'd learn though—she had claws now. She wouldn't go down without a fight.

She braced herself as she prepared to leave the lodge and realized the male werecat was just behind her. He was going with her. Somehow, that gave her the courage she needed to face the wolves in her backyard.

She padded out on clumsy feet, not at all used to walking on four instead of two. It was amazing how quickly she began to feel at home in this body. She could already scent things she never would have imagined as a human and she could see in the dark.

She saw the wolf Pack ringing her, some with their teeth bared as they growled low in their throat. She also felt the male cat beside her, and his presence gave her strength as she stood in the center of the ring of wolves, waiting for their next action.

A huge, dark wolf strode forward to face her. The rest of the Pack stayed back, watching and waiting while the big male sniffed at her, circling her. The male werecat stepped back, allowing the wolf to inspect her and she had to hold back a snarl. No sense in antagonizing them until they acted, she thought with the part of her brain that was still undeniably human while the cat essence in her wanted to claw the dog that dared sniff so rudely at her.

The wolf completed his circle, then stood facing her. She felt the energies gathering and she watched in fascination as he shifted from wolf to man before her eyes. He became a very good looking, well built, very naked man.

"I am Alpha of this Pack." He appeared to be speaking to both the wolves gathered around them and the two cats he now faced.

Make that one cat and a very huge, very naked, Grif Redstone. She knew he'd smelled familiar! Grif was her Spirit Guide. Darn it all, when and if she ever changed back to human, she'd have a few things to say to that man.

"I've claimed protection of this woman before, Alpha. She is still under my protection." Well, that was news to her. No wonder she'd felt so safe with him. He really had been protecting her all this time.

"I'm aware of that, Redstone, but this is still Pack business."

Grif stepped forward to face off with the other man. "This is *were* business, Alpha. It affects all of us."

They seemed to be staring each other down. Finally the werewolf relented. "Judging by the look of her, you're probably right. Did she intend to become a cat, or is that your doing?"

Grif stepped back as the wolf-man did and shook his head. "That's the work of the Lady, Logan. She didn't consult me. And I witnessed it all. Lindsey didn't have any idea what this was going to do to her. Her grandfather set her on this course and even he didn't know what the result would be."

"Is she *were?*"

Her eyes tracked the men as they looked down at her, but she didn't know much yet about her new body. She tried to speak, but only a hoarse whimper sounded from her throat.

"Hell if I know." Grif looked frustrated. "You know how first timers are."

She didn't like the sound of that, but she trusted Grif Redstone in a way she didn't quite understand. He'd been her protector. She somehow knew he'd be her guide in this.

The Alpha sighed. "You'd better take her on a good hard run then."

Grif nodded. "I will. As soon as our business here is finished." His expression hardened. "You have any more complaint with her? She's made up for her grandfather's interference. She was more than willing to stand in his place. She offered herself freely, and this," he gestured to her cat form, "is what the Lady we all serve decided."

"A shifter for a shifter." The Alpha nodded. "It's fitting. Though I could've wished for another wolf to increase the numbers of my Pack."

Grif shook his head. "After all the history between you, would she really have been accepted in your Pack?"

The Alpha tilted his head and nodded. "You're probably right. The Lady knows what She's doing, after all." He stepped back and faced her squarely. "So. One more cougar in the world. You'll face no threat from my Pack, Lindsey Tate. Our trouble with your family is over now, for all time. The debt is repaid." He bowed his head, though his eyes never left hers. "Welcome to the woods."

With that, he shifted back into wolf form and bounded away, howling to his Pack. They followed him, barking as they went, disappearing into the moonlit woods.

That left her alone with Grif, who stood looking down at her, apparently completely comfortable with his nakedness. The human part of her mind appreciated his rugged masculinity and impeccable body. He was powerfully built and now she knew how he kept in such great shape. He probably ran through the woods all the time, keeping himself lithe, lean and sleekly muscular.

She felt a purr lodge in her throat and was surprised by the vocalization. He quirked a smile at her as he crouched down facing her.

"What am I going to do with you, Lindsey?" He reached out one hand hesitantly, then scratched her neck in a way that made her purr grow louder as she arched into his caress. She never could have imagined how good it felt to have someone caress your fur. "I know you want to run, baby. And we will. But I have to tell you a few things first." He stood to pace away from her and she followed, still a little clumsy on her feet, but she was getting more comfortable by the moment.

"First..." He ran a hand through his hair as he looked down at her. "I have to apologize. You've got to know that I didn't mean to deceive you. I didn't think you would understand if I told you I was a werecat. It's not something I go around telling people. And I have my sister to protect. I tried to stay away from you, but after the wolves gave you trouble, I knew you needed my protection, dubious as it is."

She tried to speak, but succeeded only in creating a yowling kind of noise that didn't sound very pretty.

"Ah hell." He crouched down in front of her again. "I picked a hell of a time to tell you this. Especially when you can't talk back." A smile quirked his lips. "Maybe that's why I'm saying it now, huh? So you can't argue with me and tell me what a jerk I was."

She licked his hand, hoping he'd understand. He turned his hand to caress her neck again and she thought maybe he did. He got to his feet slowly.

"Now, watch and feel the energies as I shift. Most of our young have years to watch the members of their Clans change and learn, but you have only tonight. Watch closely, Lindsey. You'll have to change back before morning, or you might be locked in cougar form for the rest of your life."

She perked up, worried now, but he shook his head.

"I'm sorry to have to tell you that. I know it's harsh, but it's the truth. The first time you shift is the most important. You need to know so you'll work hard at regaining your human form when the time comes. I'll be there with you, but you have to do it on your own. I can't do it for you."

She nodded her head up and down though the motion felt jerky and somewhat drunken in her cat form. He seemed to understand, nodding before he started to shift. She felt the energies gather, watching the way he started shifting—from his toes to the top of his head. She imagined he was doing it extra slow for her, so she could see every moment, but still it went by awfully fast.

She was a little shocked when he stopped after he'd changed almost all the way and reversed the process. She watched avidly, trying to store away her impressions of the process for when it came time for her to do it. He stood before her, human, huge and naked, and smiled.

"I almost forgot." He moved toward the opening to the sweat lodge and ducked in, dousing the fire as she watched. "We won't be coming back here until tomorrow at the earliest," he said as he came back out. "Anything in your house I need to do before we go?"

She shook her big head negatively, and he smiled. "Good. Now watch. Shifting takes up a lot of energy. I've been doing it for quite a long time, so I can shift back and forth several times a day with no strain, but when you first start out, shifting just once will tax you. That's why you have to get your first one right."

With that, he shifted form again and she watched, fascinated as the bones compressed and fur sprouted. His ears elongated and his hands and feet reformed into huge paws. He was bigger than any wild mountain lion, and so much more beautiful, he nearly stole her breath.

When he was completely changed, he vocalized something that sounded to her like *let's go*. He nudged her with his chin and she began to move toward the woods, watching the way he moved and trying to copy him. He went slow at first, letting her get a feel for her new legs and paws, but she was getting more and more comfortable the farther they went.

When they reached a moonlit clearing, he opened up with the speed and she followed behind, only a little bit slower. She exhilarated in the freedom and the speed she had in this form, running happily after him. He looped back and snapped at her heels playfully a time or two, making her laugh inside while her new vocal chords made some odd sounds that she couldn't quite control as yet. Her spirit was free in a way it had never been before.

CHAPTER SIX

Grif watched her run and knew she was experiencing the euphoria of her first change. It was something he remembered well from his own first time. It was a special time, but it was also a very dangerous time. If she couldn't change back before the sun rose, she could lose her human side forever.

And he would lose the human half of his mate.

For that's what he now knew she was beyond the shadow of a doubt. She was his. He'd known it from the moment he'd seen her in that diner and now the Lady had put the seal on her fate. She was *were* now. There was nothing standing in his way now that she was like him. He could claim her, mate her, and truly make her part of his Clan.

And he would.

If only she could change back to her human form and prove that she really was strong enough to not lose her human side. He'd bet good money that if anyone had the strength to survive this harsh change from human to shifter, it was Lindsey. More than just her own future was riding on it. *His* future was tangled up with this small woman, and she essentially held both their lives in her hands.

As she began to tire, he nudged her toward his cabin. He wanted her there tonight, where he could watch her. He thought Belinda just might be of some help too. Belinda liked Lindsey already. His little sister would want to help.

Lindsey was exhilarated, but tired when she first scented the wood fire burning in the distance. The smell of horses came to her on the wind and she realized they were nearing a human dwelling with a barn. Judging by the direction and distance they'd traveled, she guessed he was gently directing her toward his cabin.

She'd be glad to rest, and maybe get a drink of water. She was thirsty after all the exertion. She was a fit woman, but their run across the meadow and through the woods had exercised muscles she'd never known before.

When she saw the cabin, her human side was impressed by the snug looking place nestled in the hills. It looked spacious and clean, glinting with big windows and the chimney on the roof gave off puffs of welcoming smoke from the fire that danced orange reflections in the window panes of the living room. Really, the word *cabin* wasn't a very accurate description of the architectural dream she saw before her. It was more like a masterpiece. Two stories, with multi-level roofs, a porch and what looked to be very high-end construction. It was gorgeous.

Grif surprised her by striding right up to the door in his cat form, reaching up and hitting the special latch with one giant paw, and opening the door for her. He padded inside and waited until she cleared the door—tail included—before he nudged it closed behind them. He walked with her into the front room. Belinda was there, watching them with wide eyes.

The little girl sniffed the air delicately as her eyes widened. "Lindsey?" Her gaze shot to her brother. "Grif, what happened? Is that Lindsey?"

Grif padded over to his sister and nuzzled her hand, nudging her toward the kitchen area. She apparently understood his silent command because she took off for the kitchen, returning with a big pan of water a moment later and put it in front of Lindsey.

Lindsey was never so grateful to see a bowl of water than at that moment. Using her new, obscenely long tongue, she lapped at the water, but she was less than graceful. Belinda laughed outright, and the young girl's laughter was infectious. Lindsey made a sort of snorting sound that passed for laughter, she guessed, while she was in this form, and the girl laughed louder.

"Oh Lindsey, I wish you could see yourself. You're getting more water on the floor than in you." Lindsey was glad to hear the amusement in the girl's voice, even if it was at her expense. A moment later, Belinda reached out slowly to stroke Lindsey's cheek. "It's hard when you're new, I know. But we'll help you."

Lindsey stroked her tongue gently across the girl's hand in thanks as she giggled again. All this was worth it just to put a smile on Belinda's too-serious face.

Grif nudged his sister with his head, growling something that the girl apparently understood because she got up and went out of the room once more. Grif stood in front of Lindsey, being certain she could see him as he shifted back to human form.

He was naked again, his skin glowing with the reflection from the fireplace, making her mouth even drier. Lord, the man was built!

A worn pair of jeans sailed through the air, followed by the sound of little feet pounding up a set of stairs.

"I'll dig up something for Lindsey to wear too," Belinda called down from the top of the stairs as Grif tugged his jeans on, smiling a bit at his sister's antics.

"Don't mind the munchkin, Lindsey. She's thrilled you're here. And thrilled that you're cougar now, I bet. She's missed her sister and our mother." His face hardened for a moment as he reached out to stroke her back. "I know you're tired, but you have to try to change back now, sweetheart. It'll be easier if you do it now, before you sleep off the run. The longer you wait, the harder it'll be to reclaim your human half this first time."

She licked his arm, hoping he knew that she didn't regret a moment of this, even if she had to stay a cat for the rest of her life. She'd accomplished her goal and gotten more than she'd ever expected. The Great Spirit had been kind, letting her experience this freedom at least once in her life.

"Come on sweetheart. I know this is all new to you, but you have to try." He lay down next to her in front of the fire and stroked her back as he encouraged her to shift. "Picture it in your mind. Imagine your human body and will yourself to change."

She tried to do as he said, but her strength was fading fast. He moved in close to nuzzle his face into her neck and her ears twitched as he lifted up to whisper encouragement.

"I want you to change, Lindsey. I want you, Lindsey. Shift back so I can take you in my arms and show you how much." His hands stroked her, digging into her fur and making her purr. "Do it for me, Lindsey. Do it for us."

He continued to whisper encouragement and instructions as she gathered her energy for a last effort. It was now or never. She felt it. She didn't want to spend the rest of her life never knowing what it would feel like to be loved by this incredible man who treated her so gently, curbing his natural strength for her.

She gathered her energy and thought hard about what it had felt like to change that first time. She concentrated on her human form, willing it into existence and pushing the cougar down. It was odd, she realized, the cougar spirit was now a part of her, fighting for dominance, but she was stronger—just a fraction stronger, but it was enough.

Slowly she felt her bones begin to stretch and reform. It hurt like hell, but it was also a rapture that she couldn't quite describe. The fur receded and her paws elongated into fingers and toes, her feet and hands reforming as she felt the bones in her legs lengthen. Her face itched, but it changed along with the rest of her, the effort leaving her drained in a way she'd never been before.

She felt more than saw Grif pull a soft throw off the couch and wrap her up in it as he lifted her in his strong arms. He carried her up the stairs and padded barefoot into a dark room. Her eyesight wasn't as sharp as it had been as the cat, but it was definitely better than it had been before she'd changed.

She also smelled things differently, not as strongly as her senses were as a cougar, but definitely stronger than they'd been as a regular human. She scented him all over the room he took her to and she guessed it was his bedroom. He placed her gently on his bed, tucking her under the soft covers and placing a soft kiss on her lips as he straightened.

"I'm so proud of you, Lindsey. I know you're beat. Sleep it off. I'll be here when you wake and we can talk over everything that's happened." He stroked her hair back from her face as she fought the incredible lethargy that made it nearly impossible to talk. "Things will be different for you now, but don't worry. I'll be here to guide you through the changes, and Belinda will help too. You're part of our Clan now, kitten. Under our protection. You don't know what that all means yet, but you'll understand soon, I promise. I'll explain everything, but for now, you need to sleep. Don't fight it."

He crooned to her as she drifted off, but she didn't really understand much after that. She only knew she felt safer than she'd ever felt with anyone and more tired than she'd ever been in her life.

Light against her eyelids woke her the next morning. That, and a warm feeling at her back that was intense and enveloping. She moved experimentally and discovered that the warmth was a hard, muscular, bare male chest. Grif was in bed with her. And they were both naked.

Well.

She tried to remember what happened the night before and it came rushing back to her. She was a shapeshifter! She could hardly believe it.

She was lying in Grif's bed, naked, and she distinctly remembered him tucking her in after he'd helped her through her first change. He'd been so good to her last night, she remembered. He was really one in a million.

"About time you woke up."

The sexy male growl in her ear made her stiffen. She wasn't a virgin, but she also wasn't used to sharing a bed with a naked man all that often, and certainly not anytime recently. She shivered though she was plenty warm under the blankets with Grif as he rubbed his open palm over her bare breast.

"You're beautiful, Lindsey." He nuzzled her neck as he pulled her closer in his arms, running his hands over her body. She realized he was hard as a rock behind her, his erection finding its way between her butt cheeks as if seeking her warmth.

"Grif..." She knew she meant to say something important but for the life of her, she couldn't remember what it was when his hand skimmed down to tease between her legs.

"Mmm. I like the way you say my name, sweetheart. I've waited weeks to hear that tone from you."

"Weeks?" she squeaked as he stroked her clit.

He nodded behind her, rasping his stubbly cheek against the soft skin of her nape. "I've wanted you since the first time I saw you in the diner."

"Hey, you two!" Belinda's sweet voice piped from behind the closed door. "Are you going to sleep all day?"

He growled as Lindsey stiffened and tried to pull away. "Saved by the munchkin," he mused as he let her go. "All right, we have things to talk about. But later, you're mine." His eyes held the light of promise as she tugged the sheet with her, wrapping it toga-style around her.

"We'll see about that, Grif."

He towered over her as he stood, naked and hard, and oh-so-delicious.

"Yes, we will."

Belinda was ecstatic about the change in Lindsey. The little girl was more animated than she'd ever seen her when they joined her in the state of the art kitchen. As Lindsey saw the array of cereals littered about the table, she suddenly realized she was ravenous.

"I can make some eggs or pancakes if you'll show me where the frying pan is."

Belinda's eyes lit up. "Can you do sunny side up eggs? Grif always breaks the yolks."

Lindsey smiled. "I won't break the yolks if you don't want me to, okay?"

"Can you show me how?"

"You bet." She looked over at the silent man who stood in the doorway to the kitchen. "If your brother doesn't mind."

Grif's smile was intense. "Make yourself at home, Lindsey."

He padded over to the refrigerator and took out the things she'd need while Belinda showed her where the frying pan was. Together, the three of them made a huge breakfast of eggs, bacon, pancakes and more, laughing often as they collided in the small space around the stove.

Though Grif was doing it deliberately, she well knew. He crowded her, 'showing' her how to flip the pancakes just right by moving behind her and taking her hand in his over the handle of the pan. She giggled like Belinda when he tickled both their tummies, but the swipe of his hand across her butt where Belinda couldn't see, made her shiver.

She was wearing one of his shirts and a pair of old sweatpants that had a drawstring keeping the baggy things up around her waist. She looked like a ragamuffin, but she felt surprisingly good after the ordeal of the night before.

"One of the benefits of being a shifter is increased metabolism," Grif explained as they sat at the table, consuming huge piles of food. "We use a lot of energy to shift and of course, all the physical activity we get into when we roam."

"So you're saying I can actually have dessert and not have it go straight to my hips?" Lindsey chuckled. "I think I'm gonna like this."

Grif put down his fork and just watched her. "You really had no idea this was going to happen, did you?"

Lindsey paused and met his gaze. "I thought I was ready for anything when I started the ceremony last night, but I hadn't contemplated this result. Grandpa told me that the balance had to be restored, but I guessed that in the worst case scenario, I'd have to give my life in exchange."

"You thought you would die and you still did it anyway?" Grif sounded upset, but she didn't quite understand why.

"It was a matter of honor. I'd made a promise to my grandfather. And yes, if that's what was necessary, I was ready to leave this world, but was hoping there'd be some other way to satisfy the Great Spirit. I just never counted on this."

Grif started eating again, growling under his breath, but her hearing was so improved, she heard the low sounds, if not the actual words. Her nose was more sensitive too, as were her eyes, and it was an amazing experience.

"Grif's teaching me stalking skills now that I'm getting bigger," Belinda said cheerfully. "But you're already full grown. You should know this stuff already. Will you teach her, Grif?" Her questioning eyes turned to her big brother.

"Stalking?" Lindsey found it hard to accept, but something wild and new in her roared in the back of her mind. It felt right, somehow, if totally alien. She knew it was something she was going to have to get used to now that she'd been changed.

"She's part of our Clan now, munchkin. I'll teach her what she needs to know, and we'll look out for her like we do each other."

Lindsey helped clean up the remains of their huge breakfast, then joined Grif and his sister in the beautiful living room she'd seen only through her cat's eyes the night before. The room was fabulous, with large windows that let in lots of light. In fact, the whole house was lovely, and far more sumptuous than she would have believed a handyman could afford.

"Your house is gorgeous, Grif."

"You're probably wondering how a down-on-his-luck drifter could afford to build something like this, huh?" Grif chuckled as she reddened with a becoming blush of embarrassment. "This is our retreat, Lindsey. We came here to get back to nature and let our cats run. But this isn't the only place we live." He handed her a cup of coffee he'd brought in from the kitchen for her. "Right now our brothers are holding down the fort at the homestead and running the family business."

"Family business? What business are you in?" There was no hiding her curiosity.

Grif sat on the couch next to her, sipping from his own cup of steaming hot coffee. "We do construction."

Lindsey's eyes widened in shock. "Redstone Construction? That's you?"

Grif smiled widely. "Me and my younger brothers. Even Belinda will be joining the firm once she gets old enough, won't you, munchkin?"

The little girl bounded into an overstuffed chair near them, smiling. "I'm gonna run one of the crews, once I'm old enough."

He laughed, leaned over and tousled her hair. Lindsey was happy to see the affection between this brother and sister, so far apart in age, yet so close. She'd loved her parents, though they had died when she was still quite young. She'd missed having siblings, but after her parents died, she'd moved in with her grandfather and had a good relationship with him.

"There's a lot you have to learn, Lindsey, now that you're part of our world. There are rules among the *were* Tribes, Clans and Packs. We're in wolf territory here and we abide by the local Pack's rules while we roam their lands." He focused his attention on her. "You met Logan, the Pack's Alpha male last night. He said you were free and clear of any obligation to the Pack, but you might still have some trouble with them—unofficially. Not that they'd come right out and attack you, but they could make your life difficult in little ways."

"Believe me, I'll do my best to steer clear of them."

"Now that you're werecat, you're going to learn that you have to roam. It's not something you can deny. And when you roam, you will undoubtedly come across some of the wolf Pack. Which is why I don't want you roaming alone, Lindsey." He took her hand in his, claiming possession with his tight grip. "We're going to shift and go over to your house today. Then we're driving your car back here. I want you to stay with us for the time being."

"But I have to work tomorrow."

"Which is why we're getting your car today. You could take my truck, but you need your clothes and personal stuff and we can't drag all that back here in our teeth."

Belinda giggled and Lindsey had to smile. Things were moving a little too fast for her, but she knew he was protecting her. Still protecting her, as he had from the first. She was confused by all the changes and the startling revelation he'd been watching over her in cougar form for the past days.

"Why are you doing all this for me?"

He cupped her cheek in his palm, looking deep into her eyes. "I have to believe the Lady had a plan when She made you cat and not wolf. You belong with us now, Lindsey, and you'll never roam alone again."

How he wanted to kiss her, take her down to the floor and sink into her body. But there was much to do and his little sister was watching them. Belinda was taking Lindsey's change better than he'd expected, but she was still very dependent on him and he didn't want to do or say anything that might make Belinda feel threatened. He knew that Lindsey would be part of their lives now on a long term basis, so he had time to acclimate his females to each other without tugging anyone's tail—figuratively or literally.

He stood and began removing his shirt in preparation for shifting and Belinda followed suit, kicking off her clothes without embarrassment and shifting into the juvenile body of a young mountain lion. He saw Lindsey's cheeks flush and her eyes widen and noted that she hadn't moved a muscle from her seat on the couch. His hand went to the button on his jeans and he saw her start, looking from him to his little sister and back again.

"Munchkin, I think Lindsey is probably still a little shy about shifting. We'll be out in a minute, okay? Wait for us by the barn. And not one step farther kitten, you hear me?"

A little growl was his answer as he opened the door for Belinda who was still too small to reach the handle in her cat form. She padded out, wiggling her tail and he closed the door after her.

"Nakedness among werefolk is not the big deal it is among humans," he began, scratching his head as he approached her wearing nothing but his unbuttoned jeans. "It's one of the many things you're going to have to get used to, Lindsey. But you don't have to shift in front of others if you don't want to."

"Good, then you go ahead and I'll meet you outside." A spark of defiance lit her pretty eyes as he watched her.

He shook his head, smiling. "Do you honestly think you can shift yet without a little coaching? Remember, the first time you woke in your fur the change was done to you. You haven't done it yourself yet. It takes practice to learn how to do it efficiently and quickly. We don't let our young learn to shift alone. They are supervised closely, sometimes for years, before the adults will let them shift on their own."

"Dammit." She stood angrily, turned her back to him and began removing her clothes.

When she was naked, he came up behind her, grasping her shoulders and rubbing soft circles on her skin. She crossed her arms over her breasts and he had to smile at her stubbornness.

"Now focus on the center of your being, right below your belly button. That's where the change will start. Feel the pulse of your blood as it pushes through your veins. Follow the beat and listen to the rhythm. Think of the change, call on the beast that lives within you now." He stroked his hands down her arms, gratified when he felt a little bit of silk fur starting to ripple out from her soft skin. He started his own change, keeping pace with hers as his hands began to form into paws, the palms becoming pads that rubbed over her fur.

He had to let her go as she let the change overtake her and her spine changed. He held his own change back so he could talk her through, let her know what adjustments to make, but she was doing much better than he'd expected for a first-timer.

"Think of your hands and feet, sweetheart. Think of the soft paws that will eat up the distance from here to your grandfather's house and the way they felt last night as we bounded across the meadow." He was gratified when his words helped her refocus and her hands and feet were better able to support her slowly changing form.

She groaned and it came out half moan, half screech. "I know this probably hurts, but you'll get faster as you master this skill and it won't hurt nearly as much." He stroked the fur over her spine, noting that it hadn't completely reformed as it should just yet. He instructed her gently, coaxing her to pay attention to each small detail of the shift, stroking her though the painful parts, privately loving the soft feel of her fur against his partially turned body.

Finally, she was completely changed and he breathed a sigh of relief. Her eyes were clear and she was in control of the new, beast side of her nature. He let the cougar overtake him completely and let her watch how he changed, quickly and efficiently. She would learn by watching and by doing and he would be there, he vowed, at every step to guide her.

CHAPTER SEVEN

They bounded through the trees and meadow, eventually arriving at her grandfather's house. Grif and Belinda both carried small packs in their teeth that held a change of clothes.

Grif and Lindsey both went upstairs, leaving Belinda downstairs. She stayed in her fur, puttering around the lower floor and investigating. She'd be content down there for a while, Grif knew. The girl was curious about Lindsey and how she lived. She'd be fascinated by her belongings and the scents that still lingered and said so much about her and her grandfather.

Knowing Belinda would be kept busy for a while, Grif followed Lindsey into her bedroom. He shifted shape quickly, showing her how it was done once more and coaching her through her own transformation. It was a little quicker this time, though he could tell it still pained her, as it would until she mastered the skill.

He rubbed her shoulders, hoping to relieve the ache of the change, focusing his energy on her. But the feel of her skin under his fingers was slowly driving him crazy. She had pulled a sheet from the bed over herself as her hands reformed, but her arms and legs were smooth and bare, peeking out from the edges of the fabric. She was sleek and soft, and so feminine. She made his mouth water.

He knew he couldn't wait any longer to have her. He had to claim his mate. She had been raised human and he was pretty sure that would make this a little more complicated. She had no idea what *were* mating really meant and he had to teach her. But first he had to make her his. Now.

"Lindsey." His voice was a rough purr next to her ear as his hands tightened on her shoulders. He turned her to face him and it was all he could do to keep from pouncing on her then and there. "Lindsey, I need you so bad."

Her expression was temptation itself as she looked up at him and he thanked the Lady that had sent him such a woman. Her eyes flared golden for a split second, a sure sign of her excitement and the magic that still coursed through her. She wanted him too. Lindsey was his match in every way, it seemed, even if she was afraid of her new needs and abilities.

"Oh, Grif," she whispered, drawing him closer.

He crushed her mouth against his, kissing her deeply, keeping a tight leash on his inner beast. This first time, they had to do this as humans. Not only did she not know any other way, but it was important for his kind to establish the bonds that would carry them through life in human form before tempting their darker natures by mating in their fur.

He tugged the sheet out of her hands and let it drop to the floor as he pushed her up against the wall near the door. There wasn't a lot of time to do this, but he didn't think either of them needed much to push them over the edge. And he couldn't wait. Judging by her ardent response, neither could Lindsey.

There were no barriers between them. No clothes. No fabric. Just them and the love he thought they shared. For certain there was an amazing attraction. A deep sense of belonging to each other that he'd never had with any other female. He knew in his heart this female was the one meant for him and he hoped she realized it too. If not now, he'd spend the rest of his life making her believe it.

But right now, he couldn't wait. Not one minute longer. His hands roamed over her body, loving the way she raised one leg to rub along the outside of his hip. She squirmed and moaned softly as he dipped his fingers between her legs to see if she was as ready as he was.

She was slick and hot. Everything a man could want. And she quivered against his hand as he slid two fingers into her tight opening. Her curved fingernails bit into his shoulders and he knew it was with pleasure as she kissed him even more fervently. She was in a frenzy of need and he marveled at how easily and quickly she responded to his touch. Truly, they were meant for each other. All she had to do was look at him and he was ready to take her.

As he was now. He wouldn't make either of them wait any longer.

Grif slid his fingers out of her, using that hand to guide his cock into the hidden place it wanted to go. The place it belonged. Now and for the rest of their many years together.

He slid into her in one, long, smooth move, watching her

response carefully. She was tight, but slick. Ready but fragile. He didn't want to hurt her and he judged by her positive responses, that he hadn't. She was with him and hell, yeah! It felt really good. The best. Better than he'd ever dreamed.

And that was the last truly coherent thought he had before his body took over, slamming her up against the wall, taking her hard as she scratched his shoulders and back, trying to draw him even closer.

She moaned and nearly screamed, but Grif smothered her loudest cries with his mouth, wanting her sounds for himself. In the back of his mind, somewhere, he was aware they weren't completely alone in the house. Normally, he wouldn't have cared, but he didn't want to frighten Belinda with sounds she wouldn't understand and might possibly think were scary.

She wouldn't hear them up here unless they got too loud and even in his nearly mindless state, he somehow knew enough to keep control on the volume. There would come a time, he promised himself, when they wouldn't have to hold back, and he looked forward to making Lindsey scream with delight.

And then the crisis drew near and he pushed hard into her, loving the way she gloved him and writhed in his arms. She was a wildcat and he loved her. His mate!

She came a split second before he let go and came with a muffled roar. They were together in pleasure. They were one.

Grif held her against the wall for long moments while they soared to the heavens together, then began the slow plummet back to earth. He felt tears on his skin and he drew back to look at her, concern furrowing his brow. Had he hurt her?

But no. She was smiling. They were happy tears. Or perhaps tears caused by the overwhelming nature of their pleasure. He understood. He felt the same.

Never in his life had he ever experienced anything like making love to his mate. This moment would be frozen for all time in his memory. A milestone. One of the most joyous, solemn and sacred moments of his life.

"Thank you, Lindsey," he whispered, taking her lips in a tender kiss.

When he pulled back moments later, she smiled softly. "I think I should be the one thanking you," she joked in a mellow tone as she hugged him, resting her cheek against his chest. She fit so well in his arms. They stood there for long moments, basking in the joy of being together.

And then he heard a noise downstairs. And it all came back to him. Belinda was down there and they had things to do.

Grif groaned. "Much as I'd love to curl up in your bed and do that again, we have to get moving."

Lindsey echoed his groan, though in a more feminine version. Still, he could tell, the reminder of their responsibilities wasn't popular. He had to smile. She was a good match for him. Hell, she was his perfect match. And he'd spend the rest of his life letting her know how special she was to him.

They drove back to his cabin in her car, staying in human form. Lindsey had packed up and brought enough of her things with her to tide her over for a while.

Grif installed her in his bedroom and made room for her clothes and toiletries with very little fuss. All in all, she was left with this vague impression that he was taking over her life, but she couldn't complain. He'd been so good to her since the change. And his lovemaking...well, that was in a class by itself.

She couldn't bring herself to regret what they'd done in her bedroom. She was more drawn to Grif Redstone than she'd ever been to any man. He was like a dream lover—considerate and rugged. Powerful and yet careful not to hurt her. In short, he was amazing.

They made love repeatedly through the night and every time was a new and exciting adventure. He took her in the bed, on the floor, perched on the dresser, bent over it, and then he let her ride him. She'd never really done that before, though she'd dreamed about it.

He'd stopped her at one point, gazing deep into her eyes. She thought he was just about the sexiest thing he'd ever seen. His hands were on her breasts, squeezing in just the right way to send pleasurable sparks throughout her body.

"Your eyes are glowing, sweetheart," he'd said in that soft, sexy, growly voice he seemed to reserve for when they were making love.

"They are?" Her eye color was the furthest thing from her mind at the moment.

"It's magic."

"I'm not doing anything."

He smiled at her, in a playful mood. "It's okay. It happens sometimes. Right now, I think we have more pressing matters to attend to." He pulled her down and nipped her skin, just lightly, driving her temperature upward again.

She slid onto his cock, imprisoning him within her body, just where she wanted him. Then she rode him to heaven and back again, whimpering when she came with the most amazing pleasure. A pleasure only this man had ever brought to her.

He was definitely something special.

The next morning, Lindsey had dark circles under her eyes when she showed up at work. Ed didn't say much about it, for which she was glad. She went about her morning chores quietly while Ed did prep work in the back. Today was baking day in addition to all the regular stuff, so she probably wouldn't see much of him out front until around noon.

The breakfast crowd was typical and Lindsey didn't have a lot of time to think about the amazing events of the past day or two. Toward the end of the rush, some young werewolves came in and sat down at the back of the room. They were adolescents, barely out of their teens. She could smell them now. Her senses were so amazing. She could smell things she had never noticed before.

Even the food had taken on new, sensory delights as she served it. Ed was a good cook and every plate she served smelled it.

The wolves hassled her, making her feel unwelcome, as usual. Apparently nothing had changed in regards to how the wolf Pack felt about her presence in the area. She was a cat now, though, and her inner cat was snarling and ready to hiss at the dogs. Ready to claw.

That was something she hadn't expected. Up 'til now, the cat that now shared her soul had been surrounded by others of its kind. It had felt welcome. Faced with the wolf shifters in human form, her cat arched its back in alarm within her soul. At least…that's what it sort of felt like. It was hard to describe accurately, but the cat did *not* like these inferior wolves messing with her.

Everything changed though, when the door opened to admit a familiar figure. Logan, the Alpha werewolf stalked into the place and sat by himself at the counter. She went over to serve him coffee and her inner cat seemed to recognize him as an equal. It was wary, but willing to give him a chance to prove his intentions.

They exchanged greetings and she served him a cup of coffee, passing his order back to Ed, then going back to her regular duties. The last of the breakfast crowd was on their way out, leaving only the table of young werewolves and their Alpha at the counter.

When she went back to the table, predictably, the young wolves started to hassle her again, complaining about food that was perfectly prepared—and they all knew it. She wasn't taking any of their shit anymore and was about to give them a piece of her mind when a large shadow loomed up behind her.

A growl sounded low, over her shoulder. She turned to look and Logan was there. He'd moved silently from his spot at the counter to back her up. He was growling at his Pack members, not at her.

"Apologize," he said in a low, menacing tone.

One by one, the young wolves gulped and said they were sorry to her. Lindsey could hardly believe it.

The youngsters got up, giving her more than enough cash to cover their bill and left the diner without another word. It was the human shaped version of slinking away with your tail between your legs and she would have laughed if she wasn't so surprised.

Only the Alpha remained, standing at her side.

"I'm sorry about that, Miss Tate. Please let me know if you have any other problems with members of my Pack and I'll take care of it."

"I appreciate it, Mr. Logan, but you can warn the miscreants in your Pack that I now have claws of my own and unless they want to feel them, they'll be civil." Lindsey had had just about enough of the wolves' attitudes. She'd done everything in her power to fix the debt between her family and these folks and it still didn't seem good enough for some of them.

Logan laughed at her unexpected show of spirit. "Damn, the Lady really knew what She was doing when She made you a cat. You can hiss with the best of them, can't you?" Her eyes narrowed but he didn't appear intimidated. "And Logan's my first name. You can drop the *mister*—or if you want to be formal, you can call me Alpha."

She nodded tightly. "I don't know all the protocol yet, but I'm trying to learn."

"That's okay." He held up one hand, palm outward in a show

of peace. "I'm not criticizing. I'm well aware of the drastic change that has been forced upon you, and I, for one, think you've handled it with grace." His genuine smile warmed her a little. "If you have any questions your cougar friends can't answer, feel free to give me a call, okay?"

He extended a hand in friendship and she took it after only a moment's consideration. He seemed genuine and her newly enhanced senses couldn't detect any untruth, but then she didn't really know if she'd be able to smell that kind of thing from another werecreature. She guessed she'd learn in time.

She felt a tingle when she shook his hand, but she had no idea what it could mean. His eyes sparkled down into hers and he winked before he turned and left, taking some of the sizzling energy out of the room with him.

Ed called from the back door as he returned shortly thereafter and the bustle of the lunch crowd took her mind off the earlier encounter with the wolves. She worked straight through until after the lunch crowd cleared out and her shift was finally over. A few more of the wolves had come in but they had been quiet and caused no trouble for her.

It amazed her how easily she could scent a wolf now when she'd had no idea that so many of them visited the diner on a regular basis before. She had been pretty much surrounded by them before, and never knew. It made her realize there was a whole separate world out there she had only known the slightest bit about, and that idea intrigued her. She knew she had a lot to learn, but she had always been a good student.

She drove to her grandfather's house after work, intending to spend the night there, even though Grif expected her to stay at his place. But she needed some space. After the disturbing emotions of last night and the amazing happenings of the past few days, she needed to gather her wits and that wasn't something she could do anywhere near Grif's incredibly distracting presence.

She should have known he wouldn't let her be. Within an hour of arriving home, a huge, angry mountain lion sauntered into her house. She felt his approach, scented him while he was still on the back porch, using the pads of his huge paws to turn the doorknob in a way few other cats could do. She didn't bother moving from her sprawl on the couch. She was tired, her feet—and other muscles—were sore, and she didn't want to have this confrontation right now.

Grif slunk in, his supple body making not a sound as he twined through the furniture to come to a rest facing her from across the coffee table. He sat back on his haunches, his intelligent eyes sparkling over at her, waiting.

"Go away, Grif. I need time to think."

He growled low in his throat, but she was too tired to be intimidated.

"I mean it. I need some space." She flopped her head back on the couch, closing her eyes as fatigue weighed her down.

"I'm sorry, babe. I can't give it to you. Not yet." Grif's voice was a gentle purr next to her ear as she felt the cushions of the couch dip. His warm, human presence settled at her side, not touching, but protective. She peeled her eyes open and looked over at him.

He was naked, but she guessed she should have expected that. Still, it was a bit of a jolt. The man was a work of art and she could look at him all day long and never tire of his devastating maleness. She looked up at his chiseled features and caught the slight wrinkling of his brow, the determination in his jaw and the worry in his eyes.

"What's wrong?"

Grif sighed. "You can read me well enough already to tell when I'm worried, can't you?" His gentle smile didn't quite reach his eyes. "I don't know whether to be amazed or horrified that I'm so transparent."

"You're ducking the question, Mr. Redstone." Her voice held a note of teasing but his evasion began to stir worry within her. She turned on the couch to face him. "Tell me. What's bothering you?"

Grif ran a hand through his hair in frustration. "It could be nothing, but then again, it could be something very dangerous."

"Dangerous how?"

"I told you a bit about why Belinda and I came up here, right? Well, I suppose it's time you heard the rest of the story." He seemed reluctant to speak but forged ahead anyway. "I think I told you about how my sister, Jackie, was murdered by her mate about a year ago." He looked away, his expression dark with remembered pain. "Belinda was very attached to Jackie and took her death very hard. Jackie's mate was a werecougar from back east named Bill

Timmons. We didn't know until it was too late that he was a brutal man. He beat Jackie and she ran home when she finally couldn't take it any longer. We tried to protect her but I underestimated Bill. He let us believe he would let her go. Months passed while she stayed with us. My vigilance decreased and my brothers began to roam as before. I did too and one day when I returned, it was to find Jackie dead."

Lindsey reached out to him, cuddling into the arms that came up automatically to accept her comforting embrace. "I'm so sorry." She whispered the words into his chest, kissing him gently, offering sympathy and support.

"I'll never forgive myself for failing to protect my family and I will live with the guilt for the rest of my life." He didn't give her a chance to interject, squeezing her tight while he spoke quickly. "Which is why I can't take any chances with your safety. A few times over the past weeks I've thought I caught Timmons's scent, but I always lost it. I thought it might just be a product of my imagination. Still, it's happened a few too many times now for my comfort. I called my brothers, and two of them are coming to help guard and protect you and Belinda. Timmons won't come after me or my brothers directly. He's too weak and too warped. But he will try to hurt us by hurting our women."

She didn't know what to respond to first. "Umm… I'm not part of your family, Grif. Why would he come after me?"

Grif pulled her in close and kissed her softly. "I keep forgetting you don't know our ways. It feels like you've been in my arms forever and that you always will be." He tucked a stray lock of her hair back behind her ear gently. "And you *will be*, Lindsey. You are my mate. I knew it even before the Lady changed you, but I didn't understand how a human woman could possibly be mine. Now of course, it all makes sense. You're cougar. The Lady could have made you anything, but She made you cougar. For me."

"I don't understand."

"Inside me lives the cougar, just as she now lives in you. Don't you feel them calling out to each other whenever we're together? Lindsey, my cougar knew you on first sight. I wanted you from the moment I saw you in the diner and nothing has changed since that moment, except now you can be my mate in every sense of the word. Forever."

"Grif, this is all happening so fast. How can you be so sure?"

He looked deeply into her eyes. "Listen to your inner cougar. She knows the truth of it. We were meant to be together. Once our kind mates, we mate for life. I knew when we first made love it would change my life forever. I'm yours, Lindsey. As you are mine. In the eyes of all werefolk, we're already a mated pair."

"Oh, man." She pulled back, confusion in her eyes. "Grif, are you saying we're married or something?"

He chuckled. "Something like that. We're almost there. Since I'm Alpha of a big Clan, we'll have to announce it and have a party before everyone knows we're fully mated. But you're already mine, Lindsey, in every way that counts. Mating goes deeper than human marriage. It's a bond that cannot be broken."

"But you said your sister left her mate."

He sighed. "It's very rare, but every once in a while a shifter will pair off with the wrong person, or one of us will become mentally unstable. I don't know which was the case with my sister's mating, but Timmons is definitely insane at this point. Whether it was because his legitimate mate—my sister—left him due to his violent ways or whether he was insane from the beginning is something I'll never know, but the mating went drastically wrong in my sister's case. That's not the case with you and me, kitten. Can't you feel the rightness of our joining? Don't tell me you didn't feel the connection when we made love."

"I felt something…" She was hesitant to say too much. After all, he hadn't given her the most important words she needed to hear yet. She knew deep in her heart that she loved him, but she didn't know if he felt the same.

He tugged her closer into his arms, fitting her soft body to his hard frame. He kissed her long and hard, aligning their bodies on the soft couch and touching her intimately.

"You can't deny this." He raised his head. They were both breathing hard and his eyes glowed with desire. "You can't deny we were made to pleasure each other."

She panted but her gaze was steady. "There's more to life than pleasure, Grif."

"Much more." He nodded. "We will live and grow together as the years move on. We'll have youngsters to teach and nurture and we'll share the freedom of being cougar with them and with each other."

"Children?" She gasped. "You're already talking about children and I'm not even certain I want to date you, much less be your mate."

He laughed, but she could see the worry in his eyes. "I'm sorry, sweetheart. It's hard for me sometimes to remember you were raised human." He stood and pulled her up by the arms to stand in front of him as he began unbuttoning her waitress uniform.

"What do you think you're doing?" She tried to bat his hands away but he was too quick for her.

"Getting you naked." He leered down at her comically. "The only way you're going to learn what it is to be *were*—to be part of my Clan, part of my family—is to hang around with us. You can't very well do that all the way over here, and I can't protect you alone. I'm man enough to admit when I need help and my brothers know the stakes. Even more, they know the enemy and they won't let him harm any of our family ever again. You need to come home with me, kitten. You need to meet my brothers and let us protect you and teach you what it is to be cougar."

He had valid points, she had to admit, and if there really was some kind of werecougar madman on the loose she knew she would be better off with Grif and his family. She was just too new at this to know how to defend herself, and this guy Timmons had killed before. It was probably better to humor Grif for now. She could always come home after he was satisfied that Timmons really wasn't in the area, and in the meantime she could learn a bit more about her new abilities. There was just one problem.

"What about my job?"

Grif frowned. "Are you really that attached to it?"

Lindsey had to hold back a snort of laughter. "Not particularly, but it's my only source of income. I need to pay for things somehow."

"Not if you're living with me," he cajoled. While tempting, she found it hard to give up her independence.

"How about this?" Grif seemed willing to broker some kind of deal and she'd hear him out. He hadn't steered her wrong so far, after all. "Move in with us on a trial basis. You've seen how we live. We have plenty of room and I think you realize by now that I'm not without resources. As my mate, what's mine is yours, but if you want, I'll set up a bank account in your name only and deposit what you would have made at the diner into it for as long as you stay. If things don't work out—though I can't imagine any scenario in which that would happen—you wouldn't be out anything."

"That sounds a lot like payment for services rendered," she objected.

"No, kitten. Just me, reassuring my mate." He moved closer and stroked her hair. "If I was going to try to pay you for making love with me, I'd need to rob Fort Knox, and maybe a bunch of Swiss banks to boot. There isn't enough money in the world to pay you for the happiness you've brought into my life, Lindsey."

Oh, yeah. He'd found just the right things to say to cause a melting sensation in the region of her heart. Damn. He was good.

She cared about him so much. Living with him wouldn't be any sort of hardship. In fact, it would be a joy. She'd had far too little joy in her life in recent years.

"All right. I'll go with you."

*

The predator was careful to stay upwind of his prey. It had taken a long time to return here—not the geographical location, but to the man he wanted to kill. Not just kill. Make suffer.

He wanted Griffon Redstone to suffer—as he had—before he killed him and took his place in the Clan. He deserved it.

Bill Timmons was going to be Alpha of the Redstone Clan, only he'd rename it. It would be the Timmons Clan after he took over. He rubbed one hand over the back of his neck, soothing the ache there.

But first he had to make Griffon suffer. And the way to hurt Griffon—weak as he was—was to hurt the females around him. Timmons would take Griffon's mate—just like Grif had kept Jackie from her rightful mate. Timmons would never forgive him for that. Grif'd had no right to do that. None at all.

The stupid bitch had run home to her brother and instead of sending her back, like a good Alpha should, Griffon had given her a place to live. Apart from her mate! Nothing should come between mates. It wasn't right.

A cougar's mate was his property. Timmons was her owner the moment she'd mated with him. Griffon didn't have any right to keep that worthless bitch away from her rightful mate.

He hadn't quite meant to kill her, Timmons admitted to himself. She'd just made him so mad. And something...wasn't right with him. Something…he couldn't remember what…but something had happened. He scratched the skin above his heart until his sharp fingernails brought forth traces of blood, but still it itched. And the throbbing in his temples nearly drove him mad. But the pain reminded him that he had a job to do. With determination, he set about bringing his evil plans to fruition. Redstone would suffer. All Redstones. Especially their thrice damned Alpha.

He remembered how he had stalked his runaway mate, biding his time, waiting for her to be alone in the big house the Redstones had built. He wanted to talk to her. He *needed* his mate. And they were keeping her from him. They would pay for that.

When he'd finally made his move, the stupid bitch had fought him. *Fought* him! Her defiance threw him into a rage and he'd gone a little overboard with the discipline, but she'd pushed him to it. It was her own fault, really.

She'd died at his hands and Timmons watched from afar as the Redstone Alpha fell to pieces over the loss of his sister. It was then that Timmons knew how to hurt Griffon Redstone. Hurt the weak women, and the mighty Alpha hurt too.

If that wasn't fucked up, Bill Timmons didn't know what was. Males were stronger. They ruled by might, not with the weakening compassion that Redstone displayed. It was a wonder he had ever become Alpha—or that nobody challenged him outright for the position after he showed himself to be so weak.

Timmons would challenge though. When the time was right. He'd work his way into position—a position he should have taken a long time ago, right after Jackie's death. But the Redstones had put a price on his head and he'd fled the country, always knowing that he'd come back one day and finish the job.

He'd kill every last Redstone and take over the Clan. It was what he lived for now. It was an obsession that consumed him— much like that weak bitch had consumed him for the short time they'd been together. He'd felt…things…for Jackie he had never felt before.

Killing her had done something to him. He didn't spend a lot of time trying to figure it out. If he'd been a weaker man, he would have said the mate bond all the gooey-eyed romantics talk about was real, but Timmons wasn't weak. His Alpha father had beat all weakness out of him before sending him off to find a mate and start a Clan of his own.

The old man had wanted him to build a Clan from scratch, but why should he when one of the most powerful Clans in the country was his for the taking? All he had to do was kill the Redstone Alpha and he would have a legitimate claim to leadership of the Clan and all that entailed. And wouldn't his old man be surprised by that turn of events?

For now, Timmons would watch and wait for his opportunity. He was good at stalking his prey. When the time was right, and not before, he'd strike. And heaven help anyone who stood in his way.

CHAPTER EIGHT

When Grif and Lindsey loped into the yard in front of his cabin in their fur, they were greeted by two slightly younger, but no less powerful male cougars. Lindsey had to assume they were his brothers because Grif greeted them with a boisterous tumble as they wrestled each other to the ground. She could tell they were not really attacking from the playful way they swatted at each other.

Grif tumbled with one of them while the other came over to sniff at her. Lindsey tried to sit still and allow the rather rude once over, but when the fresh male put his nose against her hindquarters and started sniffing around, she jumped away and swatted at his nose. He sat back and licked his chops, eying her as Grif came over and stood protectively in front of her. Both of the male cougars seemed to get the message as Grif prodded her to move before him into the house, the two younger males following behind them.

Belinda scratched her ears as Lindsey stopped by the girl's side for a moment. She wanted to change so she could talk, but she didn't want to be naked in front of all these people. With little urging, she bounded up the stairs to Grif's bedroom, watching as he changed first, then letting him coach her through the change that was becoming easier and faster each time she did it.

She was beat. The long day and the effort it took to change had wiped her energy.

"You want to meet the boys or do you want to sleep?" Grif held her in his arms, smoothly stroking her back as if she was still some kind of sleek cat.

"I want to meet them, but I can barely keep my eyes open."

"Tomorrow will be soon enough to meet my brothers." He tugged her down onto the bed and slid her naked body under the covers. "Sleep now, baby. I know changing is tiring when you first start to do it. It'll get easier with time." He bent low to kiss her brow and she was almost asleep before he tugged on his jeans and left the room.

*

"That's a pretty little kitty you brought in with you," Matt observed when Grif joined his brothers in the kitchen. He felt like growling but just the thought of her sleeping upstairs in his bed made him want to purr instead.

Steve elbowed his brother with a grin. "I'd say big bro's got it bad."

Grif just let them talk around him. They'd understand when they found their mates, how little everything else in the world mattered when compared to her. Keeping her and the rest of his family safe was his number one priority, which reminded him why he had called in the cavalry.

"You made good time. Thanks for coming." He looked around, sniffing slightly to see if he could locate everyone. "Where's the munchkin?"

"Out by the barn," Matt answered from his position looking out the kitchen window. "I can see her from here."

"Good. I don't want her to hear this, but keep her in your sights. We need to be wary, just in case I'm not going nuts." He ran a hand through his disheveled hair. "I caught scent of Timmons a few times over the past few weeks but it's so faint and elusive I wonder if I'm not imagining things."

Steve's eyes grew serious. "He's not stable, Grif, and he's skilled. It's wise to take precautions. I'm glad you called us instead of trying to handle this on your own."

"But that's just it. There may not be anything to handle. I might be mistaken."

Matt shook his head, his eyes never leaving Belinda out the window. "I don't think you are. I asked Slade to check with his sources a while back. You know how well connected he is in intelligence circles."

Both Steve and Grif—the only two of the five brothers who had served in Special Forces—shot their youngest brother surprised and approving looks. Slade was a newcomer to their territory, having just mated with the priestess who served the extended Redstone Clan.

Slade was not only the rarest of all cat shifters and intensely magical, but he'd been a Black Ops guy who still worked from time to time for the CIA and other Top Secret government groups. He'd devoted most of his time in the past few years to the shifter cause, helping track the ancient society known as the *Venifucus* for the Lords of all *Were*, but he still had his hand in the game and plenty of useful contacts.

"I'm actually surprised I didn't think to ask him before," Grif admitted. "Good going, little bro."

"You had a lot on your mind." Matt rose to Grif's defense, which was touching, but unnecessary. Grif was Alpha enough to admit when something had slipped past him.

That was yet another reason he was so glad to have such capable brothers sticking by him, and what was left of their family. Any one of them could have challenged him for the position as Alpha. Each of the five brothers had the tendencies and will to command, but they deferred to him as the eldest and only rarely challenged him on anything. They were his rock. The ones he relied on the most. And the youngest had just come through—picking up a thread Grif should have investigated long ago.

"You did good, Matt," Grif put the matter to rest. "What did Slade have to say about Timmons?"

"Slade's most recent information, as of last week, puts Timmons in the vicinity of Red Creek. That's not too far from here as the cougar runs."

"Damn." Grif stood and started pacing. "That's not good."

"Call Slade and ask for an update," Steve prompted the youngest brother. "Maybe he has more accurate data now."

Matt pulled out his cell phone and began punching buttons while Grif paced away. It was Steve who came over and put one heavy hand on Grif's shoulder in support.

"We're here for you, bro. He won't get away this time."

*

Lindsey stretched like a cat under the fluffy covers the next morning, waking more fully as she realized her naked body was rubbing up and down against a very hard, very aroused, Griffon Redstone. Her eyes shot open to meet his and he was smiling.

"Good morning."

Inexplicably, she blushed at the heat in his eyes. "Good morning."

"I've been waiting for you to wake so I could do this." He leaned down and licked her nipple into his mouth, at the same time delving his hand under the covers, between her warm thighs. He sought and found the entrance to her sleep warm body, heating her even further with his tantalizing touches.

She moaned as her sleepy body woke to the temptation of his intimate touch. She didn't resist when he pulled her over his long, hard body, arranging her legs so that she straddled him, his morning erection close to the place it so obviously wanted to go. She was amazed how little it took for this incredible man to get her all hot and bothered. She was so ready for him.

"Oh, baby. That's it, nice and easy." He crooned as he lowered her over his stiff cock. He was huge, but he joined with her as if he had always been meant to be there.

She chuckled deep in her throat, excitement purring through her. She felt so full, but so complete at the same time. It was an awesome feeling. Yet a little devil of mischief rode her shoulder as she stroked her hands down his muscled chest.

"Did you just call me easy?" Her eyes challenged him, signaling her silly mood. He grinned back at her.

"Just the way I like my woman, ready for me any time I crook my little finger."

"You think so?" she teased as she began a slow, seductive movement over his straining body.

"Oh, honey, I know so."

She picked up the pace. "How can you be so sure?"

He gasped as she clenched her inner muscles, tormenting him in a delicious way.

"Yeah, baby, do that again." He was enjoying it so much, she decided to indulge him. He groaned as she tightened on him again, dragging herself over him in a planned seduction that fired both their senses. "Mmm, you were made for me baby."

She stilled, watching his slightly dazed eyes. He hadn't answered her question. "How can you be so sure?" she asked again.

His eyes snapped open into hers and just that quickly his mood changed. He rolled, pinning her under his heavy body, rising up just enough so that he could meet her eyes as he began a pounding rhythm into her clasping body.

"How?" he asked, his pace increasing as his eyes held hers in a mesmerizing stare of passion. "How do I know?" He rubbed one long finger over her clit, forcing her to join him, dancing near the edge of fulfillment. She gasped, writhing beneath him as her peak came so close, she knew within moments she would be shattered.

He pushed her higher still, his eyes holding a message of need, of want, and of something deeper still. "I know," he gasped between hard thrusts, "because." Each word was punctuated by a hard pulse. "You're. My. Mate."

She came with what felt like a clap of thunder, her body shattering into a million pieces as he pushed her over the edge. He followed, his hot essence filling her. He gathered her into his arms, holding her close as they writhed together in the long, long echoes of pleasure, coming down only a bit at a time, enjoying the languor of shared ecstasy.

"I was going to wish you a good morning, but I see you've already had that." An amused male voice sounded from the doorway as Lindsey gasped. Grif stayed right where he was, on top of her, his softening cock buried up her wet pussy as if it was perfectly normal to have visitors during such moments. Her hands dug into his shoulders as her eyes widened in alarm.

"Go away Matt."

Grif threw a pillow in the general direction of the door and Lindsey followed its trajectory with her eyes, all the way to a tall, muscular man who had to be one of Grif's brothers. Lindsey was horrified when he dodged the pillow, meeting her gaze. The smile on his face was pure deviltry. He made a production out of licking his lips as his eyes traveled down what he could see of her body, roaming back up to give her a jaunty wink.

She would just bet he was the cougar who had tried to sniff her pussy the day before. He had that kind of mischievous air about him.

While she was busy being mortified apparently Grif was priming for more lovemaking. She gasped again when he started to move once more within her, hardening even as he began to thrust. Matt was still in the doorway, watching, and to her horror, another good looking man joined him with a nearly identical teasing smile.

"Aw, leave them be, Matt," the other man said loud enough for Grif to hear. "Grif won't be any use to us until he fucks her into oblivion."

"I said—" Grif paused only slightly as he addressed his brothers in a stern voice, "—get the fuck out of here." He emphasized his words by ramming into her with more force. When she would have objected, he squeezed her shoulders, forcing her eyes to meet his. "Only me, Lindsey. See only me. Nothing else matters."

He mesmerized her, that was the only explanation she could come up with later as she realized that in that moment, the entire Mormon Tabernacle Choir could be watching them and she couldn't have cared less. When Grif made love to her, he was her only point of connection with the world. He was all that mattered, just as she realized that it was the same for him. She could read it in his eyes and the loving way he touched her, rough yet gentle, never giving her more than she could comfortably bear. He was a thoughtful lover who pressed her to stretch her boundaries and reach for what she really wanted.

And what she really wanted was him. Anyway, anyplace, anytime. She wanted him regardless of who watched or didn't watch, or what happened in the world around them. All that mattered was him and the way he made her feel—cherished, valued and loved.

He increased his pace, bringing her to several beautiful orgasms before joining her in ecstasy. This time was slower, but no less intense. Actually, when Grif took his time, she realized, he brought her multiple orgasms that just went on and on. She never knew her body was capable of such, but Grif proved to her that with him, she could find pleasure the likes of which she had never even dreamed.

When she finally came back down to earth, she was glad to see the doorway was empty of Grif's brothers, but she had no way of knowing just how much they had seen before leaving. She blushed deeply, wondering how she was going to face them. Undoubtedly she would be properly introduced to the two men who had come such a distance at their brother's call. She had no idea how she was going to bluff her way through such a meeting.

"Are your brothers always so, um, mischievous?"

Grif had rolled off her to allow her to breathe, but he hadn't gone far. His hand cupped her wet pussy as he held her tight, her back against his chest.

"That's a kind word to use. Honey, they are Grade A pains in the ass sometimes." They both chuckled at the exasperation in his tone. "Don't let them bother you."

"But they saw us—"

"Fucking?" His hand rested over her pussy, reminding her of the hard use he had just put her to and the incredible pleasure he had wrung from her body and soul. "Sweetheart, you're going to have to get used to being *were*. Just as nudity isn't a big deal for our kind, seeing mates enjoying each other isn't a huge taboo either. Not like it can be in human society."

She turned in his arms. "What does that really mean?" His eyes scrunched up as he seemed to try to follow her thoughts. "You said I was your mate." His expression cleared, replaced by something that looked like joy to her.

"When a *were* of any species finds the one person in all the world who was meant for them, they mate for life. Lindsey, you're my mate." She had never seen him more serious, or happier.

"You mean you want to marry me?"

He nodded. "That's one way of putting it, but mating entails more than a human marriage. It's a deeper bond and it's already formed between us. The ceremony is just a celebration of that bond. Really, it's an excuse to have a party." His smile charmed her. "Lindsey, will you mate with me?"

"Isn't that what we've already been doing?" She couldn't resist teasing him.

He smiled gently. "What we've been doing is making love, fucking like mates. For all intents and purposes, we're mated already, but to make it official, there's a ceremony we can hold, so my Clan can welcome you."

"And have an excuse to hold a party, right?"

"Well, with all that's going on, we'll probably put it off for a few weeks, until we can gather with the Clan, but I'd like to know you'll agree to the ceremony when we get to it." He kissed her softly. "And for you to realize that I'm serious in this. You're my mate. There's no going back on that for me. The ceremony will make our mating known publicly. Plus, it would make me feel better to have some official claim on you in the eyes of the Clan. This way if anything happened to me, I know you would always have a home with my family."

"Don't talk like that, Grif." She hugged him close, unable to bear even the thought of him coming to harm.

He sighed, stroking her soft hair. "I like to be prepared for all contingencies, sweetheart. I don't intend anything to happen to me, but I'll feel safer knowing that we've made things official between us. I want to claim you for the entire world to see, Lindsey. Even those mangy wolves will have to stand up and take notice of our mating. Kitten," his eyes grew serious, "I hold a relatively high rank among the weretribes. As my mate, now you do too."

"You're kidding, right? I can barely walk on my four paws without tripping."

He chuckled. "You'll get better with practice, love. Regardless, I'm the leader of the Redstone Clan. As my mate, you'll share part of that responsibility. The women of our Clan may come to you with their concerns and it'll be your duty to listen and help when you can, and decide when an issue needs my intervention."

"Wow." She was stunned by the responsibility, unsure of her own ability to do the job, and still a little rocked by the idea that she was his mate. She knew she loved him, though she hadn't found the courage to tell him that flat out, but how could he be so sure she was the one for him?

"What's wrong, sweetheart?"

She searched his eyes. "How do you know I'm the one? How can you be so sure I'm the one person you've been looking for? Up until a few days ago I wasn't even a shapeshifter. I have no idea how to live in your world, Grif. What if I can't?"

He smiled with what looked like relief, hugging her close. "The Lady never gives us more than we can handle, sweetheart. You'll learn our ways, I have no doubt of that. And to answer your other question, I knew almost from the first moment I saw you in the diner that you were mine. Something about you called to me but I didn't understand it because you weren't cougar then." His hand stroked through her hair softly. "It drove me crazy, but I found myself prowling your land at night, guarding you while you slept, watching you through the holes in your roof, even on that first night. Sweetheart, I knew you were meant for me, but I didn't understand it until the Lady made you cougar."

She snuggled into him, needing his reassurance. "You spied on me through the roof?" She chuckled at the thought.

"How do you think I knew I could fix your roof? I did a little pre-inspection."

"In the middle of the night? Climbing up on my roof without a ladder? Grif! You could have fallen."

He soothed her though the thought of him falling off her roof made her shiver. "Don't worry, honey. Cats are good climbers and we almost always land on our feet. You'll learn that soon enough."

"I don't like heights." She shivered again as he stroked her, but whether in fear or from his tempting closeness, even she didn't know.

"It's okay. You don't have to climb anything unless you want to, but it's a good skill to learn. Most other things that will come after you in the wild can't climb well, so it's a good escape route."

"You mean other animals chase you when you're in cougar form?" She was appalled by the idea, but he just shrugged.

"Once in a while something bigger, like a grizzly, will try, but most animals give all *were* a wide berth. Most *were* forms are natural predators and with the human influence we're pretty powerful hunters. Animals sense that and most steer clear. Of course, once in a while different kinds of *were* will chase each other for fun."

"Fun?" This was certainly an odd world she had gotten herself into. She felt a bit like Alice must have felt after she fell down that rabbit hole.

"Some of the wolf Pack up here likes to play games once in a while, but it's mostly all in fun. A lot of growling and posturing but I can almost always outrun them."

"What about when you can't outrun them?" Her eyes were wide as she pulled back to watch his grinning face.

He squeezed her as he kissed the tip of her nose. "That's what trees are for. Wolves can't climb for shit."

After they were dressed, Lindsey plucked up her courage to face the two brothers to whom she had yet to be properly introduced. She couldn't help the blistering blush that stained her cheeks as Grif held her against his chest, his arms under her breasts, facing the two men.

"Boys, this is my mate, Lindsey." She heard the rumble of satisfaction in his voice and felt it against her back as he held her close in the spacious kitchen. "Sweetheart, this is Steve." He pointed her toward the slightly larger, more muscular of the two men standing at the kitchen counter, impatiently watching the toaster. "And the youngster over there is Matt."

Matt snatched the much awaited toast out of his older brother's hands. Steve went after him, making stabbing snatches at the toast, to no avail. Steve's eyes were a deep chocolate brown, holding secrets and wisdom in their depths as he gave up on the toast and faced her with an appraising look.

"Welcome to the family." His voice was pleasant, deep and masculine and his manner was friendly. He really did make her feel welcome. As Grif finally released her, Steve stepped forward and took her by the arms, pulling her close for a hug that took her by surprise.

Even more shocking was the kiss he placed on her startled lips a moment later. He smiled down into her startled eyes and licked his lips as he drew away.

"You're a sweet one, Lindsey and you've made my brother a grinning, happy fool. I say it's about time." He released her and clapped Grif on the back, both men sharing an admiring glance at her as she was swept into Matt's arms for a second smooch and warm embrace.

"Damn," Matt said as he pulled back. "Grif is a lucky man. Welcome, to the Clan."

She stammered out what she hoped was a polite thanks, realizing yet again that traditions among the weretribes were undoubtedly different than what she was used to. Being kissed on the mouth by her brothers-in-law apparently was something quite normal. She wondered and worried a bit over what else might be considered normal to these folks, but she was a shifter now, and she had better get used to it.

CHAPTER NINE

The men each packed away more food at breakfast than Lindsey had been used to eating in an entire day, but she found her own appetite had increased as well. While nowhere near the full package of bacon, dozen eggs, and multitude of muffins the men ate, she still found herself taking an extra helping here and there because she was truly hungry. The fact that little Belinda ate as much as she did simply amazed her.

Lindsey found herself grinning as she went for her fourth strip of bacon.

"What's made you so happy?" Grif dropped a quick kiss on her temple as she stuffed the last piece of crispy bacon in her mouth and chewed. He dipped down to lick at her lips, catching a bit of the flavor on his tongue. "Mmm, bacon."

She swallowed happily. "I'm amazed by the idea that I can eat that extra piece of bacon and not have it go straight to my hips."

Nuzzling her ear he whispered. "The only thing going straight to your hips, Lindsey, will be me." He pulled her chair closer to his with a loud scrape as the family watched indulgently.

Belinda jumped up from the table and put her dishes in the sink. "I'm going to check on Blaze."

"Who's Blaze?" Lindsey asked with more enthusiasm than the question warranted, embarrassed to have been caught cuddling with Grif in even so innocent a way. The last thing she wanted to do was upset his little sister—or any of his family, for that matter.

"My pony," Belinda answered with a nonchalance that reassured Lindsey. The girl wasn't upset with her, just preoccupied by thoughts of her four-legged friend. "He was limping before. Grif says I was lucky to find a pony who wasn't scared of big cats."

"Yeah, I guess so," Lindsey answered, thinking about the world in a whole new way. Belinda's easy words spoke volumes about how different Lindsey's life would be now that she was a shapeshifter like this family. She was going to have to consider things like how animals reacted to the wild side of her now.

Grif eyed his brothers and Steve stood as Belinda headed for the door. "I'll go with you, squirt. Let's see if I can help out with Blaze. I had a pony when I was your age."

Lindsey knew the girl was unaware of the silent messages passing between the brothers as Grif motioned Steve to keep a close eye on their little sister.

"Do you expect trouble?" Lindsey asked as soon as the door shut behind Belinda and Steve.

Instead of answering, Grif shot a look at his youngest brother. Both men had grim expressions on their faces.

"It could be nothing…" Grif began, turning back to her.

"But you don't think it is," she finished his sentence for him.

"Grif told you about our ex-brother-in-law, right?" Matt said from across the table. Lindsey looked over at him and nodded. "Our best information puts him nearby. The threat could be very real and we're treating it as such."

Wow. Not only did she have to deal with all the changes in her life and her relationship status, but now there might be a killer nearby, looking to kill her and hurt the Redstones. It was almost too much to take in.

But she knew one thing. She knew Grif would protect her to the best of his ability. He'd done nothing but that since almost the first moment they'd met.

She turned to him and took his hand. "It'll be all right," she whispered, hoping she spoke the truth. "I'll do whatever you need me to, but I want you to know one thing. If something happens to me, it's not your fault. I got myself into this mess. I'll take whatever consequences—unintended or otherwise—result. Becoming a shifter has exposed me to any number of unforeseen dangers. This problem with your ex-brother-in-law is just another. You couldn't have foreseen any of it any more than I could."

"You're very forgiving," was Grif's soft comment, spoken after a few moments of thought. The tension in the room was significant and she could feel Matt's scrutiny, though the younger man said nothing for the moment.

"I love you," she whispered. For her, that said it all.

Grif's hand tightened on hers and his lips turned upward in a small smile.

Anything he would've said in return was forestalled by the

opening of the door. Belinda walked in, Steve close behind her. She looked dejected as she poured a glass of water for herself from the sink.

Lindsey saw Grif look up in question at Steve.

"Munchkin's pony needs to rest his foreleg for the next day or two. She's not happy about it," Steve explained. "He was favoring the right front leg and it's inflamed. We put a poultice on it and he should be right as rain as soon as he gets a little time to recover."

"But I can't ride him," Belinda put in with a frown as she sat at the table, propping her chin in her hand and placing the water glass in front of her. "That stinks."

Lindsey couldn't help her amusement at the young girl's downcast expression. If only her own problems were so simple. Belinda probably didn't know the danger that stalked near the family. The brothers were protecting the fragile youngster from it while they could. Lindsey wasn't so sure that was a good idea, but she'd only been part of their little group for a short time. It wasn't her place to critique what they chose to tell the youngest member of their family, or not.

She'd bet that Belinda was a lot stronger than they thought she was. Sure, she'd had some terrible things happen to her recently. The loss of her mother had, no doubt, hit the girl hard. Lindsey sensed strength about her though. The strength of the willow that bent, but did not break under a heavy wind.

The somewhat poetic thought made her wonder if maybe her grandfather was sending thoughts to her. Grandpa often compared life situations to those in nature, though it hadn't really been Lindsey's way...until just lately. It seemed the older she got, the more she appreciated her grandfather's wisdom that had been passed on to her in bits and pieces. She only wished she'd had more time with him, to learn from him.

"You okay, love?" Grif spoke softly to her, reclaiming her attention. He'd called her *love*, which was about as close as she supposed he'd come to returning her earlier declaration in company. Still, the term of endearment sent a little thrill through her bloodstream, making her tingle with joy.

"Fine. I was just thinking." Lindsey searched for a way to help the brothers keep the active young girl close to home for the day. "Maybe Belinda would like to help me bake today? I thought maybe I'd make some treats."

"Baking?" Steve's head popped up and his gaze zeroed in on hers with an eager hopefulness she never would have expected from him.

But Lindsey really wanted to know what Belinda thought. Lindsey wanted to help the brothers keep everyone safe and she also wanted to become better friends with Belinda—her only female ally in this house full of men.

"I bought chocolate chips the last time we were in town," Belinda offered, a guarded sort of eagerness entering her gaze as she met Lindsey's eyes. "And there's plenty of oatmeal, raisins and brown sugar. What else do we need for oatmeal cookies?" As she spoke, her enthusiasm became harder to hide.

"Not much else," Lindsey said, rising from her chair to check out the oven. "You've got two baking sheets. That's good. We can work with that. But first, we need to clear the decks and start with a clean kitchen, so we can mess it up." Lindsey smiled and Belinda laughed, already taking dishes to the sink from the remnants of breakfast.

They'd clean the kitchen first, which would take a good half hour. Then they'd start on the cookies. That ought to fill up the morning. They could make lunch for everyone too.

Lindsey hadn't discussed the impromptu plan with Grif, but he nodded and smiled his approval and she knew she'd done well. The brothers helped clean a bit before heading toward the living room. Lindsey peeked through the open archway from time to time and saw them discussing printouts and things on the computer screen with frowns on their faces. Grif was also on the phone a lot and she could only assume he was working on locating the possible danger. He certainly looked serious enough to be tracking a killer.

The girls paused about an hour before lunch and switched from baking to lunch prep. The usual sandwiches turned into works of art under Belinda's supervision and lots of the girl's favorite side dishes were prepared and placed festively on the table before they called the boys in.

The brothers made a big deal over the 'gourmet' meal that had been prepared, peppering their sister and Lindsey both with kisses and hugs of thanks. The five of them lingered over lunch for more than an hour, talking about first shifts and teasing Lindsey in a comradely way about all the things she'd have to learn about her new life.

She took their teasing with good grace, knowing they were exaggerating some things and likely downplaying others. The brothers also lovingly teased Belinda and tried to steal cookies, but she limited them to three each until after dinner. They cajoled, but she stood firm and her laughter rang through the house, filling it with palpable joy.

After lunch was cleared away, Lindsey and Belinda went to work on a top secret project. Belinda had proposed making a cake to surprise her brothers and Lindsey was more than happy to comply. She taught Belinda some of the things her own mother had taught her about baking—a hobby they'd both enjoyed—and Lindsey found herself talking about her mother as the day wore on, drawing Belinda out about her own lost mother.

It was a day of female bonding at its best. They finished with the cake, hid it to the best of their ability in the big fridge for later revelation, and prepared a giant dinner for them all to enjoy.

Belinda and Lindsey had stayed inside all day while the men worked. It wasn't something she wanted to do every day, but Lindsey understood the necessity of keeping the youngster close to home—at least while everything was so uncertain.

All day, Lindsey had kept peeking out the archway to look at Grif. He was so darn handsome and so obviously in charge. Even among his brothers—who were no slouches themselves—Grif stood out. He had some indefinable quality that drew her like a moth to a flame. Only this flame would never hurt her. He would warm her, singe her senses with his passion, but he would also protect her with his last breath.

Each time he caught her looking at him he'd make a gesture. A wink, a nod, a playfully blown kiss. Each one made her feel special...and loved.

They hadn't been alone all day, but after dinner, when Belinda had disappeared into her bedroom with her earphones and music player, Grif took Lindsey by the hand and led her outside. They shared a few passionate kisses by the barn as he closed it up for the night and Lindsey's internal fire flared to life—much worse than before.

"Do you trust me?" Grif looked deep into her eyes in the lowering darkness. She could see a lot better at night than ever before as her new *were* senses came to life.

"I do," she answered seriously, gauging his mood.

Her body was on fire for him and she wanted to back him up against the wall of the barn and have her wicked way with him. She tried to control her impulses, but it was a losing proposition. He'd better find some real privacy for them soon, or she wouldn't hold herself accountable for the consequences.

"There's a place up in the woods I want to take you," he said, surprising her.

"Right now?" Her libido was clamoring for her to jump his bones, but she fought it. He seemed to be saying something significant, but she was darned if she could figure out why some spot up in the woods would be so important to him just at the moment.

"No time like the present," he confirmed and took her by the hand.

She'd been restless all day and had grown more so as time went on. Inside, she was still on fire and the temperature was climbing steadily. Grif's slightest touch made her shiver. It was a physical, aching need.

He led her into the last open door of the barn and started taking off his clothes. Now *that* was more like it.

She shucked her jeans and tore off her shirt, ready for anything, but when she turned back to him, he was in cougar form. Okay, so he was serious about wanting to go somewhere first. She could work with that.

Summoning her cat in the way he'd shown her, Lindsey shifted shape and followed where he led. They ran for a while, working off some of the excess energy, but instead of turning back toward the house after she'd sprinted her fill, he coaxed her upward, not too far from the house on the same mountain. It seemed he hadn't been kidding about wanting to show her something in the woods.

When they reached the top of the hill, she was surprised to find a rough circle of standing stones. Not too tall—nothing like the famous Stonehenge in England, for example—but definitely a circle of stones standing on end at the top of the mountain. There were trees all around and their branches formed a ceiling of sorts, high over the stone circle, while the circle itself remained free of trees and shrubs. Only green grass and small flowers bloomed there, around the base of the stones and the long slab in the middle that could have been a natural altar.

The moon shone down, near full, illuminating a circular patch in the center where the tops of the trees formed a circle far above their heads. Grif led her into the circle and around the altar, and there she finally spotted Logan, the werewolf Alpha, waiting for them in his human form.

He wore only a loose set of pants and his bare, muscled chest with its dark arrow of hair made Lindsey salivate.

Damn. Why was she so randy? She was committed to Grif. Should other men make her horny? Didn't she have enough? Grif should be *more* than enough for a woman who had never really slept around.

Yet there was this heat inside her. A fire that refused to be quenched.

She made a mewling sound as Grif shifted to his human form. He crouched in front of her and rubbed her neck, his gaze filled with resigned compassion.

"It's okay, kitten. I think I know what's going on. It's why I asked the Alpha to come here. You need to be made aware of some things about shifters that are not generally known." He let go of her and turned toward Logan. "Did you bring the things I asked for?"

Logan threw a small drawstring bag in Grif's direction, which he deftly caught mid-air. He opened it and pulled out a long T-shirt that was big enough to fit like a dress on Lindsey, though it would leave a lot of her thigh bare. He placed it on the slab of stone that looked like an altar and turned back to her.

"See if you can change back by yourself and put that on."

She waited only a moment to see Grif pull out a pair of sweatpants from the bag and begin putting them on. For modesty's sake, she went around to the other side of the altar, where the men couldn't see her unless they stood up, and tried to remember what Grif had taught her about shifting.

Much to her surprise and delight, she changed back quickly, with no missteps. Maybe she was getting the hang of this shifter thing after all.

She slipped the T-shirt on and tugged the hem down as far as she could before walking around the altar to join the guys. She noted the appreciation in both sets of male eyes as they caught sight of her—and the way Logan's gaze lingered on her bare legs.

"What is this place?" she asked, hoping to ease her discomfort. She was nervous and unsure of herself.

Grif motioned her over to sit next to him and she noticed the small firepit around which the men sat. It was lined with blackened stones and seemed like a more or less permanent fixture in the stone circle. Logan must have prepared wood and he leaned forward now to light the tinder he'd set up with a match pulled from the depths of the small sack he'd brought.

"Places like this exist all over the world, though very few are known by humans. As you see," Logan explained, pointing to the canopy of tree limbs, "Mother Nature does a good job of camouflaging the stone circle so we can worship Her in peace."

She'd been curious for a while now about shifter beliefs. She hadn't raised the question before, not wanting to be rude, but now that she was one of them, she needed to know more.

"My grandfather's people believe in the Great Spirit. I've noticed you all seem to refer to a goddess you call the Lady. Is she Mother Nature, as you put it, or something else?"

"She is all things," Logan answered with a hint of mysticism in his tone. "Some call Her Mother Nature. Some call Her the Lady. Some call Her by other names, but She is all those things…and probably more." Logan's lips lifted in the hint of a smile. "She gives life and magic and Light. She is goodness personified."

"The Great Spirit of the Native Americans doesn't contradict our beliefs, kitten, if that's what you're worried about," Grif added. "All shifters serve the Lady—no matter what we might call Her—if we are aligned with the Light."

"There are some, though," Logan warned, "that embrace darkness and evil. Just like humans, we have our bad apples too. So don't assume that just because someone can shapeshift, they're going to be your friend."

"That message was perfectly clear when I first arrived here, Alpha," Lindsey snapped back at him, just the tiniest bit, for the way his people had made her suffer as she tried to fulfill her grandfather's mission.

Now that her task was done and she was a shifter herself, she found the werewolf Pack's questionable *welcome* even harder to stomach. She'd been trying to do the right thing and they'd stood in her way at every opportunity. Not only that—they'd tried to run her off more than once with threats and even physical confrontations.

"Ouch," Logan laughed, taking her rebuke well. "I'm sorry for that. We had no idea what you were up to and that you'd be forever changed by the magic you called. I think you can understand that the Pack was worried you'd do something as bad as your grandsire had done...or worse. We didn't know you were trying to make amends. Or what form that would take."

"The reason I wanted to bring you here..." Grif recaptured her attention and effectively changed the subject. "Is that I think you're going to have a tough time of the transition from human to *were*. The things that our young usually have years to adapt to, you've only had a few days. I think you're going to need help—more help than I can give you alone—until things settle down."

Grif's expression was pained and almost sheepish. Logan busied himself poking the fire to get it really going into a merry little blaze.

"I thought I was handling it pretty well," Lindsey protested. Was he disappointed with her in some way? Had she already done something wrong? She began to worry over his words.

"And you are." Grif was quick to reassure her. He put one big hand on her shoulder, stroking her through the T-shirt, calming her. Even the simplest touch brought both comfort and excitement. Sexual energy zinged back and forth between them whenever he drew near. "You're doing really well for a newcomer, but kitten..." He seemed to hesitate over his words. "Haven't you noticed that you're a bit more...uh... randy than usual? Or were you always so insatiable in bed? Not that I'm complaining." He softened his words with a sexy grin that made her inner cat curl up and purr.

Now that he mentioned it—and she had to halt the automatic embarrassment discussing such a thing brought—she was like a mink in heat. Or a bunny that couldn't get enough. Some kind of horny critter that could easily fuck itself to death if stops weren't put on it.

"Um..." Lindsey knew she was blushing, but couldn't help it. The heat from the fire rivaled the heat she felt in her cheeks. "I'm sorry?" She didn't know what to think about him discussing this in front of the other Alpha. Was this some kind of sexual intervention? She didn't think she could blush any hotter.

Logan laughed out loud, making her feel even more self-conscious. Grif threw the other man a quelling look before turning back to her, taking both hands in his.

"There's nothing to be sorry for. Young shifters go through a stage during puberty where they're experimenting with sex for several years. It's a lot more...um...primal than when humans hit puberty, from what I understand. Our young—cats especially—spend a decade or more burning off the excess sexual energy. We call it the frenzy. Their eyes glow from the excess of power—just like yours have been glowing for the past day or two." He released her hands and turned toward the small fire.

Oh, no. She remembered his remarks about her eyes, but she hadn't thought anything of it. She also remembered seeing that golden glow in the mirror when she'd been in the bathroom. He wasn't kidding around. There was something wrong with her.

"Wolves go through something similar, though not quite as long or as intense as cats, from what I hear," Logan put in. "It lasts about a decade—even if they're lucky enough to find their mate early. Sometimes mating early even makes it worse. If not eased properly, the hunger can drive some young wolves mad."

"Cats too," Grif added with a grim nod.

"So this is normal?" Lindsey's inner cat wanted to yowl in relief. Finally, the human part of her was coming to understand what the feline already, instinctively knew.

Grif cringed. "Not exactly."

"Everything about your new shifter nature has been accelerated, Lindsey," Logan spoke in a quiet, almost somber voice. "Grif asked me here to help explain this and to see for myself if what he suspected was true. I can tell you right now, I can smell your arousal from over here and it's way more potent than it should be. You're mated to Grif. You shouldn't be having a reaction to me. What's worse—I shouldn't be having a reaction to you. For one thing, you're a cat. For another, you're mated. That usually means your pheromones are only attractive to your mate, not to others, though we can still scent them."

"So you think I'm in this...frenzy. And that it's stronger than it should be because I compressed a whole lifetime of learning to be a cougar into a couple of days?" Her mind was trying to focus—really it was—but the two, handsome males sitting near her were very distracting.

"That about sums it up." Grif blew out a breath, seeming resigned to the situation. "Which is why we're going to do our best to help you overcome this accelerated frenzy."

His phrasing made her jump.

"We?" She looked from one to the other and found both sets of male eyes smoldering back at her. They were both excited by her scent. Both eager to fuck her.

And she wanted them both.

Wait. What?

CHAPTER TEN

Lindsey's rational, human mind balked. She was mated to Grif. She shouldn't want Logan too. But the cat screeched inside her brain. The she devil wanted them both. She wanted every male in the vicinity to come at her beck and call—and vie for the opportunity to satisfy her sexually.

Where the heck was that kinky thought coming from? Certainly not the Lindsey Tate who had been so circumspect with her past lovers that she could count them on one hand. No, this was the cat talking. And she wanted to claw and bite. To mark her lovers and make every male want her.

Damn. Lindsey hugged herself, not really understanding how she could feel these things. The cat shouldn't have so much control over her human mind and body, should it?

"Me first," Grif explained. "I'm your mate and you *will not* forget it." His serious expression brooked no argument. "I'll do my best, but we're probably going to need some help to satisfy the frenzy. With any luck, it'll all be over soon. Everything else about your development was rushed beyond all recognition. This should be too—if we can satisfy the cat. Otherwise, I hate to think what could happen." Grif reached out and stroked her hair. She could feel his hand tremble and read the love in his eyes. He was truly worried for her.

The cat within her responded to his gentle touch, moving into his hand and sliding closer. She wanted him. Again. She would never be satisfied.

And then she realized, in one still-sane corner of her mind, that Grif wasn't kidding around. This sexual *frenzy*, as he called it, was real. She'd never felt such strong impulses in her life—not even with Grif.

She'd been attracted to him from the get go, but it was a mature, loving desire complimented by real, deep and true feelings. What she was experiencing now was blind hunger for any man with a cock. Correction—any man with a *hard* cock, ready to fuck her brains out.

This wasn't good, but there was no way around it. That little corner of her mind that wasn't consumed by the incredible hunger was being crowded out by the feline *want* that would have its way.

Grif pulled her into his arms and she went willingly, the last little bit of her sanity winking out like a light. She was aware of each touch, each caress—of the mountain breeze wafting across her skin as Grif pulled her T-shirt off and draped it across the low slab of the altar. She felt his hands cupping her breasts, pushing the fire within her blood stream to ever higher temperatures.

She went willingly when he bent her over the stone slab and entered her from behind. She ground her pussy against him as he began and slow, deliberate rhythm that sent sparks along each and every nerve ending she possessed.

A sound to her right made her turn her head. And there was the werewolf Alpha, rubbing the long rod of his cock through his sweatpants. Watching her get fucked by her lover. His gaze glued to her body and then meeting hers when he noticed her watching.

Lindsey licked her lips, the feline within her feeling like a sex goddess, satisfied with every male present wanting her. And she would let him have her. She wanted it all. Every male worshiping at her core.

The alien thoughts made that little, horrified corner of Lindsey's human mind gasp. Had she become a nympho? Why had becoming a shifter done this to her and would the shifter's deity really want such a thing to happen? Was this the real punishment then? This driving need to have every male pay homage between her thighs?

To fuck herself to death?

Was their Lady really so cruel?

Lindsey hadn't thought so, but she didn't understand any of this. She knew the guys had tried to explain, but it had been hard to concentrate with the building need distracting her. Thank goodness Grif had stopped talking and started fucking. If he hadn't, she'd have had to jump his bones. The need had become almost that desperate while he'd been speaking to her.

And now she had him just where she needed him. Between her thighs, pumping her to glory. Oh, yeah. It was coming. She needed it so bad.

Lindsey wasn't sure, but she thought maybe she'd spoken those last thoughts aloud. Grif answered with a growl, bending low over her back to get a better grip on her hips as his sharp teeth sought the tender skin of her neck.

Yes! She wanted his teeth there. His love bite. His mating mark. The cat within yowled as his teeth sank into her skin almost delicately. It didn't hurt. Her body craved it so.

She came hard and so did he, spurting within her tight core, claiming her with cock and teeth. Marking her with scent and blood. Just the way she wanted it.

Grif pressed her into the stone for long moments, holding her still while they both came down from the high he'd just pushed them to. When he withdrew, though, the fever hadn't left her. She turned to him, desperate, clinging to his strong arms, needing more.

What was this? What was wrong with her? She'd just come. How could she *need* so desperately again, so soon?

"Grif?" Her voice sounded lost and uncertain, even to her own ears.

"Ssh, kitten. This is what I was afraid of." He held her, stroking her back as he rocked her against his strong, naked body.

He was such a good man. He was going to be a great mate for the rest of her life...if she lived that long. The way she was feeling now, if she didn't get more cock in the next few minutes, she was going to die. Either that, or go completely insane.

As they had warned her. Damn. They'd been right. The little corner of Lindsey's mind accepted her fate. She finally understood Grif's fear for her and his willingness to do anything to help her be well.

She couldn't love him anymore than she already did, but her heart swelled with love. She reached up to kiss him, trying to communicate her love for him in her touch.

When he broke the kiss, she looked up into his lovely, golden eyes.

"I'm sorry," she whispered, her voice breaking with need.

He held her gaze for a long, desperate moment while the fire inside her began to burn bright once more, demanding satisfaction.

"I'm here for you, my love. No matter what happens, remember that. I'm here." He stroked her for a moment more before looking away, over her shoulder. He nodded once and then she felt the touch of the werewolf Alpha on her hip and shoulder as he moved close.

Her inner cat purred, surrounded by two amazingly handsome males, blanketed in their warmth.

And then Grif stepped away. Her heart fluttered. Where was he going? She couldn't do this without him. She couldn't live—couldn't breathe—without him.

Logan turned her in his arms and she didn't have time to think about where Grif had gone anymore. The werewolf was rougher and a little lankier than Grif, though his body was hard-muscled and sleek. Strong too. He lifted her up and placed her on the low altar, her butt protected from the rock by the soft layer of her discarded T-shirt.

"Turn her," Grif ordered. There he was. Standing behind the werewolf. He was watching. Directing.

Logan turned her so that she was sitting lengthwise on the stone slab. The T-shirt was under her back as he pushed her downward into a reclining position. Grif moved into her line of sight, off to her left while Logan was on her right side, stroking his hands down her body.

He paused at her nipples, bending over her to lap at them, then take them into his mouth one at a time. His tongue swirled and teased, making her squirm.

Logan's hands and mouth worshiped at her breasts while Grif moved closer. When Grif's hands parted her legs, she eagerly complied, spreading wide for him. She looked over Logan's head to meet Grif's golden gaze as he slid his fingers into her, pushing deep, using his thumb to circle her clit.

She moaned and Grif smiled. The smile set her off in a small explosion of pleasure. Just his smile could make her come, it seemed. As if his approval gave her permission to let the riot happening in her body carry her inhibitions away.

Grif's fingers withdrew and he stepped back. She wanted to go after him, but Logan's big body kept her exactly where she was.

"Face to face this time, Logan," Grif coached from the sidelines. "I want her to see and understand. Next time, you can do it your way."

The words didn't make a lot of sense, but the cat inside picked up on the idea that there would be a next time. More sex. More pleasure. More satisfaction for the burning need that fired her blood to almost unbearable levels.

Her legs were spread wide so there was no problem when the Alpha wolf pounced. He leapt in one smooth move to crouch, naked, between her legs. She had no idea when or where his pants had gone, but she was grateful they weren't in her way. Her body was demanding satisfaction. Again. Continuously.

She was beyond caring who fucked her, she just needed relief. But the tiny part of her mind that was still her own noticed how gentle the big Alpha werewolf was with her. He could have just taken what she was so freely offering without a second thought for her comfort, but that wasn't his way.

No, Logan touched her almost reverently. With respect. A tiny part of her heart went out to him, never to return. He was really a sweet man when push came to shove.

He joined with her slowly, drawing out the moment, holding her gaze as he made them one. It felt so *good*. And she needed it so bad.

She wrapped her legs around him and dug her heels in to urge him on, but he stayed her motions. He was in control. And beyond him—over his shoulder—she saw Grif, watching over everything, his jaw clenched and worry in his eyes.

The little aware part that was Lindsey wanted to tell him he had nothing to worry about. She was now and always would be his, but the irrational thing that had taken over most of her mind wouldn't allow speech. The cat yowled and Lindsey's hands raked down Logan's back as he finally started moving more resolutely within her.

Damn. He knew how to use those slim hips of his to full advantage. He stroked her just right, sending her into an orgasm that kept going and going… It was remarkable. Truly astounding.

And then he finished and her body still rang with climax, demanding more. How could this be? Was this the frenzy they tried to warn her about?

All she knew was that she needed more. More, her cat cried out within her soul. Ever more.

Grif came to her rescue, claiming his spot between her thighs, joining them with little fanfare and a bit more force than she'd expected. It was just the right touch, taking away the pain of need and bringing her immediately back to the peak that beckoned.

He rode her hard, stoking the fire that threatened to consume her sanity, making her come over and over until it all blended into one massively long orgasm that made her scream into the darkness. She keened her pleasure into the night sky, shouting to the stars, howling at the moon.

Well, not really howling. She was a cougar after all. Not a wolf. Still, her spirit called to the stars, dancing among them for short periods of utter bliss punctuated by moments of stark need.

Grif was always there. Stroking her. Pleasuring her. Caring for her.

Throughout the tumult, she knew his love.

In the end, it was the only thing that saved her.

The fire abated when he finally came, allowing her a brief moment of respite. Grif kissed her tenderly, whispering her name until she opened her eyes, responding to the command in his hushed tone.

"Are you okay?"

She blinked up at him. His warm body still blanketed her. His softening cock was still within. One hand cradled her cheek with tender concern and the look in his eyes... Well, it blew her away.

"I'm fine now." She wanted to reassure him but she wasn't really certain of anything at the moment. The hunger had receded, but she felt it there, waiting in the back of her mind, anticipating it's next time to strike. "Was that the frenzy?"

Grif nodded once. "Your eyes changed, sweetheart. They blazed gold with need while you were caught in the throes of the frenzy."

She tried to raise her hand to touch her eye, but she didn't have the energy just then. She would take his word for it. He seemed worried, but she couldn't do anything about that. Not yet.

She felt the fire inside her gearing up for round two.

"How long?" she gasped as the need started to creep in on her again.

"As long as it takes," he answered in a steady voice that was exactly what she needed to hear. He separated from her and helped her sit up as he stood before the low altar. "I brought you here because the stone circle offers some protection from magic. Performing this rite here beseeches the Lady to watch over you and gives Her the energy overflowing from our actions to be absorbed into this sacred place."

She thought she understood, though the shifter beliefs would take some getting used to. Her grandfather had practiced a mix of beliefs that worked for him and Lindsey had been raised in the modern world, with modern views on religion—until she'd finally spent time with her grandfather when she was a teenager.

She had learned a great deal about spirituality from the old man. She would have to learn even more from Grif and his people—if she had the time to do so.

Lindsey felt the fire approaching and knew she didn't have much more coherent time. She reached out to Grif, grabbing his forearms.

"No matter what," she gasped. "You are everything to me, Grif. Everything."

She released him and clutched her midsection as roiling pain washed over her. She needed something...some*one*. Any male would do for the pain that was plaguing her.

She saw Grif nod to the werewolf before he moved away. Large hands—not Grif's—took her by the waist, urging her to turn and bend until she was leaning face down across the middle of the altar stone. Her butt stuck up in the air, her legs spread, waiting as the fire within her fanned to painful life.

She didn't have to wait long. Logan entered her from behind and she remembered what Grif had said to him. That he'd let him have her *his* way later. Doggie style.

There were no preliminaries because none were needed. He slid into her—gentler than she'd expected—and began his motion immediately. Good. That's exactly what she needed.

Grif moved to stand on the other side of the stone, facing her. She was leaning forward, using her hands and elbows to balance her as she was pushed from behind by Logan's deep strokes. Grif's cock was getting hard again as he watched her get fucked by the werewolf Alpha. It was right in front of her.

Too far away.

But she *needed* it. She needed *him*. Lindsey reached out with one hand, nearly losing her balance in her plea for Grif to move into range.

He walked closer to steady her and then she had him. Her hand closed around his hard cock, stroking him and drawing him closer. She wanted to taste him. She *needed* to have him in her mouth while the werewolf filled her pussy. She needed it like her next breath.

Grif made a token protest, but gave up without much effort

when she took him deep into her mouth. Each stroke Logan made pushed her mouth onto Grif and she anticipated the rhythm, enjoying making both men as hot as she felt inside.

It was like nothing she'd ever experienced. It was raw. Emotional. An inferno of lust and desire.

Too much for the werewolf, apparently. He came with a howl. Too soon! Too damn soon.

She thought she heard Logan apologize as he left her, empty, aching, wanting. She held tight to Grif's cock with hands and mouth, needing the connection. Needing. So much *need*.

She felt wetness on her face and knew she cried. She was going to die. She was going to go insane. She was going to lose herself in this endless need and never come out.

"Hold on, kitten," Grif whispered, bending low to stroke his hands over her shoulders and back. "Help is coming. I know what you need."

Oh, thank heaven! He knew. Somehow, Grif knew and she trusted he would help her. Somehow. Some way. He would help her. He would find a way.

She heard a rustle of clothing behind her and then—shockingly—a new cock slid into her. Too tight. Too big. Wider than the werewolf. Thicker. Just bigger.

Her addled mind couldn't really process what was going on. All she knew was insatiable hunger. Desperate need.

And then the new man began to move, thrusting deep, stretching her wide, hitting nerves she hadn't really known about before. The slight pain of his entry was welcome in her frenzied state. It was nothing compared to the pain of being empty and unfulfilled.

She started to come almost immediately and rode the wave higher than before, longer, deeper. Climax followed climax, becoming almost indistinguishable from each other, wrapping her in one long web of pleasure the likes of which she had never before known—and would probably never know again. People couldn't feel this much and survive.

Could they? Apparently, she was about to find out.

Sanity began to return even before the end this time. Lindsey took it as a good sign. But then she started to wonder just who's cock was fucking her with such gusto. One of the other wolves? Had Logan brought reinforcements from his Pack?

She hoped it wasn't one of the assholes who'd been hassling her, even as she came again, moaning around Grif's cock in her mouth. That seemed to set him off and he pulled out as she levered herself upward, wanting his come on her breasts. The feel of his warm seed on her sensitive skin made her come again, milking the incredibly thick cock that was ramming into her in short digs from behind.

Whoever he was, he knew how to use that weapon of his to full advantage. If she hadn't been so far gone with need, she would never have been able to take such a monster, but as it was, he—whoever he was—was just what she needed.

He came and she felt the warm spurt of his seed shoot inside her. Strong, callused hands coaxed her upward to slide her back against a hard-muscled chest. Those same hands caressed her slippery breasts, rubbing in Grif's seed, tugging at her nipples as she screamed and exploded for a final time.

When she could breathe again, she opened her eyes and turned her head. She saw sandy, blond hair framing a familiar, rugged face.

"Steve?" she whispered, realizing she had just been fucked senseless by her new brother-in-law.

His hips surged, reminding her that they were still joined. He smiled and bent to gently kiss her upturned lips.

"Welcome to the family," she heard him whisper before she faded into unconsciousness. The intensity of the past hour had taken all her energy.

CHAPTER ELEVEN

Lindsey came to as Grif carried her back to the cabin. She'd been so beautiful in her frenzy, but he'd been worried. He'd never seen it take someone so completely.

"Grif?" Her groggy voice alerted him to her confused state. He looked down into her eyes, glad to see them forest green once again. The golden glow of the frenzy was gone. For now.

"It's okay, kitten. I have you." He kissed the top of her head, glad his brother and the werewolf Alpha were guarding them from a distance on their trek back to the house.

"Was I dreaming?" She squinted and the confusion on her face alleviated some of his worry. She might not even remember all of what happened. That might be best for a woman raised among humans with human sensibilities. She wouldn't understand what had to be done.

"What do you remember?"

"Logan. Then...Steve?" Her voice sounded shocked. "Was that really Steve or was I imagining it all?"

Grif debated over how to answer. Should he tell her now, while she was groggy? Or should he wait to see if the memory came back on its own? And if he waited, would she be mad at him for not telling her sooner?

"You want the truth?" he asked instead of answering her question outright.

"Always." Her answer was strong and immediate. Grif sighed. He had to tell her now.

"Yeah, it was Steve. He was supposed to just guard us from outside the circle but when your frenzy flared so high, I knew you needed more than just the two of us could provide. I've never seen a frenzy like that and I hope to never see it again." Grif squeezed her as they walked. They were getting very close now to the cabin. "I could've lost you, kitten," he admitted, not caring that his voice broke on the whispered words.

"I'm sorry," she whispered brokenly.

She had tears in her eyes and he worried about her stability after such a tumultuous night. So much had happened to this woman in such a short time. It was a lot for anyone to deal with.

"You have nothing to be sorry for," he assured her. He hoped she heard the truth in his voice.

"But Logan...and then your brother..." she trailed off.

He opened the door to the cabin with the hand under her legs and swept her inside before answering. He had to tread carefully. Lindsey had been raised human, with human sensibilities.

He carried her to his bedroom and placed her gently on the bed. Sitting at her side, he kept contact with her at all times, offering the unconscious reassurance of his touch. Her new *were* side would need that touch, which was so vital to their animal natures.

Grif stroked her hair back from her face and dipped his head to kiss away the tears that leaked out from her eyes. She looked up at him when he drew back and she looked so scared, his heart went out to her.

"Both the wolf and my brother are shifters, kitten. They've been through the frenzy. Just like me. And every other shifter. We know what it's like. And ours were normal. Yours was vastly accelerated. We can only guess what that did to you. And you need to know, you were in danger. I didn't want to scare you more beforehand, but the frenzy requires satisfaction or it can result in derangement. I've seen more than one shifter go insane and have to be either put down or locked up when the frenzy strikes. I don't want that for you. Ever."

"But I betrayed you." Her voice was a mere whisper, but it was full of shame and dread.

"Nonsense." He was deliberately curt, hoping to shock her out of her mood. It seemed to work as she blinked. Her eyes cleared and she really looked at him—studying his response. "I asked them for backup and it was a good thing I did. Your frenzy was the worst I've ever seen and although I would've tried my best, there's no way a single male could have helped you through that alone."

"I've never done anything—"

He cut her off by placing one finger gently over her lips.

"Don't you think I know that, kitten? But honestly, shifter standards are a lot different than human. We all go through the frenzy. We don't expect our mates to arrive virgin to our beds. Most cats have gotten up to all kinds of naughtiness by the time they're your age, with the full knowledge and encouragement of the Clan. It's important for us to burn off that youthful frenzy before we settle down, and repressing it can only cause problems. Serious problems. So we cats tend to play. A lot. Both before, and sometimes, even after we find our mates."

The tears were gone from her eyes, replaced by curiosity. Good. Cats were always curious and he understood that response very well indeed.

"You really don't mind?" She was still whispering, fragile, but no longer weeping, for which he was very thankful.

"I really don't mind." He had to be clear, so she understood and didn't feel bad about something he had planned for and expected once he realized what was happening to her. "I am grateful to them and to the Lady that you came through this in one piece—mentally and emotionally."

"What if it's not over?" She bit her lip, clearly worried.

"Then we'll handle it as it comes and I won't ever love you any less for what you'll be going through. It's a natural thing for us, but it's been forced on you all at once and in an overpowering way. I understand that. So does Logan. And so does Steve." He was very firm about it, making sure she understood his words and intent.

"I love you too." She'd surprised him by not asking more questions, but instead, picking up on the one part of his words that meant the most.

His woman was special, and he was lucky to have her, no matter what trials they might face in the future. With love binding them, they'd face it all…together.

Grif and Lindsey spent what was left of the night twined around each other as if the slightest space between them was not allowed to exist. He held her until she fell asleep and then followed her into dreamland, a smile on his face.

The next morning, Grif was gone from the bed when Lindsey woke. She took her time, taking a shower in the large, masculine, attached bathroom, and stole some of Grif's clothes—a crisp white button-down shirt and a pair of sweatpants—before heading toward the smell of bacon. Her stomach growled as she made her way into the kitchen.

She stopped short, finding Steve there, by the stove, overseeing a pan of sizzling meat. Grif was nowhere in sight.

"Come on in and sit down. The bacon's almost perfect. And I'll whip up some eggs next if you're in the mood." Steve's tone was light. Friendly.

Lindsey didn't know what to make of it. He'd been *inside* her the night before, for goodness sake! She wasn't used to making small talk over breakfast with acquaintances who'd fucked her brains out—by surprise, at that—the night before.

Not knowing what else to do, she took a seat at the kitchen table and watched Steve bustle around, filling plates and frying up eggs. One by one, he placed the finished products on the table.

Neither of them spoke for the few minutes it took him to finish cooking the meal. He seemed at ease with the silence, but Lindsey was growing more agitated by the second. She simply didn't know what to expect from this confrontation and she was on edge.

When Steve finally settled across the table from her, they both had big plates of bacon, eggs and toast in front of them. He dug in and she followed suit. After a few bites, he broke the uncomfortable silence.

"It's all right, you know. I could see you were in frenzy and we all know what that's about. I'm just glad I could help you." He cracked a mischievous smile before filling his fork with another scoop of eggs. "Not that I didn't enjoy it immensely." She smiled as he chewed, almost laughing as he concentrated on his plate.

"Were you watching us the whole time?" Lindsey asked, dreading the answer. She ate mechanically, not knowing how she was ever going to feel at ease in this family after what had happened the night before.

"I wouldn't be much of a guard if I watched you instead of the woods," Steve answered. Hope rose to be quickly dashed a moment later. "I could hear you, though. And I knew when you might need my help. Grif gave me a signal and I came in. Logan took my place guarding in the woods."

In the harsh light of day, sane Lindsey didn't know what to make of insane-cat-woman's frenzy. Or how she was going to deal with the ramifications of her actions the night before. This was fully outside of her experience. So far outside, it felt like she was walking on a different planet altogether.

"Just so we're clear, I'm in love with your brother." She needed him to know there would likely never be a repeat. She had never been promiscuous and wasn't about to start now.

"I never doubted it for a minute." He replied so quickly, she could feel the truth in his words. "Look, Lindsey, don't get all weird about this. Everything about you becoming a shifter out of the blue like this is strange and new. We've never had to deal with a frenzy like yours and Lady willing, we never will again. But Grif is the Alpha of a large Clan and I'm his second in command. We deal with crises of various kinds all the time. Few are as pleasurable as your situation, of course," he winked at her and continued digging through his mountain of scrambled eggs. "What I'm trying to say is that I did what I did for the good of the Clan, my brother and you. In that order." He seemed unapologetic for putting her last on his list and she found a grudging respect for his honesty taking root in her mind.

"I have no designs on you whatsoever, though I wouldn't turn down a three-way if I was ever offered the chance again. I enjoyed helping you, but that's as far as it goes. You don't have to worry this is going to cause some kind of problem within the family or the Clan. We're shifters. Furthermore, we're cat shifters. We didn't earn our frisky reputation lightly. Cats know how to have fun and we don't have a lot of hang ups about sex." He chewed a strip of bacon before resuming his revelations. "Sex is sex, and we all go through a period of frenzy when we're young. For some of us it lasts longer than others. But what you have with Grif...well...that's a mate bond if I've ever seen one. Mating is different. Mating is permanent. Commitment. Love."

She had to smile at the way he described it—and the almost-longing on his face as he stared into the distance. Maybe he did understand.

"You were in the military, weren't you?" She figured she'd give them both a break and change the subject. He'd settled quite a bit for her and she needed time to think through his words and actions.

Steve returned his attention to her and smiled. "I was a Green Beret. So was Grif, though we served at different times."

"Impressive." She didn't know much about the Army, but she did recognize the name of the elite Special Forces branch.

"Which is why he left me here this morning to guard the house while he scouted the perimeter." Steve finished his plate and put the dirty dish in the sink for a quick rinse. "Matt took Belinda into town to get supplies," he went on. "Grif is on his way back in, so we'll switch off. I'll take outside duty while you two finish breakfast." He winked at her again as he headed for door. "He didn't think you'd be up this early, but I'm glad we had some time to straighten a few things out. I'm also glad—if I haven't said it before—that you're part of the family now, Lindsey. I've never seen Grif happier, or more at peace, than when he's with you."

Steve left without another word, leaving a stunned Lindsey in the kitchen with her half-eaten breakfast. She heard the door open and then the low rumble of the two brothers sharing conversation before the door closed again. Her hearing was growing much sharper now that she was able to shapeshift.

Grif walked into the kitchen area a moment later, leaning over to kiss her hello before grabbing the third portion of eggs, bacon and toast Steve had left warming by the stove. Grif joined her at the table and ate heartily, a smile on his face every time he looked up and caught her eye.

"You're up early," he commented as he dug into his food with gusto.

"I'm usually an early riser. Or at least I have been since I moved into my grandfather's house. There's been a lot of work to do and limited time to do it."

"I know that feeling, but sometimes it's good to delegate. That's what little brothers are for." He chuckled as he chomped on a slice of crispy bacon.

"You have a big family." Even she heard the envy in her tone.

"Bigger than you realize." He squeezed some ketchup on the remainder of his scrambled eggs. "Originally there were seven of us. Me, Steven, Jacqueline, Magnus, Robert, Matthew and Belinda." Lindsey stayed quiet, allowing him to speak in his own good time. "Jackie married young to an older cat from a distant Clan. We didn't know a lot about him, but Jackie was always headstrong. I liked that about her. She knew her own mind from the time she was a kitten." He smiled nostalgically, though his expression held sorrow as well.

"I already told you, the man she married—Timmons—beat her. We didn't realize it until she came home, begging for help." Grif's voice was full of sorrow mixed with a simmering anger as he went on. "She was hiding it from us for whatever reason. Soon after they mated, she moved to live with his Clan and things went bad. If we'd seen her, we would've known something was wrong and we would have intervened. Timmons fled the country and the best trackers I could hire all over the globe haven't been able to find him. They always seem to be a day late. He's been traveling steadily, never staying in one place too long. One day though, I'll have justice. Jackie's spirit won't rest properly until I do."

Lindsey reached out to cover his hand with hers. She felt so bad for him, but there was little she could do other than offer her support and what comfort she could.

"You'll find him when the time is right." She didn't really know what else to say. It was obvious he had loved his sister and her loss had affected him deeply.

"That's the thing. The past few days..." He trailed off.

"What?" He looked so troubled, she wanted to know how she could help him.

"I could swear I've caught just a whiff of his scent a few times," he admitted. "That's why I called in the cavalry. Then we had a report that he was spotted just a short distance away. He's back in the States, but he always seems to be one step ahead of those I've hired to track him. I even asked Slade to work on the case, but he's still on his honeymoon and I didn't want to ruin it for him or his new mate."

"Who's Slade?" She wanted to encourage him to talk. She wanted to know more about the things that troubled him so that she could maybe figure out a way to help.

"Best damn tracker I've ever met," Grif answered, brightening a bit. "He came to Nevada to track my mother's killers. He found them all right. A lot faster than any of us expected him to, but then, he's got a lot of magic on his side. As does his new mate. You'll like Kate. She's the Clan's new priestess."

"They're in Nevada?"

"The Clan is based out of Las Vegas right now, though that's relatively new. I thought we all probably needed a change of location after Jackie died and there was a big construction project in Vegas that I would have to be on site for anyway. We built a development, moved in as many of our people who wanted to come with us, and set up shop. We do that from time to time. Cat's like to roam." He shrugged as if that much was obvious. "Our Clan is different from most others. It's not just cougar shifters. Well, the actual heart of the Clan is, but the extended Clan includes everyone who works for Redstone Construction. Some have stronger ties than others, but I consider them all part of my extended family."

He shrugged as if it was of no importance, but even Lindsey had heard of his construction company and had an inkling of how large it was. A whole lot of people worked for the family business and even if just a fraction of them were shifters, it meant there were a *lot* more shifters in the world than she'd thought.

As he talked, it became apparent there was also a lot she didn't know about his world. It sounded violent—his mother had been murdered, after all—but it also sounded like a truly loving and supportive environment. And she was beginning to realize that Griffon Redstone was responsible for more than just his brothers and sister. He was the head of a large, powerful and extensively connected group of shifters.

And he had trouble in his past that might still be out to get him.

"So you think Timmons might be nearby?"

Grif ran one hand through his golden hair as he blew out a frustrated breath. "Hell if I know." He had finished eating and began to clear the table. Lindsey got up and helped. "I might be imagining it, but I really thought I scented him—just the faintest whiff—a few times. Maybe I'm crazy. Maybe I just want revenge so bad, I'm manufacturing things that don't really exist."

She stopped by the sink, facing him. "Do you really think that?" she asked quietly.

His eyes met hers and she saw the serious concern and thirst for justice in his golden gaze.

"No," he answered simply. With finality. "I feel like the showdown is coming sooner rather than later. I feel that danger is closer than we think, and while one part of me rejoices at the chance to tear Timmons limb from limb, another part of me worries for everyone around me. Timmons could try to use Belinda, or you, against me. He could try to hurt or kidnap either one of you as a way to throw me off balance. Which is why I'm having my brothers guard you both if I can't be around." He placed his open palms over her shoulders, holding her gaze. "Please don't go anywhere without either me or one of my brothers. Your life could depend on it."

She didn't want to believe the danger was real, but he seemed so worried.

"I won't," she promised quickly. "But what about your brothers? Won't they be in danger too? Timmons could attack them."

"He could, but there wouldn't be as much to gain and a lot more risk involved. My brothers would take a bite out of the bastard and they are all skilled fighters. Plus, if he wants to force a fight, it's me he'll confront. I'm the Alpha. Whoever wins in a contest for dominance in my Clan and wins, rules the Clan. Sick as it is, by mating with my sister, he has some claim to position in my Clan, even though he killed her. I've renounced him, of course, but there's still that tie."

"So if he wins a fight with you, he takes over Redstone Construction?" She didn't really understand.

"No, kitten. If he kills me, he takes over my position as Alpha with the Clan. He might try to take the business too, but there are legal documents in place that would make that highly unlikely. Thing is, shifters place more stock in dominance than in money. Money can be made, dominance has to be earned."

"He has to kill you?" She was shaking at the very idea of a fight to the death. "But why? What would he gain from being dominant over a group that hates his guts?"

"Killing the old Alpha is one of the ways to establish dominance beyond the shadow of a doubt. It isn't done all that often anymore, but in the old days, it was pretty common. Of course, once Timmons killed me—which I like to believe is impossible—then my brothers would challenge him, one at a time, until they returned the favor. Still, it might be worth it to him to get the price off his head." Grif let her go and turned away. "I put a bounty on him. Only by getting rid of me and taking my Clan can he rescind it. And if he managed to get rid of me, then my brothers stand about the same chances in a one on one fight with him. We're all about equally matched. Personally, I think I can best Timmons in a fair fight, but he plays dirty. He could use you or Belinda to distract me or stir the anger of the cat beyond all rational bounds. Which is why I need to keep you both as safe as possible. If I thought sending you away would do it, I would, but for now, the safest place is with me, right here, where I can watch over you."

She went to him and put her arms around him from behind. It didn't take more than thirty seconds for him to turn around and return her embrace. He hugged her, rocking slightly back and forth, just sharing the closeness, the caring feelings. The love.

How did this man become the center of her world in such a short amount of time? Lindsey's human side wanted to question it, but the cat who now lived inside her seemed to think all was right with its world whenever Grif was near. The cat recognized him. It accepted his dominance, his partnership, his care. It wanted to do all it could to please him and bring him those warm feelings of knowing someone in the universe put you before themselves, in return.

They were still hugging when the kitchen door opened and Matt ushered Belinda in before him. The air around them was fraught with so much tension, even Lindsey could sense it. She moved back from Grif, watching the two newcomers.

Matt had a deep frown on his face and his brows were drawn together in something like anger. Belinda just looked frightened.

"What's wrong?" Grif asked before Lindsey could.

"I saw Timmons in town. Plain as day. He's definitely here."

"Sonuva—" Grif swore.

"He tried to talk to me in the store," Belinda admitted in a shaky voice. "But I ran to Matt."

"You did the right thing, munchkin," Grif praise his baby sister, dropping to one knee to catch her in a fierce hug. She clung to him like a lifeline and Lindsey saw the way the siblings loved each other and depended on each other for strength and reassurance.

"Timmons made a run for it. I saw him as he left the store. He paused by the door and caught my eye." Matt's anger seemed to boil over as his fists tightened, his knuckles showing white at his sides. "I tried to pick up his trail, but he was gone. And so many people come and go through that door every day, it's next to impossible to pick out one scent from hundreds."

Grif released his sister and stood. "Lindsey, would you take Belinda upstairs? No going outside unescorted for either of you right now. I'm sorry about that, but your lives are in danger if he catches you alone."

"It's okay Grif. I'll play inside for now," Belinda offered, her young voice trembling. She was scared and Lindsey's heart went out to her.

Lindsey reached out and put her arm around the youngster's shoulders, turning to leave the kitchen. It was pretty obvious that

Matt had more to say that he didn't want to reveal in front of the child. Lindsey didn't mind helping to shield Belinda from whatever it was that made Matt vibrate with anger, but she'd be asking Grif for the scoop the moment they were alone.

CHAPTER TWELVE

The moment Lindsey and Belinda were out of earshot, Grif turned to his youngest brother.

"What?" That's all he had to say. Matt was definitely eager to tell his Alpha the rest of whatever had happened in that store.

"When Timmons caught my eye, it was on purpose. Belinda was wrapped around me, trembling, and she couldn't see Timmons, but I could. He stopped with one hand on the door and with the other, he drew a line across his neck as he nodded at Belinda. It was a clear threat to kill her. The bastard!"

Grif seethed, but had to be calm. He had to think this through.

"He was baiting you."

"Sure he was, but the threat is still real. He's killed before. He's killed *our sister* before!" Matt was pacing now, anger almost overcoming him.

"I know." Grif was angry too, but he had to do his best to remain level headed.

He'd learned his lesson when they'd lost their mother. Not one of the five brothers had been thinking straight and they had almost played into the hands of the murderers who'd wanted them to reveal their abilities and the existence of shifters to the human world.

Grif had spoken at length to the Lords of the *Were*, Tim and Rafe, about it after the fact. They'd been the ones to send their best man—Slade—to track the killers and prevent Grif and his brothers from doing something irreparable. It had been Tim who suggested taking time away from the Clan. The cabin wasn't too far from where the Lords had their base as the crow flies, but the Rockies themselves created natural boundaries between Packs that kept them confined to certain geographical areas.

There were lots of wolf Packs spread over the Rockies. Logans' Wind River Pack was one of the smaller Packs, but he was a capable Alpha who was drawing new members to him each day.

Oftentimes, dominant, fair leaders like him would attract loners and those unhappy with their birth Packs. Logan's little group had already gained more than a quarter of its current population since he'd taken over. That was the sign of a good Alpha and a Pack that might one day become a powerhouse.

All these thoughts zipped through Grif's mind as he chewed on the problem of Timmons. He didn't want to, but they probably needed the local Alpha on this. He lifted his phone and placed the call. As it rang, he left his youngest brother in the kitchen and walked into the living room to speak with the wolf Alpha.

"Logan? It's Grif. I need your help." He exhaled his frustration. High emotion would only get in the way of rational action. He had to strive for calm.

"Is your lady still in a bad way?" Logan asked on the other end of the call and Grif could hear the concern in the wolf's voice.

"No, she's better now. The frenzy has lifted for the most part. I can handle it from here on out." He wanted that point to be crystal clear, though he'd always be grateful to the other Alpha for helping his mate stay sane when it could've gone either way. "Remember I told you how my sister was killed by her mate? Well, my younger brother saw the bastard in town today. I've been catching faint whiffs of his scent for the past few weeks, but I couldn't be sure until now. Matt definitely saw him. He's here and I believe he's stalking Belinda. I can only assume he's the next best thing to feral."

"Damn," Logan cursed. "Do you have a photo? And something to scent him by?"

"Yeah." Grif sighed. He'd brought the items with him from Nevada, hoping he would never need them, but he'd been wise to come prepared.

"I'll come over. The sooner we get the Pack on this, the sooner we can run him to ground," Logan growled. "I won't tolerate a feral shifter running loose in my territory. Especially not one that's already killed another shifter."

"Thanks, Logan. And I'm sorry we brought this danger to your territory."

Logan was silent a moment as if considering how to reply. Finally he answered.

"No sweat, Grif. It's probably not a bad thing to have the Redstone Alpha owe me one." Logan chuckled as he ended the call and Grif had to follow suit.

By comparison, Grif's Clan was much more highly placed in *were* hierarchy than Logan's. The other Alpha could benefit greatly if he called in his favor at the right time.

"You think Timmons is feral?" Matt's voice came to Grif from near the entry to the kitchen. He'd followed quietly, listening in on the call, but Grif didn't mind. If he'd wanted the call to be private, he'd have gone elsewhere.

"I've been thinking about it for a while. And it's something I talked over with Tim and Rafe the last time we spoke. We'll never know if Jackie was his true mate. Only they know the truth of that, but if she was, now that she's gone, his inner cat has to be in deep mourning. The conflict between the cougar and the man who possibly killed his own mate…that kind of thing can drive a person around the bend." Grif sighed. "Rafe tried to dig into Timmons's past, but information was hard to come by. Before joining his Clan, he was a loner. No family ties to that group, and the Alpha there isn't the strongest or most upstanding cat in the woods. He tends to attract the dregs, though before his reign, the Clan was a good one. Since he took over though, the only new members are not exactly the cream of shifter society."

"I wish we'd known this before allowing Jackie to move there."

"*Allowing?*" Grif laughed. "You're younger, but you should remember Jackie's stubbornness. We never *allowed* her to do anything. She just did whatever she wanted and asked forgiveness later. The only one who could even attempt to curb her impulses was dad. After he died, she was a wildcat. That girl was a handful. And I loved her exactly as she was." Grif had to fight the emotion that tempted to overcome him.

"So what are we going to do?" Matt's tone was deferential, but strong. He might be the youngest of the brothers, but he was by no means weak.

He could be Alpha of the Redstone Clan as well as any of Grif's brothers. They were all Alpha in nature and good men. It did Grif's heart proud to know that his brothers suppressed their natural instincts somewhat to follow his lead, and that if something happened to him, the Clan would be in good hands.

"Logan's coming over. We need to tell him what's happening in his territory." Grif's thoughts turned to the grim business at hand. "He's offered his Pack's help and I'll gladly take it. They know this land better than anyone else. But I'm also going to tell him I'm calling in more specialized help."

"The Wraiths?" Matt named the group of former Special Operators who had gathered around Jesse Moore, a werewolf who lived reasonably close by. Members of the elite shifter team had come to help after the Redstone matriarch—their mother—had been murdered in Nevada.

Grif nodded. "As many of them as will come. I don't care what it costs. The local Pack is strong, but young, and Timmons has outrun every professional tracker we've put on him. I want to run him to ground here. I want this threat over with so we can all get on with our lives and end this once and for all."

"The locals may not go for it," Matt warned.

"Too bad." Grif was in no mood for counterpoint, though he knew his little brother had a valid thought. "That's part of why I asked Logan here. We need to lay out the case for him and get his agreement. I expect you to help with that. Of the three of us, you're the one with the glibbest tongue. You could sell sand to the Arabs, mom always said. I need you to use that persuasive power on the werewolf Alpha."

"Done," Matt was quick to answer. "Anything else I can do?"

Grif clapped his little brother on the shoulder, glad of his support. "Yeah, go out and tell Steve to make the call. He and I already discussed military contingencies. Tell him to call Jesse Moore and see what kind of help he can organize and when. We need them ASAP. And while you do that, I'm going to talk to Belinda and then try to explain all this to Lindsey." He headed for the stairs. "Call me when Logan gets here."

Grif went up to Belinda's small room and found her there with Lindsey, sitting on the edge of her little twin bed. Belinda was in Lindsey's arms, clinging and shaking with remembered fear. Lindsey looked up, patting the girl's back and her eyes plead with him for a way to calm Belinda. He saw the true worry for his little sister in Lindsey's eyes and once more thanked the Lady for giving him a mate with such a loving heart.

Grif cleared his throat to announce his presence. It was a sign of how upset Belinda still was that she hadn't heard him approach. He'd taught her how to best utilize her sharp shifter senses from a young age, but she was in an emotional state of turmoil and still just a kid. He'd cut her some slack for the moment.

Belinda looked up and saw him. She moved away from Lindsey and tried to wipe her eyes and be brave and his heart broke a little more for the baby that had seen so much tragedy in her young life.

Grif held out his arms and Belinda crumpled, her tears flowing as she launched herself into his arms. He held her and rocked her, letting her cry for the moment. There would be time enough later to put on her brave face. For right now, she needed the outlet and he needed to hold her and know that, at least for now, she was all right.

He held her, sitting on the edge of the little bed, next to Lindsey, and let Belinda cry herself out. He'd done this all too often over the past few years. First when Jackie had died and then, just a few weeks ago, when Belinda had found their mother's murdered body in the back garden.

Poor little mite. She'd had a lot more death to deal with than any kitten should.

When she stopped shivering, Grif drew away gradually, stroking her hair away from her face and smiling as best he could. They both knew the threat was real and Belinda had every right to be upset. He wouldn't deny her those feelings. Her instincts were part of her and something that could only help.

Her instincts had sent her running for the safety of Matt when Timmons had approached her earlier today. He wouldn't fault that in a million years.

"It's going to be okay, munchkin. I promise," he tried to soothe her with his words and gentle hands on her hair.

"But he's here! I saw him!" She was still understandably upset, but at least the crying seemed to be over.

"I know, sweetie. But believe it or not, that's a good thing. It means he wants a confrontation and believe me, he's going to get it." Grif allowed a hint of his determination to sound through his voice. He'd been Alpha long enough to know when his people—in this case, his little sister—needed his strength more than his gentle side. "You may not realize it, but I've had people hunting him all over the world. He fled after Jackie died and that, more than anything else, tells me he was as guilty as I always thought he was. He killed her."

Grif didn't think he was telling the girl anything she hadn't already figured out for herself, though he heard Lindsey's little gasp. Shifter life was, by necessity, more brutal than human life. Lindsey would have to get used to that, and now was as good a time as any to start.

Belinda straightened away from him and dried her last tear. "You're going to make him pay for what he did."

Her strong tone in that little voice took him by surprise. Damn, he was proud of her. This might be the moment he'd witnessed the first stirrings of the Alpha he hoped lived within his little sister. She was young, but she'd always been strong. Maybe she was finding her backbone again, after all the hits she'd taken this past year or two.

Grif smiled at her, showing his teeth. "Justice may not have been swift in his case, but he cannot escape it."

"Good." That seemed to put an end to her tears as Belinda bounced back even more quickly than he would have believed.

She stood up and went to the little window in her small room and looked out from an oblique angle, not allowing herself to be seen from below. That was another move that surprised him. She was learning stealth. He and his brothers had showed her these things before, but she hadn't really been using them, except in games. Now, she was starting to act like a true shifter—still little, but more adult in her ways with every day.

"I'll stay inside as long as I have to if it means you'll get him, Grif," Belinda surprised him yet again by stating as she looked out the window covertly.

He felt his heart swell with both pride and love for his brave little sister – the only female left in his immediate family. He hadn't been a good enough protector of his older sister and their mother, but he'd give his life before he let anything happen to this brave little girl.

And now that he had Lindsey by his side… Nothing and no one would stop him from protecting his family. He'd done what he could before, but even he had to admit Jackie had been an adult and they'd all *thought* she'd been happily mated. Nobody really could have known that her so-called mate would turn on her.

The death of their mother was an act of insanity perpetrated by not one, but two evil mages who had used their magical skills to foul the trail and made it all but impossible to detect their presence. It had taken Slade—a mythical snowcat shifter—to track them. Even then, he was no match for the pair on his own. It had taken all the skills of a powerful priestess and the cunning of the Redstone Clan to bring them both to heel and serve justice.

Nobody blamed Grif for his mother's murder. Nobody, but himself.

There might have been something he could have done to protect her. He didn't know what, but *something*. Something he'd missed. Or overlooked.

He felt the same way, deep down, over Jackie's death. The guilt he carried over both deaths ate at his soul.

But he wouldn't let that stop him from protecting what was left of his family—and his new mate—as best he could. In fact, it only made him extra diligent. He wouldn't lose any more people to Timmons. Never again.

Either Timmons would die...or Grif would die trying to kill him. It was as simple as that.

If a sacrifice needed to be made to bring Timmons to justice, Grif was fully prepared to make it. He didn't *want* to leave his new mate alone, but this had been going on too long to back down now. He loved Lindsey enough to do anything to be certain Timmons couldn't harm her, or the rest of his family, ever again.

"You have to go," Belinda's voice came to him, pulling him from his grim thoughts. "The werewolf Alpha is here. Steve is walking him in right now. I'll be okay now, Grif. You go do what you need to do to keep us all safe."

Belinda turned to him and gave him a quick hug around the waist before turning away, going to the little desk with its pink accessories over in one corner. She turned on her little light and began writing in a little pink notebook, seemingly at peace.

Grif was dumbfounded by the change in her mood. His baby sister was growing up. He looked over at Lindsey and his heart was warmed by her smile. She stood and joined him, and they both walked out of the small room together leaving the girl at her desk.

"Do you really think she's okay?" Grif asked as soon as they were out of earshot of Belinda's room.

"If she's not now, she will be. That's one strong little girl."

Grif liked the admiration and affection in Lindsey's voice. It was good that his females liked each other. He hoped Lindsey would find the same affection for other members of his extended family and Clan once she began to settle into her new role as his mate. One day, depending on what the Clan thought of her, she might even step into the rather large shoes his mother had left behind as matriarch of the Clan. Only time would tell, but Grif thought if anyone could fill that role, it would be Lindsey with her big heart and daring soul.

Grif put his arm around Lindsey's shoulders and tugged her close to his side. She looked up at him as they paused near the top of the stairs.

"I'm sorry all this is happening now, but I have to end this chase with Timmons. Whatever happens, I have to keep you and Belinda safe and finish this mess with my former brother-in-law. He has to be held accountable for what he's done."

Lindsey gave him a little hug and looked up into his eyes. Her gaze with filled with understanding.

"I see how this hurts you and terrorizes Belinda. I'll help in whatever way I can to see justice served. I don't want you all to suffer this way if there's anything I can do."

"You're doing it, just by being here, by my side, kitten. I've never understood the strength a mate can give to her man, just by being there. I'm learning. And I thank the Lady every day that She made you, just for me." He dipped his head and gave her a quick kiss, wishing he had time for more, but he could already hear the downstairs door opening and Steve returning with the werewolf Alpha.

Lindsey reached up and held him there for just a moment, looking deep into his eyes. "I won't pretend to understand your world yet, Grif, but if there's anything I can do, please don't hesitate to tell me. I really do want to help."

Oh yeah, this was his mate. She was as fierce, in her way, as his mother had been, though Lindsey had only been a shapeshifter for a few days. She had the spirit of the Alpha female down pat. She would be a fierce protector and he had to respect that.

"Okay, kitten. We're partners now. For good times and bad. I'll do my best to remember that."

"That's all I ask." She let him go and they walked down the stairs to greet the werewolf.

It was more than a little embarrassing at first to be around Logan—and Steve—after what had happened the last time she'd seen the werewolf Alpha, but the men's casual attitude and Grif's reassuring arm around her shoulders went a long way toward setting her at ease as she sat at his side on the couch. The others were arrayed around the living room and they were all focused on the battle plan they were formulating.

They'd exchanged quick greetings, then all sat down. Matt had told Logan about seeing their ex-brother-in-law in town and Steve had laid out what they knew about Timmons from both years ago and recent reports. He'd also given Logan a small plastic bag that held what looked like an old bandana that apparently held Timmons's scent.

Lindsey was curious about whether her newly sharpened sense of smell would be able to let her track someone by scent, but she'd ask Grif about it later, when they had time. Right now, she was doing her best to sit back and listen. Drawing attention to herself wasn't on her agenda for the evening.

This hunt was clearly the men's purview. They'd been shifters all their lives and knew what they were capable of. By comparison, she was the rankest novice. She wanted to know what was happening, but she knew her contribution—at least to this phase of the operation—would be necessarily limited.

After Logan had been brought up to speed and had asked some questions of his own, Grif finally spoke up. He seemed reluctant at first. She felt the tension in him when he removed his arm from around her shoulders and sat forward on the couch, steepling his hands before speaking his piece. Lindsey wondered what he had up his sleeve and why he was so hesitant to tell Logan about whatever it was.

"Alpha, there's something else you need to know," Grif began. Everyone stilled and looked to the Redstone Clan leader. "While I want and need the help of your Pack on this—if for no other reason than to keep them out of harm's way—I also called in a few other resources. Catching Timmons is too important to leave any stone unturned and he's already proved he can outrun the best trackers money can buy. I hired a team of specialists to aid in running him to ground."

"Who did you call?" Logan's eyes narrowed, but he was reacting more calmly than the others appeared to expect.

"Have you heard about the group of ex-Spec Ops shifters gathered around a former colleague of mine and Steve's?" Grif seemed to be dancing around identifying exactly who he'd contacted. Lindsey figured such information was on a need-to-know basis and unless Logan already knew about the team of shifter warriors, Grif would be circumspect in what he revealed about them. Interesting.

"Jesse Moore's crew?" Logan asked, his tension easing visibly. "Hell, if you hadn't already called them, I was going to suggest it."

"You know Jesse?" Grif asked cautiously and with just a hint of surprise.

"I've known all the Moores since I was just a pup. My mother was from their Pack. I still have family there and we have friendly relations between the two Packs. Theirs is a lot bigger than mine, of course, but we get together a few times a year so the youngsters can make friends and look for potential mates."

"Thank heaven," Grif muttered with real feeling. "I was worried you'd take exception to my hiring them. This is your territory and you've been very indulgent since the little matter of Lindsey was resolved." Grif reached for her hand and clasped it warmly. "I know I'm a visitor here, regardless of how big my Clan is out west. I didn't want to step on your toes."

"No harm done," Logan assured them. "Jesse's guys will probably check in with my security team as a matter of course. They know these woods pretty well. I let them run maneuvers through my territory when they want to sharpen their skills and they've taught my guys a thing or two. The folks who make up my security team were either regular Army or Marines back in the day. Not Special Operators. Though they are pretty sharp. Still, Jesse's guys are even sharper. And younger."

"All right then. Steve called them in right after I called you. What's the ETA?" Grif looked to Steve for the information.

"Boots on the ground in about an hour. I figure they'll send someone to liaise with Logan, and everyone else will probably convene around our cabin. They'll take up guard positions in the woods and send one or two men in to strategize with us."

"Guard posts are good for now, but I'm going to want to go on the offensive. Timmons has been left loose too long as it is. I want him caught and dealt with once and for all."

"Sanction?" Logan asked with a grave expression and though the phrasing was odd, Lindsey had a sinking feeling she knew what he was asking. They were discussing whether or not they were going to kill Timmons.

Lindsey's stomach clenched. Here it was. The stark reminder that these guys were not entirely human. They were predators who occasionally dressed up in human form. But the heart of the beast was still there. The cold-blooded killer lurked in their hearts. Lindsey wasn't sure just how to deal with that aspect of her new friends.

"I want to hear what he has to say first. The evidence is there. Gathered too late to do anything useful with it – except present it to the Lords and get their ruling in absentia. They've already given me leave to deal with it as I will – up to and including the ultimate sanction." Grif's eyes went cold. "I've wanted that bastard dead so bad I could taste it, but the saner side of me wants to hear what he has to say first. If we can take him alive, then fine. If not, nobody's going to get in trouble for killing him while in pursuit."

Logan swallowed. He was taking Grif's words very seriously.

Maybe they weren't as bloodthirsty as she feared.

"Good to know," Logan said in a subdued tone.

CHAPTER THIRTEEN

Like clockwork, about an hour later, there was a knock on the cabin's front door. Logan had left earlier to gather his Pack and make sure everyone was accounted for. Nobody would be running loose until Timmons had been dealt with. Steve and Matt were both outside—Steve on the perimeter, hidden in the tree line and Matt in the barn.

Belinda had stayed up in her room. Grif didn't like the fear he could smell on her, but there was nothing he could do about it now. On second thought—he was doing the best he could to eliminate that fear once and for all by bringing the situation with Timmons to a head. Once he was gone, then Belinda might be able to lose that fear and embrace joy again. It was one of his most fervent wishes.

Lindsey had remained downstairs, only going upstairs to check on Belinda from time to time and bring her a tray with snacks and pop. Grif liked the way Lindsey supported not only him, but his little sister. Lindsey had a soft spot for Belinda, which boded well for their future as a family. And Belinda already looked up to Lindsey, quite obviously happy to have a female in the immediate family again.

Grif opened the door, knowing it had to be one of Moore's men. Nobody else could've gotten past both Steve and Matt without there being some kind of disturbance. Sure enough, the face that greeted him was a familiar one.

"Arlo," Grif greeted the man, offering his hand. "Good of you to come."

The other man didn't smile, but then, neither did Grif. This wasn't a happy reunion. Or at least, the reason Grif was seeing one of Jesse Moore's top men on his doorstep was not a happy one. Grif was relieved to have skilled backup. He knew Arlo's background and abilities. Their odds of coming out of this intact had just increased exponentially because Arlo was just the tip of the spear. He was just a single representative of a force that was most likely even now deploying into the woods all around the house.

"Glad to assist, Alpha." Arlo nodded, one hand resting on the assault rifle slung across his chest with easy familiarity. He was in cammo from head to toe and looked ready for anything.

"Come in," Grif invited, opening the door wider and inviting the ex-soldier into the cabin.

He wouldn't ask Arlo to remove his weapon. The man was a shifter. His entire body was a weapon. If he meant harm to anyone inside the cabin, Grif would deal with it, but pigs would sooner fly than Arlo would betray him. Grif was staking more than just his life on that belief, but he didn't think he was wrong.

Arlo entered and his glance darted around the room, taking in every possible threat while Grif closed the door and then led him toward the coffee table they'd been using for laptops and data collation. Arlo sat on the edge of the sofa at Grif's gesture and looked quickly at the data the brothers had collected.

"Jesse sends his regards. He's on another mission at the moment, but the rest of the team is at your disposal," Arlo reported as he read through the few reports they'd printed out.

"How many men?"

Grif felt a moment of panic. They needed every skilled hand they could get on this. Timmons we too slippery. He'd escaped expert trackers for months. He could easily slip away this time too, and Grif wouldn't allow that. This threat to his family had to end here and now.

"Two squads surrounding the perimeter of the cabin. I've got another squad out hunting with some of the wolves. If they find the target, orders are to herd him toward us here." Arlo finally looked up at Grif, having finished with the reports. "Do you have any objections to that, Alpha? I figured you'd want to witness the capture or kill."

"Witness? Hell, I want in on it!" Grif let a little of his frustration show.

Arlo quirked a smile in response. Grif knew Arlo understood how Grif *needed* to see justice done with every fiber of his being. He wanted his teeth on Timmons's neck. He wanted his claws in Timmons's flesh. The beast wanted vengeance.

"Understood." Arlo nodded respectfully and stood. "I've got eyes in the air as well as on the ground."

Grif took that statement to mean some of the raptor shifters that were rumored to be part of Moore's team were actively pursuing Timmons's trail. All the better.

"No word yet, I presume?" Grif asked as they stood. Arlo didn't seem in a hurry to leave.

Arlo tapped his ear. "Nothing worth reporting yet, but I expect some action soon. I assume the females are here. Do you want them extracted?"

"I'm not going anywhere." Lindsey's voice came from the doorway to the kitchen and Grif realized she'd been listening in. He sighed and realized she was right. He motioned for her to join them.

"Arlo, this is Lindsey. My mate. Up 'til a few days ago, she was completely human. Now, she's cougar, but not used to it. Go easy on her." The warning was couched in a friendly tone, but it was a warning nonetheless. Grif would brook no disrespect to his lady.

"Ma'am," Arlo nodded respectfully, though one of his eyebrows rose at Grif's talk of her being a newly made cougar. Still, Arlo was discrete and didn't ask the obvious question. There would be time for explanations later, if they all lived through this.

"Nice to meet you," Lindsey replied. "And I meant what I said." She turned to Grif as she stood at his side. "I'm not leaving."

"It's okay, kitten. I wasn't going to send you anywhere. I think you and Belinda are both safest with me and my brothers. I trust your people, Arlo, but I don't trust Timmons. He's escaped expert trackers too many times before. He's got skills and I don't want to take any more chances than I have to with my sister or my mate. They stay."

"Understood," Arlo nodded as if it didn't matter to him one way or the other. It was clear he was deferring to Grif as the Alpha, and Grif appreciated it.

Arlo reached into his pocket and came out with a small earpiece, handing it to Grif. He'd used many like it in his time as a Green Beret, though they'd gotten smaller over the years.

"I stopped on the way in and gave one to Steve as well," Arlo said as Grif put the thing in his ear and did a com check.

He could hear the intermittent reports from the team and it made him feel a lot better. They weren't all alone in the wilderness anymore. There was a support team of skilled fighters ready to help defend and protect…and serve up justice to a creature who had escaped it for much too long.

"I've also got one very special team working in town." Arlo's expression was a little more closed when he mentioned the last component of his group. Grif was instantly curious, but he knew enough not to ask for too many details about Moore's men. They were secretive by nature to protect their civilian identities and loved ones. "Jason's best tracker and a small support team. She's got mad skills and is working on picking up the trail from the store where your brother had contact with Timmons. She got the scent from Logan's people and is already on the job."

Grif knew his eyebrow rose as the idea of a female being allowed to work with Jesse Moore's group. The fact that Arlo had been careful to note that the woman was Jason Moore's tracker didn't escape Grif. She wasn't part of the merc team that reported directly to Jesse. Instead, she was part of the larger Pack that answered to Jason, Jesse's brother and Alpha of the Wyoming wolf Pack, of which Jesse's group was part.

"I'm going to hang with Matt in the barn, if you have no objection. Use that as my base of operation. I'm leading the four teams we brought. Logan's leading his group and liaising with me. We figured you'd call the shots from in here and we'd report up to you. Is that okay?"

"Perfect." Grif agreed with the command structure they'd come up with. It would avoid confusion among the groups and allow Grif to coordinate the effort as a whole while the subordinate commanders organized their own teams.

"All right then. I suggest you hole up here 'til we have some news. I've got a feeling for these things and I expect something within the next twenty-four to forty-eight hours."

Grif had learned to trust Arlo's feelings. He had a sort of sixth sense about when action would strike that was well documented among the small group of elite ex-Spec Ops shifters. If he said it was going down in certain time frame, ninety-nine percent of the time, it was going down within that period.

In a way, Grif was relieved to know Arlo had one of his famous feelings about this situation. It was good to know that *something* would happen soon.

In another way, it scared the shit out of him. This could all go sideways very easily. There were a lot of people in the field and any one of them could be hurt or killed trying to help. Or Timmons could somehow infiltrate too far and manage to hurt his family—again. Grif vowed not to let that happen, but he knew better than anyone that the bastard had skills. Grif tried not to take anything for granted.

He shook Arlo's hand as the other man made to leave. "Thanks for coming in on this so quickly. I owe you."

Arlo chuckled. "Just wait 'til you see the bill."

Grif laughed with him, knowing that whatever the mercs charged for their fast response, it would be well worth it. These guys were the best of the best and it was a relief to know they were out there, helping guard his family.

The rest of the day was spent indoors and when it came time to turn in, Grif made sure the second shift of watchers was on duty and ready before he tucked Belinda in for the night. He then went with Lindsey to their room, but he was too on guard to make love to her. Anything could happen at any moment. He didn't want to be caught with his pants down and too caught up in his mate to protect his family.

Lindsey hugged him and he knew she understood. She was on edge too, though they discussed how they needed to sleep so they'd be fresh and alert the next day. Grif was trusting to Moore's guys to keep them safe through the night. He'd trusted them before and knew he needed to trust them now so he'd be rested when it came time for action.

As it turned out, action came a lot sooner than he expected.

"Red Alert."

Grif woke to the sound of Arlo's soft voice in his ear. He hadn't removed the earpiece and he could hear tension in the team leader's voice as he spoke.

It was about three in the morning. Grif and Lindsey had been sleeping, but he came instantly awake, careful of making too much noise. He had to figure out what was going on before he started stomping around. It was too late not to wake Lindsey. She was rubbing her eyes at his side as he sat up in bed. He scanned the dark room and found no immediate threat, so he took the chance to communicate with Arlo through the earpiece.

"Sit rep," he demanded in a low rumble.

"My tracker just followed Timmons's trail to your front door. I think he's in the cabin. We're moving in. Will enter from all points on the first floor." Grif could hear the soft sounds of fast movement on the other end. "I'm sending men to the roof as well. They'll be at every window within the next three minutes. Get ready."

"I'm going to check Belinda," Grif reported, already out of bed and going for his weapon. He'd gone to sleep in his T-shirt and sweats. He'd be able to shift without too much trouble if he needed to and he had a loaded .357 Magnum in his night stand.

A moment later it was in his hand as he headed for the hall. Belinda's room was two doors down on the hall and he cursed the distance between them. He didn't see anyone in the hall, so he moved closer on swift, silent feet, knowing Lindsey was following behind. He could smell the scent of fear and concern, but she was staying with him, showing more courage than he would have imagined.

He didn't really want her with him, but he also didn't want to let her out of his sight. In the end, he figured it was better to have her where he could see her and handle any threats first-hand.

A noise came from behind the closed door to the room on the other side of the hall. Grif stilled, motioning to Lindsey to continue on to Belinda's room while he checked the noise.

He waited 'til she was past him to throw open the door and bring his weapon to bear. He checked himself, seeing one of Arlo's guys entering a little too noisily through the window. Grif cursed. This guy had to be a newbie—or maybe just unlucky. He'd have words with him later. For now, Grif was just glad he hadn't opened fire without checking who it was first.

A scream pierced the night. Lindsey's scream, coming from Belinda's room.

Grif cursed and ran for the child's room, his heart in his throat.

Lindsey had pushed open the door to Belinda's room as quietly as she could, surprised to find it ajar. But then she realized someone was there before her. A man's form stood over Belinda, looking down at the sleeping girl.

And then she saw the knife.

She screamed. She didn't know what else to do. She screamed bloody murder, knowing Grif and everyone else would come running.

As she screamed, she moved out of the doorway and into the

room. Timmons turned to face her. It had to be him. Nobody else would be carrying an unsheathed knife in Belinda's room.

A number of things happened simultaneously. Belinda woke up and jumped into the corner of her bed, crouching and changing into her cat. Good girl. Timmons whirled toward Lindsey and raised the knife, stepping toward her.

Then Grif ran into the room and took Timmons's attention off Lindsey. Grif was followed by another big man, dressed all in black. Grif tackled Timmons while Lindsey went to Belinda, her cat form shaking in fear.

While the men struggled in the small space, Lindsey looked for a way out. The men were blocking the doorway. That left only the window. She didn't like it, but Grif had said cats were good climbers. Seemed like now was the moment to find out how much truth there was in that claim.

Lindsey pushed the window open as quickly as she could and beckoned Belinda over. The little cat didn't need any coaxing. As furniture crashed behind them and men cursed and growled, tearing up the place, Lindsey looked out to find Arlo on the roof along with two cougars she recognized as Matt and Steve.

She pushed Belinda out the window first, then squeezed through the small opening herself, in human form. The roof was relatively wide at this point and not too pitched. She'd be able to cling to it for a little while. At least long enough for things to settle down inside Belinda's bedroom.

Arlo met her. He was in human form too. Belinda was rubbing up against Matt, both in cat form. Steve was heading toward the window at a fast clip. He clearly wanted in on the fight.

"My men are below. They'll help you down from the roof. Go with Freddy. He'll take care of you," Arlo instructed, handing her off to another human-shaped, black-clad operative.

Lindsey was torn. She didn't want to leave Grif, but she knew he wouldn't want her anywhere near the bad guy. And there was Belinda to look out for.

With a last look back at the dark window where crashing sounds could still be heard loud and clear, she followed the man named Freddy toward the edge of the roof. She wasn't quite sure how she was going to get down, but she watched Matt jump from one level of the roof to another, then to the porch roof, Belinda right behind him. Lindsey did the same, but wasn't quite ready to jump off the porch roof the way the cougars had. She'd probably break a leg if she tried that in her human form and she wasn't comfortable enough as a cougar yet to try it either.

She sat on the edge of the porch roof, dangling her feet over the side. Looking down, it seemed much too far to the ground for her comfort.

Freddy touched her shoulder. "I'll go first and catch you. All you have to do is slide down. I'll grab your legs and take you the rest of the way."

That sounded a lot better to her. Lindsey swallowed hard. "Thanks."

Freddy squeezed her shoulder once before hopping off the side. He landed on his feet, his knees bent to absorb the shock. He made it look so easy, but he was clearly a shifter, and had been his whole life. Lindsey didn't know what her newly-changed body could and couldn't do just yet. She wasn't about to chance jumping off a roof anytime soon.

She followed Freddy's encouraging gestures and slid slowly off the roof. There was a scary moment where she was in freefall before the solid man caught her around the thighs and stopped her descent. True to his word, he lowered her carefully to the ground and she did her best not to let her knees buckle. She didn't want to appear any weaker to these shifters than she already had.

"Where's Belinda?" she whispered, aware of the dark shapes of people and animals all around them. There were many men carrying weapons and kitted out like commandos. She could only assume those were the guys Grif had called, finally showing themselves *en masse*.

"She's with Matt, heading for the barn," the man she knew as Freddy answered in a low, gruff tone. He pointed and Lindsey could easily see the small cougar in the shadow of the larger one, loping toward relative safety.

"What about Grif?" Her thoughts turned to the chaos she'd left inside Belinda's bedroom.

She watched Belinda's tail disappear into the dark opening of the barn door and breathed a sigh of relief, knowing she'd be safe for the moment. Then her gaze switched to the upper story of the house behind her. Grif was still in there. She looked over at Freddy and saw him touching his ear, probably to indicate he was listening in on whatever was going down inside. He had one of those little earpieces.

"They're coming out now," Freddy reported after a slight pause. "Target is subdued."

A sigh of relief escaped her as she moved toward the house. She took Freddy's words to mean they'd captured Timmons, not killed him. She thought that was the best result. Her new, inner cat wanted blood, but her human side was glad it hadn't been spilled inside the house.

The front door opened and the man she'd only seen in shadow in the bedroom came out snarling. Grif and Steve were right behind him. They had each held one of his hands and one shoulder as they marched him out the door.

Lindsey stood watching and realized she'd made a big mistake as everything seemed to move into slow motion. She saw how close she was to the steps and tried to move back. Her movement must've captured the prisoner's attention because his eyes locked with hers as he screamed. The scream started out human, but quickly morphed into the scratchy yowl of an enraged cougar.

He shifted shape faster than she'd ever seen anyone change, slipping free of both Grif and Steve's holds. Even encumbered by the shreds of his clothing hanging off his body, he was able to launch himself down the stairs, crashing into Lindsey on his way down.

But she didn't fall. She'd expected to be pinned under a cat. Instead, she was held in the hairy arms of a creature that was some kind of weird cross between a cat and a man. And it was larger and deadlier than either.

What the heck *was* he? She didn't know enough about shifters to know what was happening. Until she'd changed into a cougar, she didn't even know there were more than werewolves in the forest.

A massive, clawed hand wrapped around her throat as Timmons—in monster form—got behind her. Oh, dear lord, he was using her as a shield.

Time resumed its sickening tempo as Timmons backed away from Grif and Steve, left angrily holding air as Timmons slipped away from them. Her eyes met Grif's and she saw the anger and pain in his gaze as he met hers. She wanted to reach out to him but the bastard behind her had her pinned.

"You won't get away with this, Timmons," Steve growled,

pacing closer while Grif held back, watching and clearly both angered and worried by developments.

She'd ruined this for him. She'd been in the wrong place at exactly the wrong time, taking what should have been his triumph over the bastard that had killed his sister away in one moment of stupidity.

Dammit! She wasn't going to let this end badly. She'd screwed up, but maybe she could fix things. Somehow. She grasped for ideas but came up empty.

"I'll rip her throat out," Timmons growled too close to her ear. She tried to shy away but the claws at her throat pierced the skin slightly, drawing blood. She could smell the tang of it in the air. Dammit. She had to think!

"Don't do it," Grif warned in a low, deadly voice.

He was seething with anger and she thought maybe he was up to something. He was hanging back, letting Steve take point. But could she wait for him to do whatever it is he was planning? Or could she help in some way?

"You lower yourself to lie with a human?" Timmons seemed appalled, judging by the tone of his growl. She could see his teeth and they weren't normal human teeth. They were pointy, sharp, two inch-long fangs. Damn.

Grif didn't answer, only mirroring Timmons as he backed toward the trees, dragging her with him. Steve followed, only a few paces away.

Steve shifted as he walked, but didn't turn into the cat she was familiar with. Instead, he stopped halfway—sort of—and became like the monster who held her. It was scary as hell. Steve was a big son of a gun when he was in human form. In this half-shifted monster shape, he was absolutely terrifying.

He stalked them, matching Timmons move for move as he continued backing toward the trees. She tried to see Grif, but Steve was blocking her view. What was he *doing?* Why wasn't he doing *something?*

CHAPTER FOURTEEN

Lindsey realized then that this was all part of the strategy. The brothers were working together. Steve was presenting a clear threat so Timmons would focus on him, but Grif was still in the background. Still in human form. Still dangerous.

But for whatever reason, they were hesitating to act. Probably it had to do with the way Timmons had her by the throat. She had to do something to alter her position... And then it came to her. She was thinking like a human, but she was a shifter now and apparently Timmons didn't realize it.

She wasn't sure why he couldn't smell it on her, but maybe he just assumed any cat scent he picked up around her was from one of the Redstones. That had to be it.

If she shifted, she'd have to do it faster than she'd ever done it before. She had to take Timmons completely by surprise. Could she do it? Lindsey thought maybe she could, but it would take all her courage to try. Still, she had to. She had to give Grif an opening to take down his sister's killer. She'd messed this up by being in the wrong place at just the wrong time. She needed to fix it.

She tried to catch Grif's eye, but Steve was most definitely in the way. She settled for winking at Steve, hoping he'd figure out what she intended and somehow let his brother know.

Lindsey gathered herself and sought the change, almost begging for it to take her fast this time. Fast like lightning. Faster than Timmons could close his claws on her shifting throat.

And just like that, she dropped to the ground, on all fours. She bounded away and a split second later, she heard shots ring out and a dull thud behind her. Her cat eyes looked for Grif and she found him standing with his legs spread, his handgun smoking in his grip. She looked back to where Timmons had been and he was on the ground, the sharp scent of his blood wafting stronger by the moment through the still night air. Grif had shot the bastard and he wasn't moving. Thank goodness.

142

Her legs threatened to give out, but she needed to be strong. Her little nightshirt was bunched around her furry body, but she didn't care. She padded up to Grif and rubbed her head along his legs until he bent down to caress her head with his hands. The scent of spent gunpowder tickled her sensitive nose, but she did her best to hold back the sneeze that threatened.

Grif wrapped his arms around her and lifted, carrying her to the porch as dark-clothed soldiers moved in on Timmons's body. He sat on the steps with her in his arms and she could feel the tremors running through his body. It wasn't obvious to the casual observer, but he let her feel how deeply affected he'd been by the past few minutes.

"Change back," he whispered in her ear and the raw emotion in his gravelly voice would not be denied.

She shifted, not really caring if she flashed everyone. They were shifters. They were used to seeing each other naked, she was sure. But she needn't have worried. Her stretchy sleep shirt fell back into the right place when she resumed her human form with a few tugs from Grif's big hands.

She sat on his lap, his arms around her. She turned, wrapping him in her embrace as well.

"I'm sorry I almost screwed everything up. I shouldn't have been so close to the steps," she whispered, wanting to come clean and clear the air between them.

He drew away and looked into her eyes, seeming to be surprised by her words.

"Sweetheart, this was all my fault. I should have anticipated what he'd do once we got outside. If not you, he'd have grabbed the first vulnerable person he saw. He gave up too easily inside. I should have realized he had something else up his sleeve. Can you forgive me?"

She cupped his stubbly cheek and smiled. "Oh, Grif. There's nothing to forgive. Let's just forget all about it, okay? I definitely don't blame you and I'm just relieved you don't blame me, but you can be sure I've learned a valuable lesson here tonight."

He leaned in and kissed her. His kiss tasted of desperation as well as gratitude and when he moved back and let her up for air, his trembling had ended. So had hers, as a matter of fact. They had helped each other over the rough spot and were ready to move on…together. As it should be.

"You were amazing, Lindsey. I've never seen you shift so fast. I doubt any natural born shifter could have done better." His praise made her feel even better.

Steve was tugging on his shirt as he approached them. He'd been over by Timmons's body for a while but since he wasn't moving and nobody was fussing over the guy, Lindsey figured he was a goner.

"Nice shot, bro," Steve said with a grim smile.

"Thanks." Grif didn't sound pleased, but she would have been appalled if he'd been happy about killing someone. The Grif she knew valued life. He shouldn't take it lightly.

"Timmons will never bother us again. He's dead," Steve stated, looking from Grif to Lindsey. "You did good for a beginner, Lindz. I wouldn't have believed it if I hadn't seen it myself. You're cool in a crisis and that makes me even gladder to know you're part of the family now. We don't look for trouble, but just lately, it's been finding us all too often. It's good to have someone at Grif's side to ease his many burdens who can also be relied upon to be cool under pressure."

Wow. She felt the weight of Steve's approval and it felt good. Grif squeezed her waist and she took it as agreement with his brother's words.

"Thanks. I'm just glad it worked." She would have said more, but she was at a bit of a loss. Arlo's arrival next to Steve saved her from having to figure out what to say.

"We'll clean up if that's agreeable to you, Alpha," Arlo offered.

"I'd be obliged. Can you send his remains to Las Vegas? I'll send him on from there to his home Pack, but I want our priestess to take a look at him first. We've had dealings with mages recently and I want her to check him for magical taint."

"Can do. I can also ask Millie to take a look. She might sense something. She's the Pack's new tracker."

"She's the one who tracked Timmons here, right?" Grif asked and Lindsey could hear the curiosity in his voice.

"The very same." Arlo looked behind him and signaled toward the barn.

A moment later, a woman emerged from the structure, Belinda at her side wearing a man's very large T-shirt. The woman was beautiful, even at a distance. She had black hair, light eyes and a figure that made Lindsey feel a pang of instant envy.

Matt walked behind them, clad only in what had to be borrowed pants that were a little short on his lanky form. Both were barefoot, but the woman was dressed stylishly in a black cat suit and soft soled black boots.

Grif let Lindsey move off his lap. If she was going to meet a woman who looked like that, she didn't want to do it from such a compromising position. She was strong. She had to *be* strong in front of all these badass shifters.

She took a seat at Grif's side and she liked how he reached out for her hand, closing his big fingers over her smaller ones and drawing it to his side. He seemed disinclined to let her hand go and she didn't mind one bit. After what they'd all been through that night, she needed the contact probably way more than he did. That he'd realize that and see to her need without being asked or told meant a lot. He was one helluva guy. And he was all hers.

She tried not to feel too smug about that, but she was proud to have him at her side. In her life. In her bed.

"Millie," Arlo made the introductions as the woman neared. "This is the Redstone Alpha. Grif, this is Millie, our Pack's new tracker."

The woman reached out her hand and Grif took it for a businesslike shake. He then turned to Lindsey and introduced her before they went any further.

"This is my mate, Lindsey," he said, his voice strong with just a hint of emotion as he looked at her. He wouldn't let go of her hand so she couldn't shake Millie's, but the smile the other woman gave her said she understood and even found his possessiveness as amusing as she did.

"I think you know my brother, Slade," Millie said, surprising them. Lindsey felt Grif jerk, just slightly. It probably couldn't have been seen, but she felt it, close as she was to him.

"Slade is a great addition to our Clan," Grif replied somewhat formally. "Can I assume you have his rather unique abilities as well?"

"For the most part," she answered. Something was being said between the lines here but Lindsey didn't quite know what it was. Still, she felt Grif relax slightly and realized the woman held secrets that Grif somehow was privy to because of their mutual knowledge of this guy Slade.

"Thank you for your work here tonight. Without your

warning…" Grif got choked up as he looked at Belinda, standing with Matt and Steve off to one side.

She was all right, but she wouldn't have been if they hadn't gotten the warning in time. Timmons would have killed her first, then moved on to do more damage. It had been so close. Lindsey sucked in a breath, realizing what a close escape it had really been for the girl.

Lindsey squeezed Grif's hand in silent support.

"My pleasure, Alpha. I'm only glad I found the trail in time. He was very good at evasion."

"You can say that again." Grif sighed. "He kept ditching the best trackers I could hire all over the world. Thank the Lady you were here tonight, Millie. I can never thank you enough."

Millie ducked her head modestly. "It is my calling, Alpha," she said simply.

There was something very exotic about the woman and Lindsey found herself fascinated by her despite the lingering, petty jealousy at how beautiful she was. She was also brave and skilled and that only made Lindsey admire her more.

"I know it's distasteful, but would you be willing to take a look at the body?" Grif asked. "We've had dealings with mages recently and I'd like to have him examined by my Clan's priestess—who I guess is your new sister-in-law," Grif said with a hint of irony in his tone. "The more who look at him, the better I will feel. I'd be particularly interested in any magical tattoos that would be invisible to me, but that someone with your background might be able to detect."

Millie's eyes narrowed. "I understand your concern. I'll see what I can do, though I do agree that you should get Slade and his mate to examine him too. Not all of us see things the same." Millie's lips tightened as she turned toward where Timmons still lay, surrounded now by armed soldiers who seemed to be awaiting orders.

She walked away without further discussion, leaving Arlo as she picked her way through the thick grass toward the body.

"When did she join your Pack?" Grif asked Arlo in low tones.

"Not long ago. She just showed up, gave my brother Jason a letter from the Lords which began a round of teleconferences with them and their mate, and the High Priestess. After all was said and done, she'd been welcomed into the Pack. Next thing I know, she's offered her tracking services to Jesse and damned if he didn't take her up on it. She's on-call with our team for cases requiring her special skills." Arlo watched her as he talked. She was by the body now, crouching low, apparently giving it a thorough going over. "This is the first time I've worked with her and I can tell you, I'm really impressed."

"Me too," Matt said, joining the conversation, leaving Belinda to Steve, who had her in a bear hug. "That trail was stone cold. I didn't think anyone could pick up Timmons from the store where I saw him, but she did. She's got serious skills. Just like her brother."

Arlo turned his attention back to Matt and Grif. "I've worked with Slade a few times. He's intense," was all he said, but both men nodded in agreement.

Lindsey was intrigued and wondered when she would meet the guy they all seemed to be in awe of. He was part of Grif's Clan, so she supposed if and when they went back to Las Vegas, she'd get her chance to make his acquaintance. If his sister was anything to go by, he would probably be a very interesting character.

As they watched, Millie straightened and visibly winced. She held her hands outward, palms facing down over the body and spoke a few words they couldn't make out. To Lindsey it looked like a prayer or a benediction of some kind.

Millie walked back to them, a grim expression on her face. Silence held until she stood in front of Grif and found her voice.

"I don't see anything obvious, but there's a feeling…" Her brow furrowed in thought, but she shook her head, apparently unable to find the right words. "It would be best if a full priestess handled this. They see things I cannot."

"Thank you for trying," Grif said respectfully, though Lindsey could tell he was concerned.

"We'll prepare the body and send it on to your Clan." Arlo put in, already making hand gestures that sent a few of his people into action.

Lindsey saw one unfurl what had to be a body bag, though she'd never seen one outside of television before. It impressed her how these soldiers had come prepared for just about anything.

Millie walked away after a solemn nod of farewell, but Arlo remained. His expression was dark.

"Alpha, I'm to blame here for what happened and I'll accept your judgment." Arlo's words surprised Lindsey. "The target should never have been able to get that close to your family."

"How did he?" Grif seemed more curious than angry and Lindsey could see Arlo relax just a tiny bit.

"He took out four of my men in rapid succession and I'll be damned if I can figure out how he did it." Arlo growled in frustration as he ran one hand through his hair. "But you can be sure we're going to find out. Nobody takes out our people. Not that easily."

"Where were they positioned?" Grif stood up and Lindsey went with him. It seemed the time to start getting answers had begun.

Arlo began walking and they followed. He gestured with his hands as they came around the side of the house.

"It was a pretty straight line through our perimeter, on target with your sister's window." He pointed in the direction that led out from Belinda's second story window into the woods. "We found Mick and Jerry on the ground at twenty and thirty yards. Pepe was down at forty-five yards out, but the target had stashed Billy in the crook of a tree on the outermost ring, which is something I guess big cats do with their kills."

"Are they dead?" Lindsey felt the need to ask. It sounded like there had been terrible violence not only in the house, but all around it that night.

"All critical. We won't be sure if they'll make it for a few hours. Our medics are working on them in the barn. Steve suggested we set up triage there." Arlo looked at Grif, seemingly for confirmation that it was okay.

Grif nodded, staring at the woods. His expression was hard to read. Lindsey reached out to him, putting one hand on his arm and standing at his side, letting him know without words that she was there for him.

He seemed to make a decision and come out of the deep thoughts he'd been engaged in, turning to look at Arlo. Simultaneously, he took Lindsey's hand in his and squeezed lightly, reassuring her that she'd done the right thing. He knew she was there and he seemed to be glad she was.

"Whatever you need for them, let me know. I don't want anyone else dying here tonight if I can help it," Grif declared in a strong voice.

Arlo seemed impressed, nodding. "Thank you, Alpha."

"See to your men. We'll talk in a couple of hours unless you need me for something before then." Grif was already moving back toward the front of the house, Lindsey at his side and Arlo following close behind.

"Understood. I've pulled everyone in and will station them around the house. Nobody will intrude without our knowing."

"Good. We'll convene in the living room at dawn, if not before."

"Roger that." Arlo left them by the front door and jogged toward the barn.

Grif turned and took Lindsey into his arms, hugging her close and just standing there for a moment, in the darkness of the porch, resting his chin on top of her head as she listened to the steady beating of his heart. She loved this man. So very much. He'd been through hell that night and she was glad they had all lived to tell the tale. She wouldn't know what she'd have done without him—or Belinda—or even Matt or Steve, for that matter. This family had come to mean so much to her in such a short amount of time.

The door behind them opened and light spilled out from inside the house onto the porch. Matt stood at the door, looking out at them. Grif let her go and they walked into the house as Matt stepped back to allow them to pass.

Belinda was in the living room and she ran to Lindsey when she caught sight of her. She looked like she was holding up well as Lindsey hugged her close. Strong arms came around them both— Grif on one side, Matt on the other. They just stood there for a moment, the family sharing a group hug that made everyone feel better.

Maybe there was something to this shifter need for touch after all, Lindsey thought. Even after the hug ended, it was clear Belinda didn't want to go too far from her brothers or Lindsey.

Touched to be included in the family, Lindsey sat on the big sectional couch with Belinda close beside her. The little girl snuggled into her side while Matt and Grif talked with Steve who had just walked in the door.

The guys looked like they were talking business. Steve was probably talking over the events of the evening from his perspective. There was a lot of back slapping and serious looks.

"You okay now, Belinda?" Lindsey asked, putting her arm around the young girl.

"Yeah," she replied with a muffled sniff.

"You were so brave when you went out that window and jumped all the way down to the ground. You're going to have to teach me how to do that without breaking my leg one of these days." Lindsey squeezed Belinda, offering comfort and encouragement.

"It's not that hard." Belinda looked up at her and gave her a shaky smile. "I can show you sometime, if Grif says it's okay." She looked over at her brothers and Lindsey realized the men were pretty much done talking.

"I think we all need to spend a few hours as a family," Grif said to his brothers, knowing they were still as shaken as he from what had almost happened to the girls tonight. "And we all need a few more hours of sleep."

Both Steve and Matt nodded agreement and Grif turned to where his two ladies sat together on the big, sectional couch. He'd bought it with comfort in mind and he'd slept on it more than a few times, both in his fur and in human form. It would do.

"What do you say we camp out down here until morning? To tell you the truth, I don't want to let either of you out of my sight." Grif crouched down to look at Belinda's pale face.

She'd had a terrible fright tonight, but she was holding up well enough. Still, he didn't want to send her back to her bedroom—or to any room where she'd have to go to sleep all alone. She wouldn't sleep, and he wouldn't blame her. Better that they all stay together for now. At least for the few hours they had until dawn. Maybe some of them would be able to rest as long as they knew everyone was safe and accounted for—and less than a few feet away.

"What do you say, munchkin? Maybe we'll put a mellow movie on and try to catch up on our beauty sleep down here for what's left of the night?"

Belinda launched herself into Grif's open arms and clung to him. He worried at first, but he felt her smile against his chest. She was okay. Or she would be, given enough time to get over tonight's shock. She drew back after a few moments and smiled up at him.

"Thanks, Grif. Can I pick the movie?" She let him go and danced backward, toward the rack where they kept a bunch of DVDs.

"Sure thing. Matt, get the milk and cookies. Steve, get some pillows and blankets from upstairs." He sent everyone off on errands, then collapsed on the big couch, next to Lindsey. His arm went around her.

Damn, it felt good to have her close. Just having her near calmed him and made him realize once again how lucky he was.

His family had been fractured by the losses of their sister and mother, but they'd come through it. And now they'd finally ended the threat that had hung over them like a dark cloud. They could move forward from here.

The first step would be going back home. Grif was already formulating plans to close up the cabin and head back to Las Vegas. He hadn't talked it over with Lindsey yet, but he had hope that she'd be eager to start their new life together in Nevada. She knew his Clan was based there and that they'd have to return sometime. Now that Timmons had finally been dealt with, it was a good time to go back.

"Milk and cookies?" Lindsey asked, chuckling at his side.

"What? Cats like milk. Belinda will drink a couple of glasses and be asleep before you know it. Just you wait and see." He nuzzled her neck, making her giggle.

He liked hearing his mate's laughter. Things could have gone terribly wrong so easily tonight. He was thankful that everyone he cared about had come through this all right. Even the injured guys on Arlo's team were out of danger and would recover. Steve had told him when he'd come in and Grif was relieved.

The only casualty was Timmons and as far as Grif was concerned, justice had finally come to the man who'd murdered Jackie. Late, but it had finally been served.

Belinda chose a movie and slipped it into the player. She climbed over Grif's lap to snuggle in between him and Lindsey. He didn't mind. Belinda was still a child. She had to be feeling especially vulnerable after what had happened earlier. Grif would cuddle her for what was left of the night if he had to, to reassure her that they were all okay and that life would get back to normal. She was safe. They would all be as safe as they could be—together.

Steve and Matt returned as the opening credits started playing to an animated movie about the panda who did martial arts. It was one of Belinda's favorites and Grif had to admit, it had beautiful art and a nice message. He didn't mind that they'd already seen the movie a few dozen times. Tonight was about comfort. If watching something familiar and amusing would bring comfort to Belinda,

Grif didn't mind at all.

Matt poured glasses of milk for them all and passed around the plate of cookies as everyone settled into place. Steve sorted out pillows and blankets and Lindsey helped Belinda make a little nest in the center of the huge couch. Grif snagged a pillow and stuffed it under his head, lifting his feet using the built-in recliner function that was hidden in certain parts of the sectional sofa. Lindsey had her own on the other side. He watched her figure it out after seeing his chair's transformation.

Matt and Steve each had their own recliners on either side of the couch. Steve was closest to the door and Matt had taken the chair to Lindsey's right, between her and the window. His brothers would probably snooze, but they'd be on guard too, should anything threaten the family.

Though Grif seriously doubted anyone or anything would get through the contingent of soldiers stationed very visibly all around the house. They were out in the open now, as he'd noticed when he glanced out the door and window earlier. They'd been shamed by the failure of their perimeter earlier. Grif understood the pride they usually took in their work. They'd be hyper vigilant now after the earlier breach.

As predicted, Belinda downed a couple of cookies and two glasses of milk before nodding off in her little nest of blankets and pillows. He watched her for a few minutes, lowering the volume on the television with the remote control. Lindsey smiled over at him and he knew she understood.

He saw the love in her gaze and his breath caught. They were going to have such a great life together. He'd make sure of it. He'd protect her from whatever dangers might come and teach her all about being *were*. She'd done well tonight. She'd helped get Belinda to safety and performed better under pressure than he'd had a right to expect.

He was damn proud of her. Damn proud to call her mate. And he knew his people were going to love her. She might not have been born a shifter, but she had heart to spare and a sense of honor that went deep into her soul. She would grow into the role of Alpha female, but he thought maybe she had the makings of a great matriarch already. Her love and compassion would be a gift to his Clan and he knew they were going to love her. The rest would come in time.

And at least now, he was much more confident that they'd have that time. The biggest threat to his family had just been dealt with and it was a load off his mind. For the first time in years he felt able to breathe more easily.

There would be other challenges, he knew, but this particular danger had been dealt with—finally. Grif, for one, was relieved.

CHAPTER FIFTEEN

When Lindsey woke, light was streaming in from the window to her right and she was alone in the big living room. She could see armed soldiers standing guard near the windows, facing the forest, on alert for any hint of danger. She knew it was probably overkill, but she was glad of their presence after the events of the night before.

She stretched and heard quiet movements from the direction of the kitchen. Then she noticed the scents of frying eggs and bacon. Oh, yeah, she was hungry. Her stomach rumbled as she stood, but she had other pressing needs at the moment.

She tiptoed quickly upstairs to use the bathroom and find some clean clothes. A few minutes later, she emerged from the master bath to find Grif there. He was freshly shaven and just tugging on a clean T-shirt.

When he saw her, he opened his arms and she went to him, loving the feeling of his warmth, his sexy, muscular body pressed against her. He kissed her and she tasted the mint left by his toothpaste mingling with her own. Yeah, this was a nice way to start the morning. Especially after the fright of the night before.

"Good morning, my love," he whispered as he let her up for air.

"Good morning yourself," she quipped back, though she hugged that little phrase—*my love*—close to herself. How had she gotten so lucky to have captured this man's heart?

Of course, he'd captured hers. Probably back when he'd been prowling around her grandfather's property as her Spirit Guide. Or more likely, before that, when he'd fixed the old generator. Maybe it was when he'd come to her rescue in the diner, back when they'd first met. Yeah, that was probably it.

He was such a great man. Someone who'd come into her life and swept her off her feet even while she was engaged in clearing the debt of honor left by her grandfather. How had he managed to capture her heart when her whole life had been turned upside down? All too easily, actually. He was just that kind of guy.

"What?" He smiled down at her, those amazing smiles of his coming much more easily this morning, it seemed.

"I was just thinking how lucky I am."

"Luck? I prefer to think it was fate," he teased, swooping in to place playful kisses on her lips, her cheeks, her forehead. "They say the Lady works in mysterious ways. I think She made you a cougar just for me. And I, for one, think She knows what She's doing. You're perfect for me, Lindsey. And more than that, you're even perfect for my family and I know the Clan will feel the same."

Mention of his Clan made her bite her lip with a tiny bit of worry. "I hope you're right about that."

Grif leaned in and freed her lip only to capture it with his own in another searing kiss. It would have gone further, but a knock sounded on the door.

"Breakfast is ready. Get it while it's hot," Matt called out from the hallway. "We're feeding the army outside today too, so if you don't come now, there might not be any left."

Lindsey laughed as Grif groaned. "Dammit, he's probably right. The team brought some provisions with them, but we're going to supplement as best we can until the stores open up in town and we can send someone down for supplies. They didn't expect to bivouac here this long." He released her and headed toward the door, opening it and waiting for her to precede him. "Speaking of which, I've been meaning to talk to you about going home."

Lindsey felt a little weight settle in the pit of her stomach. She knew he wasn't a permanent resident here, but she'd hoped to avoid the possible trauma of meeting his Clan until she felt a little surer of herself. She kind of dreaded what they might think of her. Maybe they wouldn't approve of someone like her—someone who was only just learning how to be a shifter—for their leader. So many things could go wrong. She was more than a little scared of how they would receive her.

"I guess there's nothing to keep you and the family here anymore, huh?" she admitted as they walked toward the stairs together.

"This is our vacation place. We come here a few times a year, or whenever we need to get away, but there's work to be done at home now that Timmons has finally been stopped. And I think the Clan atmosphere would be best for Belinda right now. Plus, I want them to meet you. I know they're going to love you as much as I do." He paused at the top of the stairs and leaned down to place a reassuring kiss on the top of her head, accompanying it with a quick hug.

He let her go and they started down the stairs. She lagged behind a bit, still not quite feeling the same level of confidence in her ability to win over a whole Clan of shifters.

"I hope you're right," was all she said in reply.

Grif smiled at her over his shoulder. "Of course I am. Trust me. I've known most of them all my life. They're going to be very happy for us both."

She sighed as they arrived on the ground level. "If you say so."

They walked toward the kitchen arm in arm and were just in time to snag breakfast before Matt started to feed their guests outside. Nothing more was said about the impending trip to Nevada, but Lindsey worried about it for the rest of the morning.

Timmons's body was already on a plane heading for Nevada, Grif learned as Arlo briefed him about the team's activities after the family had retired. Arlo had been in contact with Slade and he was meeting Arlo's guys at the private airstrip in the desert that they used when they wanted to fly under the radar, so to speak.

Slade and his priestess mate, Kate, would examine the body as soon as possible. Grif congratulated Arlo on his fast work and started laying the groundwork for withdrawal from the area for both the team of soldiers and his family.

The majority of the fighting men would go back to their homes elsewhere in Wyoming—on that mountaintop where Jesse Moore had managed to gather the retired elite of the top military units. A small contingent would stay with the Redstones until they were home, traveling with them to Nevada on the private plane Grif had asked Arlo to call in.

Grif and his brothers would close up the house and take care of any last minute details as pertained to their property. The team would see to the grounds and barn they'd used. All in all, it wouldn't take long to be ready to roll. Grif hoped they'd be able to pull out that very afternoon, in fact.

He understood Lindsey's hesitancy, but he knew in his heart that she had nothing to worry about. He had faith that the Lady wouldn't have given him a mate who couldn't handle the role she would be expected to fulfill in the Clan. If it turned out to be too much for her, he could always step down.

He was fully prepared to do just that if he realized Lindsey was overwhelmed—or, less likely, if the Clan rejected her. His mate was more important to him than the Clan. That was a statement he never thought he'd make before finding her, but now that she was in his life, he understood the harsh truth of that simple fact. If they didn't like her, he'd leave. Simple as that.

There were four other Redstone brothers who all could be just as effective as he in running both the company and the Clan. He'd leave it to them and take his mate back to Wyoming. He could easily live in the cabin and he knew she liked the area as well.

He had a solid Plan B if things went south, but he really didn't think they would. Lindsey may not be everyone's idea of a kick-ass, take-no-prisoners Alpha female, but there was a lot more to being Alpha than fighting skill. In fact, among cats, Alpha females tended to be the nurturers, not the fighters.

It was different for other kinds of shifters, but his mother hadn't really been able to fight her way out of a paper bag, yet she'd been the beloved matriarch of the Clan for as long as he'd been alive. Grif knew Lindsey had the same capacity for love, understanding and compassion. He'd seen it in action with Belinda and he knew once she got to know the people of his Clan, her big heart would expand to encompass them all as well. Just as it should. The Alpha female of the Redstone Clan had always been someone who could love the whole Clan and treat them all like family.

He just needed Lindsey to understand that. It was something he had a hard time putting into words, but she'd understand once she met some of his people. He just knew it.

And if it didn't work out, there was always Plan B.

Grif knew Lindsey wasn't particularly happy about it, but she took the idea of leaving for Nevada that afternoon with good grace when he discussed it with her right before lunch. She'd been helping Belinda put her room back to rights after the minor battle that had taken place in there the night before.

Matt had carried out all the broken furniture but Belinda had wanted to wash every last item of fabric—including the curtains— and Grif really couldn't blame her. He didn't want one shred of

Timmons's evil scent left behind to remind her of what might have happened.

He'd scrounged up a shop vac and some rug cleaner and helped the girls scrub the carpet for a while. They'd taken care of everything else and within a couple of hours, the place looked and smelled a lot better. Grif had also given Belinda the option of picking another room for the next time they stayed at the cabin. He knew any of the brothers would be willing to switch with the girl, but so far she'd refused, and Grif thought that showed a lot of courage on her part. He left the option open though. He made sure she understood she was welcome to change her mind later. He wouldn't make her sleep in a room that held possibly terrifying memories.

After lunch, he drove with Lindsey and a couple of Arlo's people over to her grandfather's place. He'd helped her pack up and shut down the house. It didn't take long to put her suitcases in the back of his truck and they paused for a moment, facing the old structure.

"Would you mind if I sent some guys out here to fix this place up? It really is a beautiful setting and we could spend time here on our own once in a while. The house could be restored to its former glory relatively easily," he offered, already thinking of ways they could either restore or replace some of the old, detailed woodwork. It was a little different from anything he'd worked on before, but he'd love the opportunity to try.

"I think my grandfather would have liked that," Lindsey replied quietly. He looked over at her, standing by his side and he could see the tear in her eye even as she smiled.

"I'd only let them make the structure sound and maybe replace the generator and some of the broken appliances. Maybe put in a higher efficiency heating unit. Things like that. We could pick out the new stuff and do some of the more detailed work ourselves when we're here. I think it would be fun to restore the fussy gingerbread trim on the porch and stuff like that. What do you say?"

His enthusiasm for the project was growing the more he thought about it. The house was Lindsey's legacy and he wanted to fix it up for her as a sort of mating gift. If she wanted, they could keep it and spend time alone there, and maybe someday, they could give it to one of their children. Oh yeah, he liked that idea. He loved the thought of a future—and children, if they were so blessed—with Lindsey.

"Sounds expensive," was her only comment.

Grif turned to her and took her by the shoulders. "I'm not poor, Lindsey. And I've never had a mate to spoil before. Please let me."

She seemed to think about it for a moment before giving in. "Okay. I guess that would be nice." She smiled wistfully and looked over her shoulder at the house. "I have good memories of this place."

"And we'll make even better ones in the future. That, I promise you." He dipped his head and kissed her because he just couldn't help himself.

Time stood still until he heard a very obvious and loud throat clearing behind them. It was Freddy, the guy who'd helped Lindsey down from the roof the night before. He'd led the small team that accompanied them to her grandfather's house.

"Everything's shut down and should be good for a few months," he reported when Grif looked over at him. "If you want to make your flight, we should be getting on the road, sir."

Grif had known Fred for more than a few years. In fact, they'd been in the same unit for a while when they were both still in the service. The grin on his face belied his polite words. No doubt about it, Fred was getting a kick out of seeing how distracted Grif was by his new mate, but Grif really couldn't hold it against him. He was in too good a mood with Lindsey by his side to let anything much bother him today.

"Thanks for the reminder and for the help with the house. I know it's a little outside your usual duties." Grif let go of Lindsey to shake Fred's hand.

"No problem, Alpha. You'd be surprised how domestic some of us have become up on Moore's mountain." Fred let go and Grif saw the rest of his people already mounted up, sitting in the vehicles they'd arrived in, waiting. "Now, sir, let's get you and the missus to the airport."

Grif agreed wholeheartedly and though he knew Lindsey still felt a little anxiety about going home to Nevada with him, he also knew it was best to get it over with. She'd learn soon enough how little she had to fear.

Sometime just before midnight, they pulled into the long driveway of a lovely house in a well manicured housing development on the outskirts of Las Vegas. It had nice homes with much bigger property lines than Lindsey was used to. She tried to see as much as she could from behind the glass of a luxury SUV that had been waiting for them at a private airstrip.

She'd been a little overwhelmed since leaving the cabin in Wyoming. Instead of the airport terminal she'd expected, Grif had led them all to a private hangar where a very luxurious private jet waited for them. Lindsey had never flown on a private jet before. In fact, she could count on one hand the number of times she's flown anywhere at all. And those trips had always been on a commercial airplane, crammed in with lots of people in the economy section of the plane.

The house was huge. Not quite a mansion, but certainly larger than anything she'd ever lived in. And it was beautiful. From the outside, it had the same charm as the cabin, without the rustic setting. The yard was filled with native plants and succulents that did well in the arid climate.

When Grif shut off the engine, everyone piled out of the vehicle. Steve carried Belinda up to the front door, which was opened before they got there. Lindsey saw light spilling out but couldn't make out whoever had been waiting.

Nerves assailed her. It had to be more of Grif's family. Or maybe close members of his Clan. She worried about what they would think of her. She tried to brush the wrinkles out of her shirt. They'd been traveling for hours and she probably didn't look her best, but it couldn't be helped.

Grif came up behind her, his arms wrapping around her waist as he bent to whisper in her ear.

"Don't fret. They're going to love you as much as I do."

Lindsey didn't get to reply because Grif lifted her into his arms, carrying her up the walkway and into the house, right past a surprised man who had to be another of the brothers, judging by his looks. She laughed as he made some joke about carrying her over the threshold and it felt good to see him in such a playful mood. He hadn't been this lighthearted with her in days. Possibly, she'd never seen him this joyful. It made her heart lift to join his. She liked that she could make him happy. And she felt like just maybe, things would work out after all.

Grif deposited her in the middle of a spacious living room and kissed her for all he was worth. For a moment out of time, only the two of them existed in the entire world. And then she heard the wolf whistles from the hallway by the door.

Grif let her go and they turned to find Matt, Steve and the new guy all grinning from ear to ear, stomping their feet, clapping and cheering them on. Lindsey had to laugh at their reaction. Not only did it take away some of her nervousness, but it also made her feel almost giddy with reflected joy.

"Kitten, that's my brother, Bob," Grif introduced the new man, then called to him. "Where's Mag?"

"No idea. He's been scarce since he took that lady vamp away." Bob frowned for a moment, but his expression quickly cleared. He moved closer as Grif let Lindsey go completely. "Nice to finally meet you, Lindsey. I've heard lots of good things about you. Welcome to the family." Bob gave her a big hug that felt truly welcoming and she lost a little more of her nervousness.

"Thanks," she whispered, a little overwhelmed by having four of the Redstone brothers in such a comparatively small space. The room had looked really big when she'd entered, but these guys were all huge and they took up a lot of room.

"You guys must be tired after all the traveling. I'll bring in the luggage and see you in the morning if you turn in before I'm through," he said, already heading for the door. Matt went with him outside, pitching in, while Grif escorted Lindsey toward the staircase.

"I'll show you around and where we'll sleep. I have to check a few things before I join you. It's always tough coming back when I've been away for a while. There are a million details," Grif began as they walked up the wide staircase.

"It's okay. I understand." She smothered a yawn. "I'm pretty tired, so finding a bed sounds like a really good idea."

Grif steered her down a hallway, pointing out who the various doors belonged to. It seemed every one of the brothers had a room of his own in the house, as well as one for Belinda.

"This one," Grif paused outside the second to last closed door. He had to clear his throat before he continued. "This was my mother's room. Nobody's been in there since she was killed, but I think, in time, you might be able to learn a little bit about who she was and her role in the Clan by seeing how she lived. She made me take the master suite when we moved in to this house, hoping I'd bring a mate home sooner or later, I guess." He closed his eyes briefly and hung his head. "I wish you'd gotten to meet her. I think she would have loved you, Lindsey."

His voice was a whisper that went straight to her heart. Lindsey moved closer to his side, putting an arm around his waist and leaning into him.

"I wish I could've known her too. She had to be a very special woman to raise such a wonderful family."

Grif leaned down and kissed her. "Thanks." They stayed there for a moment more before he turned to resume their walk down the hallway.

He threw open the last door and then surprised her by lifting her into his arms again, carrying her over the threshold into the master suite. It was a big room. Bigger than any bedroom she'd ever slept in. And she could see a luxurious bathroom through the open door off to the right.

But Grif didn't give her much of a chance to take in the sights. He kicked the door shut and made straight for the huge bed, depositing her gently on its plush surface and following her down. She barely had time to breathe before he captured her mouth in a devastating kiss.

Clothes disappeared quickly as Grif went after what they both wanted. It had been too long since they'd been free to come together. Too much had happened that had almost driven them apart forever. It was time to reaffirm the love that continued to blossom and grow between them.

Lindsey welcomed him into her body gladly, meeting his thrusts with eager cries. She vaguely wondered if maybe the others in the house knew what they were up to, but then Grif touched her in just the right spot and it didn't seem to matter anymore. Let the men envy their love. Knowing the brothers, they'd keep little ears away until it was safe. The Redstones could be relied upon to protect their little sister. She knew that for a fact.

Grif brought her to peak after peak as he stroked deep within her body. He hadn't taken time to do much but get her naked and lower his pants enough to get inside her, but she didn't care. The rough rasp of his denim jeans against her calves was a sensory delight that reinforced how strongly he wanted her. It also reminded her how impatient she was to take him as well. They were well matched and she would spend the rest of her days proving it.

She shouted his name as she came for the final time, taking him with her. She felt the magic of their union, the heat of their joining, the beauty of their love, with everything in her.

She must've dozed for a bit, for when she woke, she was under the sheet, a pillow tucked under her head. Grif had taken care of her when she was too stunned to do so.

"Now that's the kind of welcome home I like," he said, leaning over her and placing a lingering kiss on her lips.

He was dressed once more—which is to say, he'd pulled up his jeans and buttoned his shirt. It was a little wrinkled, but they'd been traveling all day, so maybe the wrinkles had come from sitting in various vehicles and not from the way she'd been fisting the cotton in her hands as he'd taken her. Yeah, that could be it. She had to laugh at her own musings as he lifted away from her.

"You're not coming to bed?" Damn. She sounded even more needy to her own ears than she'd thought she would. She didn't want to be too clingy. Men hated clingy women.

"Not yet, though I wish I could. I have to make certain of a few things before I'll rest easy. Most of the Clan is still awake. Many of us keep late hours. Nighttime is the best time to prowl." He chuckled as he gave her a last, quick kiss before rising from the side of the bed. "Get some rest. I'll be back in an hour or two and then we'll see about round two." He winked as he left her and she had to laugh at his naughty words.

She was already looking forward to round two, as he put it, but she didn't quite know if she'd make it. She hadn't been able to sleep on the plane and the night before had been one of the most dramatic of her life. She was exhausted and already yawning before he closed the door behind him.

She took only a minute to use the bathroom and clean up a bit before climbing between the soft sheets once more and drifting away into a blissful sleep.

CHAPTER SIXTEEN

When Lindsey woke, Grif was in bed with her. In fact, he was naked and she was spooned in his arms. It was a lovely way to wake, but the sun was shining behind the gauzy curtains in the window. He hadn't woken her in the night for round two and she was concerned he hadn't come to bed until the wee hours of the morning.

She didn't want to wake him, but she needed to get up. Creeping out of bed wasn't her strong suit, but she somehow tiptoed into the master bath without making too much noise. Grif had grunted when she'd left his arms, but she didn't think he'd woken up. She wanted to let him sleep since he probably needed the rest.

Besides, Lindsey had been eyeing the decadent bathtub he had secreted in that giant bathroom last night. It had water jets and looked big enough to fit two. She wanted to try it and if Grif woke up and found her there, well, who knows where that would lead?

That happy thought in mind, she turned on the faucets and let the tub fill while she took care of other things. By the time she was ready, the bathtub was steaming and full enough to at least get started. She stepped in feeling very lavish and extravagant. And she had to smile when she hit the switch that turned on the jets.

"Is this a private party or can poor, lonely mates join in?" Grif's voice came to her from the door to the bathroom, through a fine mist of steam generated by the water.

"I thought you'd never ask," she replied, feeling playful.

Grif joined her a moment later, shutting off the taps as the water level rose dangerously high with the addition of his large body to the giant tub. They both laughed as he opened the drain to take out a little bit of the water for safety's sake. It wouldn't do to flood the place on their first morning together.

"My brothers would never let us live it down if we needed a mop to clean up in here when we're through," he said, adjusting the water level until he was satisfied. "I've never had company in here."

"I find that hard to believe," she replied quickly, rethinking her words as she spoke them. Grif wasn't the type to expose his family to temporary affairs, even though she was certain he'd had many.

Cats were frisky, he kept telling her. She couldn't blame him for sewing wild oats. She just hoped that now that they were a couple, those days were over. They were for her and she had to believe it was like that for him as well.

"I'll admit I had my share of fun," Grif said, coming close to her and putting his arm around her shoulders. He lifted her legs, one at a time with his under the water, settling her half-on and half-off his lap. "But once we shifters mate, it's for life. You're the only woman who will share my bath and my bed and wherever else we make love, for the rest of my days." He sealed his words with a tender kiss.

"Likewise," she whispered, almost unable to speak once he let her up for air. She was dazed by his ardor, spellbound by his passion. And the fog in the air all around them gave the whole scene a magical, mysterious feel.

Grif lowered them both into the water until just their heads rested against the sloped sides of the tub, just above the water line. His hands and even his feet teased her skin, rubbing all over, slipping and sliding against each other under the bubbly water.

He let her ride him when she pushed him back against the back of the tub and they made waves together, riding each one higher and higher until they both came in a shower of light and pleasure...and water.

They were both laughing later as they used big towels to mop up the evidence of their exuberance from the bathroom floor. Lindsey promised to sneak the wet towels into the laundry while Grif distracted his brothers later that day. It was fun to conspire with him on something so innocent and lighthearted. She didn't really care if they got busted for making a mess by his brothers, but it was kind of cute that he would care for her feelings. It was clear he wanted to spare her embarrassment. She doubted he would give a damn what his brothers thought of his mating habits.

Heck, they'd probably seen it all before.

And on that scandalous thought, Lindsey headed out of the bathroom to find some clothes. She found that her suitcases had been delivered to the hall outside their room sometime during the night and Grif had brought them in while she'd been in the bathroom. As a result, she had her full wardrobe to choose from.

She chose a colorful outfit of knit separates that didn't wrinkle no matter how long and how tightly they'd been crammed into her suitcase. When she was finished dressing and doing her hair, she looked neat and if not professional, then at least she looked friendly.

Her clothes weren't anything special or expensive, but she thought she looked okay for meeting people. They'd have to accept her as she was because she had never been rich and didn't pretend to know how someone with the kind of money the Redstones apparently had, usually acted. The brothers had been friendly and kind around her. She hoped the rest of their people would be the same.

Grif dropped a kiss on her lips as he met her near the door to the hall. He was dressed in jeans and a nice white dress shirt. He looked good enough to eat, but she knew spending the entire day in his room making love wasn't really an option. It would only postpone the inevitable and she'd done that long enough as it was.

Besides, she was hungry. Her tummy growled as Grif opened the door and they both laughed as they went downstairs. They followed the source of cooking smells to a light and airy kitchen at the back of the house.

It was like a gourmet's dream kitchen and Lindsey couldn't believe she would be allowed to use the state of the art appliances, if she wanted. She loved to cook and this room was like a showplace, full of wonder and what she hoped would be hours of joy to come.

"Wow," she breathed, walking through the kitchen. Grif was beaming at her side.

"I designed the kitchen with my mother's input. She chose the appliances and we went from there. What do you think?"

"It's gorgeous, Grif." She twirled to take in the whole space, getting a three hundred and sixty degree view. Matt was finishing up at the stove and Bob was ferrying plates into the room next door. "It's really awesome."

"Glad you like it."

He put his hand at her back and ushered her into the next room, which proved to be a spacious dining room that looked out through large windows and a glass door to the backyard. She could see an orderly garden back there. A green oasis in the middle of the desert. It was almost magical.

Grif seated her at the large table. Belinda and Steve were there before her, along with two other people she hadn't met.

"Lindsey, this is the Clan's new priestess, Kate, and her new mate, Slade. I asked them to join us this morning so you could meet them first," Grif said as he claimed the seat at her side.

She nodded uncertainly at first at the other couple, but they seemed open enough to her senses, so she began to think what she'd heard about them. She knew their names. The soldiers had discussed them with Grif a few times.

"We met your sister, Millie," Lindsey offered with a small smile as she shook Slade's big hand.

"Yeah, I heard." He frowned a bit, causing her to wonder if she'd said the wrong thing, but the woman at his side reached around him to shake Lindsey's hand.

"Don't worry about him. He's not happy his sister is working with a bunch of soldiers. Apparently she didn't run it past him before she took off for Wyoming and he's still miffed."

Lindsey liked Kate's open manner and firm handshake but she didn't quite know what to say in response.

"Dig in while it's hot," Bob broke in, seating himself as Matt joined them with the last heaping platter of food.

There were eggs, bacon, sausage, pancakes, waffles and oatmeal. More food and variety than she could really handle. But the men dug in with gusto while she and Kate shared humorous looks. Kate seemed really nice and as breakfast commenced, the conversation was kept to light topics. Lindsey was able to get to know the new couple, as well as Bob, a little better. So far, so good.

When they'd decimated the platters and Belinda and Matt had started to ferry the empties back into the kitchen, Grif suggested he and Lindsey take a little walk with the new couple and Steve. Lindsey guessed they were going to talk business away from Belinda's little ears, so she got up and joined the group headed for the backyard.

"What news do you have for me?" Grif asked as soon as the back door had shut behind them. They all drifted toward a picnic table set up in the shade of the biggest bird of paradise plant Lindsey had ever seen.

"Nothing good, I'm afraid," Kate began. "Slade and I examined the body. He had tattoos, Grif. Magical ones that only we can see. *Venifucus* tattoos."

"Fuck," Grif cursed. "I knew that bastard was getting help from somewhere. He couldn't have evaded all my trackers for so long if he hadn't had support. Were they on his wrists?"

Grif had told her on the plane ride about how some of the evil agents of the ancient organization known as the *Venifucus* were marked with magical tattoos over the pulse points on their wrists. They'd talked about why it was so important to have the body checked and a lot of other things to pass the time on the flight home. She was glad now for the knowledge.

"One on the left wrist," she confirmed. "And a few more. Alpha, they were in strange places." Kate swallowed as if what she was about to say was painful. "There was one over his heart that radiated pure evil. We think it encoded some kind of spell." She turned to her mate, probably seeking his support.

"We think it might be what caused him to kill his mate," Slade stated with no sugar coating. "He also had one on his right temple and one at the base of his skull. Neither of us have ever seen anything like it. I called the Lords and their mate earlier because this might be too important to let sit, and they had no reports of anything like this either. It's a mystery. And they've asked us to ship the body to them for further examination. With your permission, of course, Alpha," Slade added, almost as an afterthought.

"They can have him, provided they promise me that after they're done with him, his body will be burned and consecrated by a priestess. I don't want his shade coming back to haunt us, if such things are possible. With all the ancient stuff that's coming back now, I don't want to find out those fairytales are true as well."

"Neither do we," Kate said with a touch of vehemence in her tone. "I'll ask the High Priestess myself and make sure she understands, though I think they'll be thinking along the same lines once they see the evil in his marks for themselves. It's palpable. And for someone like me, they cry out to be cleansed," Kate added.

"I'll want you to accompany the body, Slade. I don't trust this to anyone else. And one of my brothers will go with you. I don't want you to let it out of your sight. Timmons had support from the

Venifucus. I don't want one of their agents taking him back, even in death." Grif's tone brooked no argument.

"Understood, Alpha. And I concur," Slade replied very seriously.

This was a guy who didn't mess around. Lindsey thought he was very much like some of the soldiers she'd met in Wyoming, but even more deadly, if that made any sense.

They were all quiet for a moment when a thought occurred to her.

"If the *Venifucus* was supporting him, then where were they when he came after us at the cabin? Did he just escape their control? Or were they still helping him? And is that why he was apparently able to take out four of those soldiers and get into Belinda's room without anybody noticing?"

Grim faces turned to regard her and Lindsey felt uncomfortable under their scrutiny for a moment before she realized they weren't angry at her, but at her words. They didn't like contemplating the danger to the Redstones any more than she did. She'd found common ground with the new people, but none of them really liked the basis for it.

"All good questions," Grif replied after a quiet moment. "And unfortunately I don't think we have the answers, but you better believe we're going to find out. If you're right, the *Venifucus* have been targeting our family in particular for much longer and more thoroughly than I thought." Grif looked angry with a hint of terror in his golden eyes that only Lindsey could see. "If they really caused Timmons to turn on Jackie, as you believe, their interference goes back years longer than I anticipated. And if they were there, in Wyoming, helping Timmons, then we might not be as safe as I thought."

"And don't forget mom," Steve said softly, but with a determined growl to his voice. "Those two who murdered her were supposedly rogue elements, but they definitely had *Venifucus* ties. Maybe they weren't so *rogue* after all. Maybe doing damage to our family is all part of some deeper plan."

"I don't like this," Grif spat. "Not at all." He turned away and paced for a moment, coming back a few seconds later. "We need to operate as if the threat continues. We've seen what they're capable of now. We need to guard against it. More than that," he pounded one fist on the picnic table. "We need to go on the offensive."

"Amen, brother," Steve muttered under his breath but they all heard him. Slade just frowned, but he also had that determined light in his spooky grey eyes.

"From this moment forth, I'm declaring the Redstone Clan at war with the *Venifucus*. We will hunt them where they live and we will end the threat against our family and against our Clan, or die trying."

Even Lindsey felt the weight of his words as Grif declared his private war and she knew in her heart they were doing the right thing. They'd already lost too many innocent people to the evil cult. She didn't want to see any more of the Redstones taken out by an enemy that didn't fight fair.

"I'm sorry I brought you into this at such a time, Lindsey," Grif turned to her and took her hand in his. "I'd send you away, but I can't. I need you like I need my next breath." She put her hand over his mouth to forestall his next words. She understood.

"I wouldn't be any other place than at your side, Grif. The Great Spirit changed me and put me here for a reason. I know that deep in my heart. I will help you and your family to the best of my ability. I don't know what I can contribute, but I'm here and I'm not going anywhere. I love you."

It was just that simple. Love made her brave when just thinking about the danger that possibly faced them should have made her tremble.

Grif kissed her in front of everybody, but she didn't mind. Let them witness the power of their love.

"This is as it should be," Kate said softly after Grif let Lindsey go. "The Alpha is stronger for having a mate and the Clan is stronger for having a matriarch. You will grow into that role in the fullness of time, Lindsey. I have no doubt about it. Let your love guide you and the Lady will show you the way." Kate raised her hand and for a moment, Lindsey thought she saw little rainbows of light dancing around her and Grif, like some kind of magical benediction. "Whatever comes, you will face it together. Now and until the end of time."

Lindsey liked the way that sounded. Apparently, so did Griff. He bent her back and laid a kiss on her like something out of a fairy tale. Dimly she heard laughter and even a little applause from those gathered around them and off in the distance...she thought she heard the flapping of great wings, as if an angel watched over them and had suddenly taken to flight.

# # #

A WORD FROM BIANCA D'ARC
ABOUT HER PARANORMAL SERIES

Since I started writing paranormal romances in 2005, much has happened behind-the-scenes to affect the way in which these stories have been released. Originally, there were two very separate series—the *Brotherhood of Blood* for vampires, and the *Tales of the Were* for werewolves and their werecreature friends.

The main reason for this separation was that each series was with a different publisher. The publisher that originally had my vampire short stories and novellas went out of business some years ago and I began the process of bringing those stories over to a new publisher that had been publishing some of my *Tales of the Were* novels. I took the vampire short stories and novellas, expanded them—in some cases significantly—and republished them with that publisher, where they remain as of this writing. Those stories are: **One & Only, Rare Vintage**, and **Phantom Desires**.

I have since added to that series with the novella **Forever Valentine** and the crossover novel, **Sweeter Than Wine**, which is the point where it became quite obvious that all of these stories happened in the same contemporary paranormal world. Matt Redstone plays a significant part in that book.

Those five stories are united by the fact that they follow the love stories of five female college friends. All five find that they are mated to vampires. But there is a sixth college friend and her story is told in the *RT Award* nominated novel, **Wolf Hills**. She is mated to Jason Moore, who is mentioned briefly in the book you just read. He is the Alpha of a large werewolf Pack in Wyoming, and his brother, Jesse, heads up the team of ex-Spec Ops shifters who comes to the aid of Grif and his family in Wyoming and beyond.

At this point, the *Brotherhood of Blood* series will begin to follow the story line begun with **Wolf Hills**, and the next novel in the series, the upcoming, **Wolf Quest**, is Jesse Moore's story. It will be out in December 2013.

There is quite a bit of crossover now between the *Brotherhood of Blood* and the *Tales of the Were*, but the timing is tricky. The internal chronology of the stories has been, at times, difficult for me to reconcile because of all this confusion in the way the initial stories came out, went out of print, then were re-released.

The *Tales of the Were* series will branch off from this point and follow the five Redstone brothers in the sub-series I'm sub-titling *Redstone Clan*. You'll notice a little graphic to that effect on the cover of this book and the subsequent four books in the series.

We'll learn more about Steve, Bobcat, Mag and Matt. With any luck, these stories will come out every few months during the rest of 2013 and into 2014. Where we go from there, I'm not sure yet, but I can guarantee, it'll be a wild ride!

OTHER BOOKS BY BIANCA D'ARC

Now Available

Brotherhood of Blood
One & Only
Rare Vintage
Phantom Desires
Sweeter Than Wine
Forever Valentine
Wolf Hills

Tales of the Were
Lords of the Were
Inferno
The Purrfect Stranger
Rocky
Slade

Tales of the Were – Redstone Clan
Grif

Jit'Suku Chronicles
Arcana: King of Swords
Arcana: King of Cups
Arcana: King of Clubs
End of the Line
Sons of Amber: Ezekiel
Sons of Amber: Michael

Guardians of the Dark
Half Past Dead
Once Bitten, Twice Dead
A Darker Shade of Dead
The Beast Within
Dead Alert

Dragon Knights
Maiden Flight
The Dragon Healer
Border Lair
Master at Arms
The Ice Dragon
Prince of Spies
Wings of Change
FireDrake
Dragon Storm
Keeper of the Flame

Resonance Mates
Hara's Legacy
Davin's Quest
Jaci's Experiment
Grady's Awakening

Gifts of the Ancients:
Warrior's Heart

String of Fate: Cat's Cradle

StarLords: Hidden Talent

Print Anthologies
Ladies of the Lair
I Dream of Dragons Vol. 1
Brotherhood of Blood
Caught by Cupid

OTHER BOOKS BY BIANCA D'ARC
(continued)

Coming Soon

Tales of the Were - Redstone Clan #2
Red
September 2013

Tales of the Were - Redstone Clan #3
Magnus
November 2013

Brotherhood of Blood
Wolf Quest
December 2013

Tales of the Were - Redstone Clan #4
Bobcat
2014

Resonance Mates
Harry's Sacrifice
2014

Tales of the Were - Redstone Clan #5
Matt
2014

EXCERPT

TALES OF THE WERE: RED
REDSTONE CLAN #2
BY BIANCA D'ARC

CHAPTER ONE

"Hey, Red! How's it hanging?"

"Damn. I knew I shouldn't have answered the phone." Steve Redstone's smile belied his gruff tone. The call was from one of his oldest and best Army buddies—Derek "Deke" Morrow—an entirely human soldier, but a great guy nonetheless. He was also one of the most skilled warriors Steve had ever known.

"Man, I've got a big favor to ask you." Deke's tone was serious and Steve sobered.

"Spill, bro. You know I'll do what I can for you."

"Thanks, man. Knew I could count on you. Thing is, my baby sister is heading your way. One of her girlfriends decided it would be fun to have her bachelorette party in Sin City. It's not that I don't trust Trish, as much as I don't trust her friends. This is an accident waiting to happen and I need some backup. I can't go. She'd kill me if I showed my face, but she doesn't know you and you're local."

"So you want me to show her a good time?" Steve relaxed. Babysitting, he could do. Teasing his friend just came naturally.

"You do, and I'll break both your legs." The tone said Deke was only half-joking.

"Relax. I've got you covered. What hotel are they staying at?"

A few minutes later, the call ended and Steve had all the information he'd need to track down his good friend's wayward sister. He'd establish a bit of surveillance first. Check the lay of the land and see what kind of mischief the girls were getting into.

If necessary, he could call on some members of his Clan to help him keep an eye on things, but he didn't really think that would be necessary. How much trouble could a few young human girls get into, after all?

Steve cursed himself for even thinking that a few hours later as he leaned against the wall of a dark club, watching the half dozen women who had stormed the Las Vegas strip with the way-too-gorgeous little sister of his friend. Trisha Morrow was a knockout. That was something Steve hadn't counted on.

When Derek talked about his kid sister, he always made her sound like a teenager. The woman currently knocking back an entire row of colorful—questionable—test tube shots at the bar was no teenager. Far from it. She was an adult and as lovely as her brother was deadly.

Steve's first sight of her had nearly knocked him off his feet and his reaction hadn't tamed any in the two hours since. He'd followed the gaggle of women out of the hotel where they were staying and tailed them to this club. They were enjoying the live band, some dancing and a whole lot of drinking. Too much, by Steve's standards. Some of the girls were getting sloppy drunk, but Trish Morrow seemed to be able to hold her liquor with a little more dignity than her friends. That was something, at least.

He knew she was just as shit-faced as the other girls, though. She was unsteady on those sexy high heels and the way her short skirt rode up when she tried to get on the barstool had nearly given him a heart attack. She was tall for a human woman. Just a little shorter than her brother, who was about six feet. Trish had to be about five-nine or so. A nice height to match Steve's six-foot-two.

And he really shouldn't be thinking thoughts like that. No, not at all. Her brother would kill him if he even *thought* Steve was thinking about his little sister in an inappropriate way. It would end a friendship Steve valued, and he wasn't willing to give up that relationship over a woman. Even a woman as knock-out gorgeous as Trisha Morrow.

Steve kept watch from afar. He didn't want to know her scent. He stayed well upwind so he wouldn't accidentally smell the sexy, feminine scent he just knew would rev his engine to full throttle. It was bad enough seeing her. He didn't want to know the intimate details her scent would reveal to him.

If he wanted to keep his friend, it was better that he didn't know. Even though his inner cougar clawed at his insides to learn more about the pretty female. The cat appreciated Trisha's beauty and its innate curiosity pushed at Steve to learn more about her.

But he couldn't. He was a babysitter. That's it.

Steve was so busy watching the woman and thinking about how he mustn't get too close to her that he almost missed the danger when it struck. One of Trisha's friends—the bride-to-be, in fact—went out onto the dance floor with a creature Steve recognized. A creature he had no respect for and would not let interfere with this particular group of women.

He had to act. Pushing away from the wall, Steve strolled onto the dance floor and positioned himself opposite Jorge, a Peruvian vampire who'd moved to the area recently. He was already treading on thin ice with the local Master of his kind for preying a little too openly on humans. He hadn't killed anyone yet—that they knew of—but he'd been warned repeatedly to be more discrete in his feeding.

Steve made sure he caught Jorge's eye and with a grudging sort of compliance, Jorge finished the dance and escorted the woman back to her friends. He left her with them and glanced over at Steve, cocking his head. Steve looked toward a quiet corner and Jorge nodded almost imperceptibly.

They both moved toward the corner. Steve stood for a moment while the vampire did one of his magic tricks and dampened the sound so they could talk. It was amazing what some of the older vamps could do. They had a weird sort of magic all their own, very unlike anything Steve had seen human magic users do.

"Handy," Steve mused. "Thanks for the moment of quiet."

"You wanted to talk with me?" Jorge prompted, clearly annoyed, but Steve didn't give a shit.

The Redstone Clan was the most powerful group in this city and even the Master knew it. This guy should show a little more respect, even if he was a few hundred years old. Steve could still crush him like an egg. And he wouldn't even need backup from his Clan to do it. Jorge just wasn't as tough as he apparently thought he was.

"I'd like you to leave those women alone." Steve didn't owe the vampire any more explanation than that, though he sensed Jorge was going to be difficult.

"Why should I? They are human, are they not?" Jorge looked over the small group who went on talking, laughing and drinking, unaware of the discussion in the corner.

"Yep. Human," Steve agreed. "And under my protection. Got

it?" He leaned forward, doing his best to intimidate the shorter man.

"What's in it for me if I do you this favor?"

Steve had to stifle a sigh. This little twerp really didn't understand the gravity of the situation and he certainly didn't know his place in the hierarchy around these parts. But Steve didn't want to be the heavy. It wasn't necessary and it would take too much time.

"I would be grateful. And I won't tell Tony that you've been sniffing around the tourists again. I heard he warned you off...what was it? Three times, already? You should know better by now, Jorge."

Antoine de Latourette was the local Master vampire. His friends called him Tony. He was more than seven hundred years old and not someone to cross lightly.

Jorge finally got the message and straightened from his insolent slouch against the wall. He looked miffed, but Steve didn't care. It was time somebody taught this little pipsqueak a lesson.

"Instead of harassing me, maybe you ought to put a leash on some of your own." Jorge sneered as he looked pointedly over at the group of women.

Steve looked too.

"Shit." Things were getting more complicated by the moment. He turned back to Jorge. "Do we have an understanding?"

Jorge nodded, dropped the barrier he'd held that kept the blaring sound of the club at bay and turned to go without another word. It was disrespectful, but Steve didn't care at the moment. The group of seven women had been joined by a small Pack of wolves he knew all too well.

What was it with Derek's little sister that she—or her group of friends—were drawing all the Others tonight? It couldn't be helped. Steve was going to have to find out for himself.

He set out across the crowded room just as a fight broke out. The violence quickly spread toward him, but he had his objective clear in mind. He wasn't going to let anything stop him from making it to the small group of women. He'd promised Derek he'd take care of his sister. Letting her get hurt in a bar fight was not going to happen on his watch.

Somebody threw a punch at Steve. He barely paused to return the favor, sending the stupid human flying several feet back, out of

Steve's way. Another idiot tried to block his way with a barstool. Steve made short work of him but he started to wonder why seemingly disinterested bystanders were suddenly keen to stop him from getting to the women.

Steve whistled and one of the wolves perked up, looking through the crowd. Steve caught his eye and gave him a silent signal. *Guard. Protect.* Instantly the stance of the young wolves went from merely protective of the women, which they'd been already, to on guard. Good dogs, Steve thought with a fleeting moment of humor as yet another human tried to block his path.

One of the wolves made as if to come help him, but Steve signaled him back. *Protect the women,* he sent via the hand signals everyone in the Redstone Clan knew. This group of wolves was part of one of the construction crews and they were mostly reputable. A little young, and rough around the edges maybe, but good men all. Steve was sort of relieved to have them here now that the situation had taken an unexpected turn.

Steve paused momentarily to parry a few punches aimed his way but he didn't let the concerted attacks slow him down. He kept his eyes on the prize, making his way one opponent at a time, toward Trisha Morrow.

The club was great, but when the fight broke out on the other side of the packed dance floor, Trisha sobered enough to realize they probably should leave. Only there were a bunch of handsome men—big bruisers, most of them—flirting with the girls and none of her friends seemed sober enough to realize there might be danger if the fight kept escalating in their direction.

Trisha looked around and her gaze was caught by one man. A big, muscular man. He was as big as her brother, Deke, and just as good in a fight. He was walking toward her, but kept getting waylaid by idiots who wanted to fight. Why they tried to hit *him*, she'd never know. Even she could see he wasn't interested in the melee. He was just trying to get from one side of the club to the other, and he didn't really care who he had to mow down to do it.

There was something so elemental about the way he moved. Like a panther on the prowl. He vanquished one opponent after another—sometimes more than one at a time—sweeping them out of his way as if they were nothing. He sent a few guys sailing through the air. Some went down hard on the grimy floor. A few turned away when he growled at them.

He actually *growled*. She could hear the low rumble of it, even across the distance that still separated them. Why in the world did she find that sexy?

"Hey guys?" Trisha tried to get the attention of her drunk friends while her gaze remained on the warrior.

That's the only word she could think of to describe him. He had to be like Deke, and most of the men in her family. Military. Spec Ops. If not, then some kind of mercenary or professional killer.

That last thought almost made her giggle with nerves as their eyes met. And held.

Even as he threw two more would-be fighters aside, he kept his gaze on her. When he had to look away to throw a punch or block a barstool being thrown at him, it was only momentary. As soon as he'd dealt with the obstacle, he looked straight back at her again.

It was about that time she realized he wasn't just moving across the room. He was actually aiming for her table. For *her*.

Her foggy mind didn't understand the animal attraction that reared up and made her want to purr when she realized that hunk of dangerous manhood was making a beeline to her side. The rest of the raucous room faded to nothing as she watched his muscles bunch and flex as he dealt with one miscreant after another. Damn. He was hot.

Hot and dangerous. The ultimate bad boy. *Rawr*.

"The fighting is getting worse," she heard one of the men who'd come to chat with her friends say to the other over her head.

One part of her fuzzy mind wondered at their calm. The men had come to flirt and her girlfriends had happily obliged, but when the fighting started, the men had stayed with them, taking up what looked like guard positions, now that she thought about it. She'd seen it often enough with the guys in her family in the past. It didn't take much to bring out the legendary Morrow protective streak. She'd dealt with it all her life.

Sometimes annoying, it was often nice to have a bunch of big, strong guys to watch your back and catch you if you fell. She'd relied on her dad and brothers for a lot of years to do just that. Though, to be honest, she hadn't needed rescuing in a long, long time.

"Steve said to stay here," the other man answered, still over her head as she watched the warrior get closer.

"Yeah, all right. But not for much longer. If he doesn't haul ass, we're going to have to start knocking some heads together. It'd be easier to just take the women outside, where it's safe," the first one said.

"You notice something funny about the fight? They're going after Steve," the second one observed. "It's subtle, but it's there. Could be, the ones who started the brawl *want* us to go outside. There's only four of us."

"Not for long," the first one replied. "I just called in the cavalry." Trisha heard a phone beep next to her. The first guy had called someone and she could only hope he was on the right side of all this mayhem. Based on what she'd overheard, he probably was.

For whatever reason, a guy named Steve had told these guys to stay and watch over the girls. That didn't make much sense. She didn't remember any of the men being introduced as Steve. Had this Steve instigated the fight? It didn't sound that way, but the question remained... Who was Steve? And why would he tell these men—perfect strangers—to protect her small group of friends?

Unless...

Oh, no. He wouldn't have.

But she knew he would. Dammit. She could smell her brother's interference in this. He had friends all over the place and she'd just bet one of his old Army buddies lived in Las Vegas. It didn't take much to imagine Deke calling ahead once she'd told him where the bachelorette party was being held.

Well. She could either get mad or be grateful that her big brother cared enough to get someone to keep an eye on them. In the normal course of business, she would have been pissed. But she was drunk and the fight was getting seriously out of control. Even she had to admit, she and her friends probably needed a knight in shining armor right now. Maybe a few of them.

Still, she knew she'd be mad at Deke later, when everything was sane again. When there were no flying beer bottles or bar stools, and no big men trying to beat the crap out of each other ten feet from where she stood.

"You guys know my brother?" she asked of the men at her side, proud when her words slurred only a little. She really shouldn't have had that row of test tube shots. She didn't even know what had been in them. But they were yummy.

"Sorry, doll. We don't know your brother," the guy on her left answered in a somewhat condescending tone.

"I don't like you," she blurted out, unable to filter her words in her drunken state. "Sorry," she apologized belatedly, but she heard laughter from both of the guys that flanked her.

"It's okay. He gets that reaction a lot," the guy on the right guffawed at his buddy's expense.

"So who's Steve?" She really wasn't very subtle when she was drunk.

"Heard that, did you? You mean you don't know him already?" The guy on the left seemed recovered from her insult and a little more respectful this time when he spoke to her.

"No. Should I?" She almost looked at them, but the man who'd been casually fighting his way to her was almost upon them. She couldn't tear her eyes away from him. He was even more good looking, the closer he got.

"Yeah, judging by the way he just cleared a path to you, I kinda figured you two were already acquainted," the guy on the left turned as the fighting drew nearer. He was watching the crowd, but she only had eyes for the man who stopped right in front of her.

"You must be Steve," she stated. Damn she was drunk. She was just blurting out whatever came into her mind, no matter how inane.

The gorgeous warrior cocked his head to the side, clearly puzzled. "I am. And you're Trisha, right?"

She nodded, making herself dizzy in the process. "How do you know my name? We weren't introduced. I'd remember."

He had the greatest smile. She was glad she was still leaning against the barstool because her knees were in serious danger of melting when he flashed that crooked smile at her. His eyes actually twinkled. And glowed.

Wait a minute. Glowed?

She must be even drunker than she thought. That round of test tubes was starting to roil in her stomach and slide right into her bloodstream. Things were getting blurrier, not better. What had been *in* those things?

Damn. Steve smelled drugs. The chemical-metallic tang of something bad came off her in waves—and not much else. The chemical scent was so strong, it was overpowering her normal female scent.

"Trisha, do you feel all right?" Steve hated this. She might've taken the drugs or she might've been slipped something. Right now, he didn't know which and the fight was too close for comfort.

"No," she admitted in a wobbly voice as she leaned heavily on the bar stool.

Steve paused to push two of the fighters behind him farther back. So far, the small group of wolves had been keeping the fighting at bay around the drunk women, but he didn't know how much longer they could keep the status quo. Things seemed to be escalating instead of dying down.

And that didn't seem right either. Something strange was definitely in the air tonight.

"Steady now," he said in as soft a tone as he could manage over the loud noise of the fight. "Do you normally use drugs? Weed, crack, heroin?" He tried to be matter-of-fact about it, but he hated asking these questions.

"Piss off," she cussed him, making him want to smile. "I'm not a druggie. I'm just drunk."

"Do you *feel* just drunk, as you put it?" he challenged. Damn, he liked her spirit. She was feisty for a human.

She paused for a moment and her tongue peeped out to run over her lips. The sight of that little wet, pink muscle made his dick rise. Damn.

"Now that you mention it..." She paused to try to bring her hand to her face and missed. She was definitely not all right. Her coordination was shot. "Those shots must've been stronger than I thought," she finished lamely. "I'm higher than a kite." She smiled, then frowned. "I don't like it."

She made him want to laugh again, which surprised the hell out of him. She was kind of cute and very frank when she was out of it. It was a charming combination.

"I just got a text. The rest of the Pack is waiting for us outside," Jed Robinson reported from Trisha's right. He was the most senior of the dogs that had been flirting with Trisha and her friends. "There was some trouble out there, but they've neutralized it."

Damn. He thought he knew what the wolf was trying to say. There'd been an ambush waiting for the women. But why? Steve didn't like this at all and he didn't understand what it was about this group of women that had attracted all this attention, but he would. Before this night was over, he'd learn why they were such a target.

"All right, let's get out of here. The fight is more than the bouncers can handle and the cops will probably be here any moment. Unless you want to spend the rest of the night at the police station, you should probably come with us, Trisha."

She looked at him again, giving him a good once over.

"You've got to be my brother's friend," she surprised him by stating. "If anyone here was his goto guy, it would be someone like you. You've got the look. Okay." She paused, seeming to need to gather her wits. "I'll go with you. If you can convince me that you served with him."

How she knew her brother had called for backup in Vegas, he didn't have to guess. Deke was pretty protective of his family, but Steve respected that about the man. Now he just had to prove to his cautious sister that he was the inside man.

"Deke and I served in Afghanistan together." A few other places too, but those were classified. "My name is Steve Redstone."

"Shit," she cursed under her breath, but he heard it. "You're Red."

"At your service," he replied, knowing they really didn't have time to dally. The fight was really out of control and moving ever closer, though the wolves frowning presence kept most of it at bay. "Now can we get out of here?"

"Sure thing." She tried to stand but her legs clearly wouldn't support her. Still, she gave it her best shot until she managed to stand, leaning heavily on the small table.

She put one hand to her lips and an ear-splitting whistle issued from her mouth. Her friends—most of whom were as drunk as she was, or worse—immediately looked at her. Well that was one way to get the ladies' attention.

"This is my brother's friend, Red," she shouted to her friends. "We're getting out of here."

Slow nods and a few worried looks answered her pronouncement, but the women did start moving. Purses were gathered, short, tight skirts were pulled downward as they hopped off bar stools. Flirtatious hands sought the werewolves for support, but they all managed to stand, though several of the girls swayed alarmingly.

Steve put his hands out to catch Trisha as she nearly fell over, but she managed to right herself and take a few steps before she nearly slid to the floor. Steve caught her on the way down and put one arm around her waist, supporting her as she took wobbly steps toward the door. He would have carried her, but she was still able to walk and he wanted at least one arm free to fight, if need be.

"We took cabs here," Trisha babbled as they headed toward the door. She fit nicely against him.

"I know," he admitted, watching everything carefully.

The wolves were flanking the group of women, with Jed on point and Steve bringing up the rear. It was as good an arrangement as they could manage until they got outside. Luckily, the door wasn't that far away.

"I guess I shouldn't be surprised." She kept talking while they neared the exit. "How long have you been following me? Since I landed, I bet. Deke probably called you the moment we left home."

"Not quite. I only picked up your trail about two hours ago. Deke held off calling as long as he could, but the guy's always had a sixth sense for trouble. Guess he was right, eh?" Steve paused long enough to deliver a back kick to the guy about to attack them from the behind.

She gasped as the man went flying and didn't answer. Steve hustled her out the door and into the protection of the wolf Pack that was waiting outside. Jed was organizing the women into waiting vehicles. It was a measure of how far gone the women were that they didn't really question who the guys were or where they were going. It was more than obvious to Steve that they'd all been dosed with something that not only altered their scents, but also decimated their better judgment.

The way to the three vehicles had been cleared and kept that way by the wolves. Steve tossed the keys to his Harley to one of the younger guys, knowing he'd follow on the motorcycle. Steve wasn't letting go of Trisha. She'd been drugged and nearly abducted. She wasn't leaving his sight until this was all sorted out.

Steve helped her into the back of the last vehicle, a big SUV driven by the wolf Pack's Alpha, Pete, whom Steve both liked and respected. Pete had been in the Marine Corps for a while. He'd left the Corps and learned his trade as a stone mason. In fact, he was one of the finest Redstone Construction employed and in charge of many of the really finicky projects that clients loved. He held rank not only within his own Pack of wolves, but within the larger

Redstone Clan that encompassed everyone who worked for Redstone Construction—almost all of whom were shapeshifters of one kind or another.

The moment the doors were closed, Pete took off. One of the other girls was sitting next to Trisha, who was in the center of the back bench seat. Pete's youngest son, Jeremy, was in the front passenger seat.

Steve's sensitive hearing picked up the sound of his beloved Harley bringing up the rear. They made a neat little convoy as they headed out of the city and drove toward the development on the outskirts of Las Vegas where the Redstone Clan had settled.

Steve checked their back trail, as he knew the others were also doing. So far, there was no sign of pursuit.

"Where are you taking us?" Trisha's head lolled against the back of the seat, as did her friend's. The only difference between the two women was that Trisha was a little more awake.

"To safety," Steve was quick to assure her. "You can call Deke, if you want to make sure we're on the level."

"Are you kidding?" She shot him a look that was full of disbelief. "I'd sooner paint myself green and stroll naked down Main Street. No, thank you." She was carefully enunciating each of her words and Steve guessed it took a lot of effort.

He admired her grit and he had to laugh at her reaction to calling her big brother. Steve would think long and hard before he made that call. On the one hand, Deke had always been a great man to have on his side in a fight. On the other, Deke probably wouldn't be all that rational when it came to his sister. And there was the paranormal aspect of all this to consider. As far as Steve knew, Deke had no idea there really were such things as werewolves, vampires and all the rest, much less that Steve himself was a werecougar.

"So we're going to your place?" Trisha insisted on picking up the thread of the conversation, such as it was. "Is it big enough for all of us?"

"We can take them to the Pack house," Pete volunteered from the front. "There's plenty of room there for all of them."

Steve realized that was probably the best plan. Wolf Packs tended to enjoy the company of their Pack mates a lot more than other kinds of shifters and they often built big Pack houses where the entire Pack could congregate for meals or events. It was also a rooming house, of sorts, designed to help out Pack members or friends in need. There were probably enough suites in the place this Pack had built to give every one of the women a place of their own.

"Sounds good," Steve agreed with Pete, then turned back to Trisha, who was now leaning against him. She was a nice, warm bundle at his side and Steve was sorely tempted to put his arm back around her. "Trisha, I'm not sure how much of this you'll remember, but the man driving is my friend Pete. His son, Jeremy, is the one who helped your friend into the car. He's in the passenger seat. They have a bed and breakfast. That's where we're going. Okay?"

Steve tried to keep it simple and at the same time wanted to reassure her that she was in safe hands. She seemed calm, but that could be a byproduct of whatever drug she'd been given. He didn't want to cause her any more distress.

She nodded, then clutched her stomach and made a face that Steve understood all too well.

"You'd better pull over quick, Pete," Steve instructed, taking Trisha's free hand.

"The lead car just pulled over too," Pete reported as he rolled to a stop on the side of the desert road. "One of the gals is barfing all over a cactus."

Get your copy of *Tales of the Were: Red* wherever books are sold starting in Setpember 2013.

ABOUT THE AUTHOR

Bianca D'Arc has run a laboratory, climbed the corporate ladder in the shark-infested streets of lower Manhattan, studied and taught martial arts, and earned the right to put a whole bunch of letters after her name, but she's always enjoyed writing more than any of her other pursuits. She grew up and still lives on Long Island, where she keeps busy with an extensive garden, several aquariums full of very demanding fish, and writing her favorite genres of paranormal, fantasy and sci-fi romance.

Bianca loves to hear from readers and can be reached through Facebook, her Yahoo group or through the various links on her website.

Website
WWW.BIANCADARC.COM

29996070R00112

Made in the USA
Lexington, KY
15 February 2014